THEO...

THE ONLY THING STANDING BETWEEN ME AND EVERYTHING I needed was through the doors in front of me. All I had to do was follow a few simple rules.

Rule 1: First rule of billionaire fight club was that one did not speak about doubling the billionaire to anyone.
Rule 2: Draw no attention to yourself.
Rule 3: For the next thirty days, *be* Derrick Arlington.
Rule 4: At no point could I ever reveal who I was.
Rule 5: See the Inline Tech acquisition through to the end.
Rule 6: Follow the script. Do not deviate.
Rule 7: Only call the SOS number in case of dire emergency.
Rule 8: Stay the hell away from the royal family.

If I could manage those few simple rules, I'd have everything I needed for my family. I'd risked so much to be here. Now was not the time to get cold feet. Everything was within my grasp.

I just had to be someone else for thirty days.

"Why did I let you talk me into this again?"

"Because I'm damned persuasive," my best friend, Kyle Winters, chuckled. He was the exemption to rules one and four. He'd been there when the whole thing started, so there was no real concealment from him. Besides, he was my right-hand guy and the only person, besides my mother, whom I trusted implicitly.

This is a bad idea. Everyone will see. Everyone will know you're an impostor.

"Your pretty-boy face got you into this trouble, so you're just going to keep doing what you're doing. *Be* the billionaire. *Feel* the billionaire. Besides, you need this. We need this. You pull this off and all our troubles are over. You can take care of your mom. And PhilanthroApp will have the funding it needs. It's just 30 days. Be the billionaire, man."

I hated that he had a point. I had a damn good reason for being there, for taking this job. "I swear to God, if you say billionaire one more time, I'll kick you in the nuts."

"Dude, I'm just saying, Derrick Arlington is literally made of fucking gold, and he's hired you as his double to do bullshit events like this. It's all about *being* him. Because if you don't believe it, no one else will."

Kyle had a point.

"I know. But I'm pretty sure this guy is a grade-A dick. Did you see the workout schedule he left me? Not to mention the list of shit he won't eat. It was nu—" My brain was suddenly robbed of the processing power it needed to finish my sentence. Damn thing stutter-started when my gaze landed on the woman by the bar...

She was tiny. She might have been five-two, maybe, with

CHAPTER 1

hair the color of midnight. And when she turned to smile at whoever it was she was talking to, I couldn't fucking breathe. It was like her mere presence alone sucked all the air out of my lungs and held them captive. All the blood in my brain headed south, and I couldn't fucking think.

Kyle snapped his fingers. "Earth to Theo. Let's grab some champagne. Mingle," he muttered as he ogled one of the bridesmaids.

I shook my head in an attempt to clear it. "Low profile, remember? We need to be seen but not stand out."

He rolled his eyes and headed for the bar. I didn't follow. I couldn't seem to find any brain cells to force my legs to follow him. Who the hell was she?

Like you really have time for this shit?

Somehow, it didn't matter. I mentally willed her to lift her gaze to meet mine.

Oh yeah, genius, what are you going to say? 'Nice to meet you. I'm Theo?'

Fuck.

For tonight and the rest of the month, I was *Derrick Arlington*, billionaire extraordinaire and one of *People* magazine's sexiest bachelors. For all I knew, she hated Derrick Arlington, which meant she might hate me. So any attempts to talk to her would be futile, especially if she knew him already.

Over the last several weeks, Derrick had schooled me in all things related to him. I'd learned his preferences for food, music, sports, all of it. All so I could take over as him for a few weeks.

It felt like a life sentence, but a few weeks and I'd be free. And then I could go back to my life, my family, and the things I needed to get done.

Kyle came back with champagne. "Okay, who has put that

look on your face? Tell me it's the hot blonde, because if she turns you down, maybe I'd get spill over."

I swallowed hard. "No, not her."

Kyle groaned. "Dude, I don't think you understand how this double thing is supposed to work. You're supposed to enjoy it. Have fun while you work if you get what I'm saying..."

I had to chuckle as I sipped my champagne. "Yeah, I get it. And I don't think you understand who I am. I'm going to user my doppelgänger powers for good. This is a job, not an excuse to go stupid buck wild and get some ass. Besides, rule two of billionaire fight club is don't draw attention."

"I know. But I mean, if we're here anyway, you might as well get some ass and have some fun in the process."

Ever since Derrick had approached me back in New York, Kyle had been like a kid in a damn candy store, completely all-in on this *my best friend is a double* thing.

The whole idea was ridiculous to me. The idea that there were people so rich in the world that they could hire other people to *be* them for an indefinite amount of time...

Right now, you are *one of them.*

Six months ago, the real Derrick Arlington had walked into my office with a proposition. He'd found me because of my work with Kyle on the PhilanthroApp, our platform for charitable giving. I first thought it was a joke Kyle had cooked up. He looked exactly like me, minus the beard and attitude. If I was being honest, I'd thought he was someone crazy until Kyle looked him up. He wasn't crazy.

He'd had an offer for me. Just not the one I expected.

One month of being him.

To pull that off, I'd had to learn everything about him. I'd get all-expense-paid travel to the Winston Isles, an expense account, and two million dollars just to be him for thirty fucking days.

I had said no, of course. Because that shit had seemed insane. Who the fuck said yes to a proposition like that? Give up my life for his?

But then Kyle had reminded me that the stakes were too high to say no.

I had an offer I really couldn't afford to refuse. So there I was at a wedding for an earl and a princess, like I fucking belonged there.

"Listen, Theo, you just need to relax. Try and have some fun."

"Yeah, I hear you." My gaze drifted back to the brunette and stayed. Again, I willed her to look at me, but instead, her gaze skittered to the right. Then she saw something in the crowd. Something that made her turn around. Something that scared her, or maybe she wanted to avoid someone, because she turned quickly, her hair flying over her shoulder as she shoved her way through the revelers.

My chest squeezed. Was she leaving? Something primal in me wanted to find her and drag her back. I found her through the crowd again, and luckily, she wasn't leaving. Instead, she was hiding behind— Wait, seriously? Was she hiding behind the pillar?

Next to me, Kyle laughed. "Oh, I see her. Oh yeah, she's cute. Definitely way out of your league."

"Shut up." I muttered.

"She may be out of Theo Coleman's reach, but she's definitely in Derrick Arlington's league."

"How many times do I have to tell you we're going to get through this making as few ripples as possible? Hooking up with someone random equals a giant ripple. Besides, what? I'm going to stand by and let her call somebody else's name during sex? That's not going to work out."

Kyle was silent for a moment. "Yeah, you have a point there. But I mean, you could go seriously method with this whole acting thing."

I shook my head, because with Kyle, that's usually what I did. But I also wanted to shake the image of the brunette stepping between the pillars.

As long as I was pretending to be Derrick Arlington, my life wasn't mine. So I might as well not even go there. Besides, it was only thirty days. Thirty days to do the job and get out. Thirty days to get my soul back.

TWO

ZIA...

DEEDEE: *911...*

Those three little dots flickered away, letting me know, my sister, DeeDee had a lot more to say about her emergency *du jour*. But I turned my phone off. I was going to have one night where I didn't have to worry about her.

Another emergency SOS from my sister. Earlier she'd called me because she was hungry and had somehow run out of money on her campus card that I'd just filled on the first. It was only the tenth. She had two weeks to go before I was going to add more money.

Someone needed to tell my sister that texting 911 would get her nowhere.

Are you sure about that?

I supposed I'd trained her that texting would get me to come running. Whether it be a bird in the flat—though to be fair, that was scary—or a bathtub flood, or a news report of a burglar, prompting a three-night sleepover, I'd taught her that if she asked, I'd run in to the rescue.

Well, not tonight. Tonight, I was not the responsible one. I was not *Miss Fix Everything*. Tonight, I was going to have fun.

"Christ, those two seriously make you believe in love. And considering I don't believe in marriage or happily ever after, that's saying something."

I slid Tamsin a happy smile as I sipped my appletini. I knew they were passé, but they were delicious. Was she judging me?

"They are perfect. They make it look easy. But remember that whole *people were trying to kill her thing* from last year? None of that shit was easy."

Neela Reynold's, Jax's wife, raised her glass. "From someone who's also had people shoot at her, that's the truth. If someone is trying to kill you, it sucks. But the heightened adrenaline makes the sex *way* hotter, so I certainly hope that they are enjoying every dance."

Princess Jessa Winston dragged her new husband across the dance floor. While she looked elegant and effortless, Roone stumbled several times. As it turned out, *the* Roone Ainsley, all-around badass, earl, and best friend to the king *couldn't* dance.

Well, you couldn't win them all.

Tamsin raised her glass. "I know she is. Have you seen that man's posterior? She is a lucky girl."

I grinned at my friends. "Here's to a night off. For the love of God, I feel so naked without my gun. I have the tranq gun, but it doesn't give you the same feel good buzz. You think anyone can tell?"

When was the last time you were naked anyway?

Tamsin snorted a laugh, throwing her head back, her long blonde hair curling behind her. "I forgot my underwear. Which one of us do you think is having a better night?"

CHAPTER 2

I snorted. "You know what? It might just be you. I'm not sure."

Neela started having a coughing fit, and I assumed part of her drink went down the wrong passageway. As if by magic, her husband appeared from nowhere and clapped her on the back gently, murmuring, "There you are."

He crooned low and whispered something in her ear that made Neela's tanned skin flush, and then she gave him a heavy-lidded, *let's get out of here and go bone* face.

I knew that face. Hell, I have occasionally even made that face to other people. Okay, just the one.

How long ago was that?

It had been a *while*. A year, in fact, but I *had* made that face before, and I was happy for her. Jax loved her in a way that was palpable and tangible. And it was good to see that kind of love existed.

"Hey, we're having a Royal Elite women's congress here."

Jax lifted a brow, his lips tipping into a smirk. Christ on a cracker, the man was handsome. We all noticed. At work, he and Trace were the kind of man candy that made Mondays, and just about any other day of the week, tolerable. Shit, if I were Neela, I wouldn't be able to look at him head-on. He was *that* pretty.

He chuckled as he kissed his wife. "Want to clue me in on what's so funny?"

I leaned in and whispered dramatically. "We're talking about how awesome Roone's ass is."

Jax stumbled back as if he'd been burned. "Ugh, Jesus. He's my mate. Have you women no shame?" He shrugged. "Besides, my arse is definitely fitter."

Neela grinned at her husband. "Are you sure sweetheart?

I'll have to do my own inspection. Besides, he is fit, and we're not dead. We can look."

Jax just shook his head. "You recognize that I have seen that bare ass on more than one occasion, right? It's not pretty."

Tamsin shook her head and raised her glass in tribute. "It looks perfectly fine from here."

Jax rolled his eyes. "If you women are done ogling, I'd like to borrow my wife for a moment."

Neela laughed. "I know what *borrow* means. Borrow means you want to take me into the coat room and—"

She didn't get to finish because Jax leaned in and kissed her shoulder, lingering in the crook of her neck. His lips murmured something that I couldn't hear, but there was another flush from Neela. She drained her glass, slid it back onto the bar top, and gave us a delicate wave.

Tamsin sighed. "God, I need to get laid."

"Me first. I think I've gone without longer than you."

She lifted a brow. "How long for you?"

That question burned.

Ever since I'd been unceremoniously dumped for my boyfriend's side piece, I had avoided romantic entanglements.

It was safer that way. Sure, falling in love was great... for other people, but I'd learned my lesson. Hell, I had avoided a job I was perfectly suited for just so I wouldn't have to see my ex. "It's been a year."

Tamsin's eyes went wide. "Okay, I'll shut up about my six-month dry spell then. That's outrageous." She leaned in closer. "Come on, pick a guy. Any guy. You look amazing tonight. You're one of those girls who's petite and sexy. You're adorable. Vaguely ethnic looking. Those lashes, I would literally kill you for. You could pull anyone." Her arms stretched out over the crowd. "Do you want me to pick for you?"

I shook my head. "No. You will not be picking my next bone. I know we're close and all, but I don't think we're *that* close."

"Oh, we're *that* close. If I can pick you up a box of tampons, I can pick someone for you to do."

I shook my head. "No. Absolutely not. No way, no how."

"What happened to that British guy? You know, the one from London. Roone's cousin? Jessa works for him. I saw him hitting on you earlier."

"Ben Covington?" I laughed. "No thank you. I'm done with playboys." Ben Covington was another *hotter than sin and knows it* kind of guy.

"You haven't had sex in a year, and you're avoiding a perfectly hard man?"

"I'm avoiding said hard man because his nickname is *Big Ben*."

Tamsin grinned. "I know. That sounds delightful."

"No, it's not delightful. If that's his nickname, you know full well he had to have *earned* it. Which means that there are many, many women who have seen the goods. Many women who will attest to the size, shape, dexterity, and stamina, and I'm not really into that. No playboys, thanks. I want a nice, normal, average dude."

Tamsin snorted. "No thanks. Why take average when you can have billionaire badass? I mean, do those even exist? Romance has taught me that billionaires are beyond hot, with bodies that are sculpted from stone. I *know* they don't exist, and you know they don't exist, but I will dream and pretend that they *do*."

I shook my head. "Nope. I want none of that. I just want a

normal, nice guy. One who won't leave me for the skanky girl he swears is just his friend."

She winced. "Jesus, I'm sorry."

"Nope, it's fine," I reassured her.

But Tamsin kept talking, and I could only half hear her because something had me looking up and around. I was being watched.

I couldn't explain it, but the sense was as potent as if someone had reached out and touched me, stroking a finger down the column of my neck into the hollow of my lower back. I looked up and glanced around, but I couldn't find the source. The caress was hot. Powerful. It made me tingle with awareness.

I slid my gaze to the right, scanning the whole crowd and looking for someone watching me, but I couldn't find anyone. When I swung my gaze to the left, I— Oh, fuck. I froze. *Oh God.*

Oh God. Oh God. Oh God. Oh God.

"Uh, I'll be right back," I muttered to no one in particular.

I didn't know where I was going. I just knew I had to be away. Away from there. Away from *him*.

So I ran.

Yes, cowardly, but completely understandable. When you saw your ex, the same one who left you naked in your bed after just telling you that he'd been fucking someone else, you ran. That was the appropriate response. Anyone would run. When you saw the person who had been your commanding officer and who you weren't supposed to be sleeping with in the first place, running was *justified*.

I didn't know where I was going. Everywhere I turned there were people, dancing and drinking and reveling. I couldn't even

CHAPTER 2

escape to the balcony. It was too crowded. Finally, I didn't know what else to do, so I picked a set of columns off to the left on the outer edge of the dance floor near the other bar, and I stepped between them.

With my back to the wall, if I pressed in *just so*, no one would see me, and I could... breathe. Hands shaking, I turned my phone back on. I had a meditation app on there. Tamsin swore by it every time she was trying not to kill someone.

I had fucking run. Like a coward.

I had run from my past, from the shame. I had run from it all. Jesus Christ, what the hell was wrong with me?

All around me, people laughed and danced and enjoyed the wedding reception. Ariel ran by, chased by Prince Tristan.

My boss, flaming red hair, bright smile, twinkling green eyes, was in love. Of course, she was in love. After all these years, she and her first love had gotten it together. And from the looks of it, they were about to go and have their own little quickie. She would never run and hide between columns.

She was a badass.

I, on the other hand, was decidedly *not* a badass.

My phone vibrated in my hand, and I glanced down at it.

Tamsin: *Where are you?*

I wasn't sure if I should answer that, but I did.

Me: *Behind the pillar.*

It took her a moment, but then she replied.

Tamsin: *?*

I leaned out from behind the pillar, met her gaze at the bar, and waved. When she saw me, she poked Neela in the ribs, and the two of them came marching over.

Oh yeah, that was smart, draw attention to why you're hiding.

When they found me, both of them stood, arms crossed, staring at me. But it was Tamsin who spoke first. "What in the world?"

"Okay, I know this looks crazy, but I saw him."

"Who?"

"Garrett."

Neela frowned, not quite getting it, but Tamsin understood immediately.

"Where?"

"We were at the bar and I just— I could feel someone watching me. I saw him and I know he saw me, and I turned and ran like a moron. Now he thinks I care about him, which I don't. Just so you know."

"Of course, you don't. You don't care about turds."

"Exactly. He is a turd."

She nodded.

Neela laughed. "Someone catch me up."

"Her ex," Tamsin blurted. "She saw him, so she figured hiding between these two pillars was a good idea."

"Hey!" I slapped her arm. "I had few options, okay?"

Tamsin shook her head. "But why are you hiding? You didn't do anything wrong."

"I know. I just... I don't know. I had no other choice. I saw him, and I freaked out, okay?"

Neela's gaze volleyed between Tamsin and myself and back again. "Zia, I have never seen you like this. Do you want us to get you out of here?"

I shook my head. "No, before I saw him, I was having fun. And come on, we were invited to the princess's wedding. You don't get invited to a cool-kid party and then take off because you saw your ex, who is a commander in the Royal fucking Guard."

Neela shook her head. "I understand how you feel. I'm so sorry. I know what it's like to have a turd of a boyfriend."

Oh yeah, before Neela and Jax, there had been Neela and some idiot. He'd taken her whole company, so she did understand. "How did you get over it?"

"Well, you find someone bigger and better to give you many, many orgasms."

My mouth hung open. And then I laughed.

I laughed at myself, at my situation, and I laughed at Neela because she was right. Why was I hiding? I hadn't done anything wrong. I had been awesome. *He* had chosen to cheat on *me*. He had chosen to leave.

I was perfect.

As I headed back to the bar with my friends, I glanced around. I still felt like I was being watched, but I had no idea where it was coming from.

Whoever it was, if the intensity was that strong with their eyes, I could only imagine what it would be like if they touched me.

THREE

THEO...

I HAD LOST KYLE IN THE CROWD SOMEWHERE. BETWEEN glasses of champagne and dancing with bridesmaids, he was having far more fun at this thing than I was. It was okay though. Because I had something else to occupy my brain. The brunette. Who would send her hiding? Was she okay? The fact that I wanted to go over there and fix things for her was ridiculous.

First of all, she likely didn't need anyone to fix anything for her. Second of all, that fact didn't stop the nearly gravitational pull attempting to yank me into that position. I'd seen her talking to the queen earlier at the wedding. And then the princess. She knew them. *Personally.*

And I had strict instructions. Stay away from the royal family. If nothing else, they, at the very least, could identify me. Derrick was, after all, Sebastian's cousin. While not a prince, he was an earl. So, that way, danger lay.

Danger or not though, that didn't stop my brain from sorting, running through the myriad of conversations and ice breakers I could use to talk to her. It didn't stop my body from tensing at the sight of her, or the blood from rushing and roaring in my head, making it impossible to form two fucking thoughts. It didn't stop my increased heart rate. It didn't stop that hitch in my breath like she'd fucking stolen it like a thief in the night.

Knowing what I wanted to do and what I *couldn't* do didn't stop me from wanting it.

Wanted or not, there were more important things to consider.

What was it about her? Yeah, she was beautiful. Glossy dark hair, the tanned complexion to her skin, wide, dark eyes that were cat-like. Her makeup was minimal, save her bright red lipstick. She wore her hair lose around her shoulders, bangs side-swept. I wanted to dig my hands into it. Feel it between my fingertips. Smell it. Tug it. Use it like a rope.

Easy does it.

I turned away and forced myself to inhale deeply.

You have a job to do. You have a job to do. You have a goddamn job to do. Do your job. Stay away.

I needed to find Kyle and get out of there. We had sufficiently mingled. Anyone who needed to pay attention would have seen that we were there. It was time to go before I did something stupid. Something I couldn't take back. Something that would have me either howling at the moon or running back to New York empty-handed with my tail between my legs and nothing to show for it.

Get it together.

I'd come all this way for something. Now I had to show that it was worth it. I'd spent the last couple of months learning everything there was to know about a man with my face.

That shit still weirded me out. Arlington had walked into my office without so much as by your leave and told me he had a job proposition for me.

Like an idiot, I thought he wanted to be an angel investor. But that's not what he wanted from me. He'd wanted thirty days. Thirty days for me to be him. There was nothing more jarring than seeing the spitting image of yourself, what you could have been before you fucked your life up, and not necessarily liking it.

If my life had gone exactly right, I would have been him. Young, rich, with more money that I knew what to do with. But I *wasn't* him. I had made an entirely different choice in my life. Oh yeah, and he was born rich. Me, not so much. He'd been given access to all the best things and opportunities. I only had my mother. But she was enough.

Everything I'd done, hopefully, made her proud. But this, what the hell would she think about this?

When I couldn't find Kyle in the crowd, I pulled my phone out and typed a message.

Theo Coleman: *Time to go, where are you?*

I waited, but there were no little dots.

Where the hell had he gone? Had he vanished with that bridesmaid? The blonde one. Pixie haircut. What was her name? I'd been introduced. It started with a J or something. Jessica? It was unusual. I couldn't remember. I'd been told the name in passing. The thing about my photographic memory was that I only remembered shit I saw written down. A passing name was too difficult. My brain always disregarded that kind of stuff. So anything I wanted to remember, I wrote down. It made my life a lot easier.

There was a rustle behind me, and before I could turn, there was something pressed into my back.

"Easy does it, Theo. We wouldn't want to make a scene."

I froze.

CHAPTER 3

Theo.

No one here knew me as Theo. I swallowed. "I'm sorry. I think you have the wrong person."

"No, I have the right person. What you're going to do for me, Theo, is you're going to finish your champagne and smile at no one in particular. And then you're going to march nice and easy right to the outer doors. Then you and I are going on a little trip."

"I'm not going anywhere with you. I know better than to get in a car."

"Okay, well, that's up to you. But if you choose not to get in that car, something disastrous is going to happen to dear, sweet old Mom. That's right. We have people watching her in New Jersey. That yellow Craftsman house is cute. Is that where you grew up?"

I tensed. Fuck. They had someone watching her. "What do you want?"

"I told you what I want. Start moving."

"You don't have to do this." *Think, man, think.*

He snickered. "Don't I though? Start moving."

I did as I was told. I drained the glass, depositing it with a passing member of the waitstaff. I frantically searched the crowd for Kyle, and then I remembered the phone. There was an app, an SOS beacon to whoever was in your emergency contacts. He was mine, so I hoped to Christ he was paying attention and would eventually see it.

Asshole, find me. Find me quick, because sooner or later this motherfucker right here is going to make me toss my phone. This was Kidnapping 101. GPS could ruin everything.

"Move." He growled through his teeth when I didn't move quickly enough.

"I'm moving. Relax. No need to leave a mess. Not in this pretty ballroom."

"Shame for you, you're not going to get to enjoy it."

"Yeah, why don't you tell me what all this is about?"

"Shut up, Theo."

"All right, if you already knew I'm Theo, then you know Arlington would pay dearly if this is what that's about. He'll pay whatever ransom and demands you want."

I had no idea if Derrick would pay to get me back. I had no idea what the final end-game plan was. He'd left me instructions and told me to use the emergency contact when I absolutely needed it. This felt like one of those times.

"I'm not sure what this is about, but I'm not getting in that car." I turned around to face him. "So either you're going to have to shoot me here or walk away. Because right now, it's not happening."

And then there was movement behind him. Icicles formed in my veins as I froze. It was *her*, the *brunette*. She was coming outside.

No. No. No. No.

This asshole would not hesitate to shoot her. *No.* I willed her to go back. "Fine, let's get in the car."

But the brunette called out. "Sweetheart, there you are. Are you being naughty and sneaking a cigarette?"

I shook my head at her, silently signaling for her to back off. But the guy with the gun had already paused and turned around. "Oh, is this a friend of yours?"

I turned him around to face me. "Nope, focus on me, asshole. She has nothing to do with this." And then I realized my mistake. Showing that I cared about this anonymous woman in any way, had actually put her in danger.

CHAPTER 3

Zia...

NOTHING LIKE SIGHTING an ex to put the end to revelry. But I wasn't going to leave. I'd already run and hidden once. I'd dressed up and the whole thing. I wasn't packing it in. There was absolutely nothing appealing about going back to my room at Royal Elite... *alone.*

If I did that, there would be vodka. And ice-cream. And Ariel would know I couldn't keep my shit together. No way was I letting that shit happen. Besides, I wasn't weak.

I could handle my shit. I was the one who handled everything. I was the one people called to handle *their* shit. I was not vodka-and-ice-cream weak.

So I threw myself into dancing, but I cooled it on the champagne. I wasn't going to get sloppy drunk and say something stupid.

It seemed though, that Roone's cousin Ben had not made the same resolution. He was making an ass of himself asking me to dance. He wasn't being disrespectful, he just thought he was a comedian. And while his British accent was indisputably charming. So far, I couldn't find the humor in his attempts.

"Come on, darling. I can tell that under that buttoned-up exterior, you know how to do a mean running man."

I wrinkled my nose. "Do *you* even know what the running man is? What makes you think I can do that in heels?"

His gaze slid over my body. I saw the interest. *Sorry playboy. Players need not apply.* I could almost count the swarms of women he'd been with as clearly as if their names had been etched on his forehead.

It emanated off of his aura in flashing neon letters. *I am a player. Beware all who tarry on this cock.*

I had zero problem with handsome, and Ben Covington had the handsome gene in droves. He was Roone's cousin after all.

I had no problem with rich, and from what I understood, he was a billionaire. I might be down with someone who I didn't have to look after financially.

I just had a problem with players. Guys who were ruled by their dicks. And I had no desire to be some playboy's plaything.

"Don't you have someone else to go and bother?"

He leaned against the bar. "Well, the way I figure it, you should always aim for the most beautiful woman in the room. You never know when she'll say yes."

Lord, he was slick. "Okay, what if I tell you it's a resounding no?"

His brows furrowed as if he'd never heard the word before in his lifetime. "A no?"

I couldn't help but grin at that. "Yeah. Nope. No thank you."

He drained the rest of his scotch, something worth more than my salary for the week, no doubt. His brows were still drawn down as if completely confused that a woman wouldn't want him.

"What? Is it because I'm not James Bond? I know you work at Royal Elite. You prefer rough and tumble? Someone who knows his way around a gun? Would it change your mind if I told you I happen to be good at hand to hand combat?" He winked.

I couldn't help it. That was almost kind of witty, and I snorted a laugh. "No, it wouldn't change anything."

He sighed. "Fine. Might I ask why? Because earlier, I thought we had a moment."

"You mean when I met your gaze and smiled?"

He nodded as if that said everything. "It's a hell of a smile."

I rolled my eyes. "Just because I smile at you doesn't mean I want to shag you. I'm allergic to playboys."

His mouth formed an O as if he was shocked, and he crushed a hand to his heart. "Oh, you wound me."

"As if. You *know* you're a playboy. How many women have you shagged exactly?" I turned to face him and leaned my elbow on the bar.

He could barely contain his smirk. "A gentleman never tells."

I couldn't hold the giggle. "You sir, are far from a gentleman."

"The lady sees the truth."

Again, he made me laugh. "I'll let you in on a secret. I'm far from a lady."

And I had to give him credit, because his gaze did not falter from mine.

"Then I think maybe you don't see enough."

Something about his statement heated my skin and made it flush. It was the first hint of something honest out of his mouth.

Out of my periphery, I watched as Jessa and Roone twirled around the dance floor again. But it wasn't them I was aware of. I finally knew who had been watching me. A man at the far end of the ballroom. His gaze didn't waver from mine but instead held me captive, refusing to let go until I'd spilled all my secrets.

Hair the color of midnight, piercing smoke-gray eyes. He leaned against the wall by the door to the balcony.

He was focused. Intent. Unwavering. And Jesus Christ, the jolt of awareness was hot, piercing, and I couldn't shake it. His look was like a blast from a furnace.

I wasn't trying to get distracted. Screw distraction.

No, seriously. Screw distraction. It's been a year since you got laid.

I tried to avert my gaze, but it took longer than it should have. When I finally managed to tear my eyes away, I turned my attention back to Ben and his brows were raised.

"So, I guess I'm out of luck. You found someone else more interesting."

"What makes you say that?"

"The look on your face. You certainly didn't look at me like that." He shrugged. "And to the winner go the spoils."

I retorted back immediately, "Who said I'm a spoil?"

His grin was slow, sexy, confident. The player was back. "Who said *you* were the spoil?"

If I'd been the kind of girl who hadn't had her heart broken by someone playful and fun, someone who exuded that same kind of confidence, I could've fallen for someone like him. But I had already been burned by a playboy, so Ben Covington wasn't on the table.

As I walked through the ballroom, I headed to the balcony to find Tamsin and shook off thoughts of the heated gaze. When Tamsin saw me, she smiled. "Ah, I see Ben finally gave up."

I rolled my eyes. "If only he'd been half serious. That is probably one hard man to shake when he wants something."

She laughed. "Count me in as one woman who's willing to be first in line. I bet they don't call him Big Ben for nothing."

I snorted a laugh. "Oh, he is all yours. I'll give him one thing. He sure is pretty."

"I mean, he and his friends, Bridge and East, walking in together was like an orgasm waiting to—"

I lost my train of thought as Tall-dark-and-melt-your-panties walked by the open door. This time, he was with a man who spoke intently to him as they walked briskly past. I couldn't lie... the view from the back was just as good as the front.

The hairs on the back of my neck stood at attention. Something was off. The other guy was dressed the part, but he looked off. Like maybe he was too rough around the edges to be wearing that tux.

"Hey, give me a sec," I muttered. "I'll be right back."

Tamsin frowned at me. "You okay?"

"Yeah, just following a hunch." I ran back in and followed both men out of the ballroom, into the hall, and to the stairs leading to the side entrance headed to the north parking lot where the valet had been parking the cars. *Faster. Faster. Do not lose them.*

Outside, the too big, too rough guy was speaking intently to the man with the gray eyes right next to a car. The passenger door was open, and no one else was in the car that I could tell.

They were arguing and gray eyes had his hands up. Was this the time to butt in? What if my hunch was wrong?

What if it's right?

Yeah, fuck it. I ran up to them both. "Sweetheart, there you are. Are you being naughty and sneaking a cigarette?"

Stormy gray eyes met mine, and he gave me a sharp shake of his head. I ignored him and turned to Mr. Too Many Muscles. "Oh, is this a friend of yours?"

The guy was shaved bald. He had eyes that were dark and too closely set together, high cheekbones, and a forehead and nose that suggested he was maybe Eastern European.

When he spoke, it confirmed my impression that this scenario was nothing good. "Get rid of her, or she comes with us."

"I'm not going anywhere, buddy." I jabbed him in the chest in an attempt to create more space. In close combat with this guy, I'd lose. Sure, I was faster and nimbler. But one good hit and I'd be down.

His sharp, slashing brows drew down. "Suit yourself. I know what to do with someone like you."

I'd bet he did. And none of those things included me sleeping in my warm cozy bed tonight. "Babe, come on the royal family wants a photo."

Gray Eyes arched a brow. "Darling, you go ahead I'll meet you there." His voice was sin and bad decisions mixed together.

I stood my ground. Now was no time for him to be noble. "Oh, I know King Sebastian insists."

"I'll have to pass, love."

"Yeah, you heard him, he'll have to —"

He was talking and also raising his right arm. All I saw was the black gleam, and I acted, launching myself in the air and slamming against Gray Eyes. Toppling him over and covering his body with mine, tranq gun raised.

Wasting no time, I squeezed twice. The asshole about to shoot at us was big. Who knew if two doses would be enough? But I was prepared to run.

The muscle-bound brute fell to his knees. I rolled on my back, ready for anything.

But I didn't need to worry. Two hits with the tranq had done the job.

I sucked in a shuddering breath.

When I turned to my bed of muscles, he was glaring at me. "Do you have a bloody death wish?"

His voice had lost some of the sin quality. It was colder, like he was pissed.

I pushed to my feet. "What? You wanted me to let you go with that asshole? He was going to kill you."

"I promise you, I'm quite capable."

Unbelievable. "You could have fooled me. Men wielding weapons and shoving you into a car are generally bad news."

His gaze narrowed as he glowered at me. "I had it under control."

I crossed my arms. "Oh, so you're delusional. Okay then. Goodbye, crazy. And P.S. You're welcome."

"You generally only say thank you when you're glad someone did something."

I shook my head. "For fuck's sake. Next time I'll let you die then. Pity. You look expensive, like someone would miss you, but it's no skin off my back. I'll just let the homicidal asshole kill you when he wakes up."

"You could have been hurt. Did you pay attention to what just happened?"

"You mean besides me putting on a display of badassery the likes of which you've never seen? I also made this couture look damn good. Oh yes... and *saved your ass.*"

"My ass didn't need saving, princess."

"I'm not a princess, asshole. I'm a King's Knight. I don't need anybody to save me. Have a nice life." As I strutted off, I flipped him the bird.

Not my most mature moment, but he was an ungrateful prick. Let him deal with the body. The dickhead was going to wake up at some point, and he was going to be all kinds of pissed off. But neither one of them was my problem anymore. No good deed went unpunished.

Boy, I sure did know how to pick 'em. But at least I'd never have to see Gray Eyes again, the ungrateful prick.

FOUR

THEO...

That fucking woman, she could have been killed. She said she was a King's Knight. What the hell was that? And why had she had a tranq gun?

I turned to find my would-be kidnapper. But there was no body. I nearly gave myself whip lash as I whipped my head back and forth searching for him.

Fuck. Fuck. Fuck.

He'd used my goddamn name. That motherfucker had called me, *Theo*. Only Derrick knew who I was. But Derrick needed me here. So what the hell was going on?

With swift, jerky movements, I grabbed my phone out of my pocket and dialed the number Derrick had left me for emergencies. It was pretty safe to say that this qualified as an emergency.

It went straight to voicemail.

That didn't stop me from leaving a message though. "Hey, Arlington. You know who it is. We need to talk. Someone just tried to grab me at your little party. News flash. Someone knows."

Christ. I needed him to respond quickly. That jackhole's

CHAPTER 4

words sent a chilling spike through my blood. That had been enough to get me moving out of the reception.

Denying it had done no good. He'd known. And where the hell was Kyle? We needed to get out of here. More importantly, where the hell was Arlington? I needed some damn answers.

I could still feel the blunt edge of the gun he'd pressed into my back. Then we'd been outside in the balmy air with the sounds of the ocean in the distance. He'd been leading me to the car and then Little Miss Loud Mouth had turned up and, everything had gone to shit. He knew who I was. What the hell had happened to my goddamn life?

I had to think things through. I ran my hands through my hair and tried to force my brain into action. Great idea, taking this job. So fucking smart. That was me, too goddamn smart for my own good.

I thought I could handle this, be what everyone needed, be all things for all people. But if I wasn't' careful, I wouldn't only fail, I'd fail the people who needed me most.

So get your shit together.

I turned back to the ballroom. I hadn't been able to take my eyes off of the woman, but maybe that was the point. Considering we were in the playground of the rich and famous, was she part of some kind of con?

Focus. You don't have time for that shit. Someone out there clearly knows that you are an impostor. If you don't get your shit together, the whole situation is going to crumble around you.

And worse, the one person that could pull the plug and tell me what the fuck I was supposed to do about it wasn't immediately available.

I could go back to the party, or go back to the penthouse, or go back to New York and resume my life. Pretend none of this had ever happened.

If you go back, you'll be empty-handed.

Going back to New York wasn't an option, so I had to stay and figure this shit out. I wasn't going back to the party. Besides, if I did, there would be the chance of running into the king and—

"Derrick?"

Fuck. Slowly, I turned. I squinted, and my gut knotted. It was the one person I was hoping to avoid. "Sebastian."

He frowned. "Did you just call me Sebastian? You haven't called me anything but Seb, since we were fourteen."

"Sorry, I just uh—It's been a long night. Roone and your sister know how to party."

The king studied me closely as if trying to figure out what was wrong, what was different, what wasn't adding up. I knew my English accent was impeccable. My mother was English, so I'd learned from the best.

Clearly, you've done something wrong. He's looking too closely.

"I'm just going to head back in. You know, kiss the bride again. See if one of the bridesmaids wants to dance with me."

"Most of them are taken. Are you all right, Derrick? You look off."

"I'm fine." And then I tried to deflect. "Shouldn't you be out here with security?"

"Christ, you sound like Penny. I came to give her a shawl because now she's cold, even though for weeks she's been talking about how she's going to crawl out of her skin from the heat. That was something I could take care of. I was going to send someone to do it."

"You're the king. You should take better care with your life."

"Trust me, there are security personnel that you can't even see out here."

I didn't know how I felt about that. "Well, if you're sure."

I tried to pass by him, and he frowned. "Derrick, what the hell is that on your tux?"

I glanced down at the dirt. It must have been from when the brunette knocked me down. All one hundred and twenty pounds of her. But she'd done it valiantly trying to save my life or something. "Uh, it's just some dirt. I fell."

Sebastian watched me closely. He frowned. "You want to tell me what's up?"

How much choice did I have? If he was right, and there was security out there, that indicated there were probably security cameras too, which meant he would see for himself anyway.

Tell as much of the truth as you can.

"Someone inside the party cornered me with a gun."

Sebastian's eyes rounded. His lips pressed firm into a thin line. "For fuck's sake. Can't this family get any fucking break?"

"It's not your concern, Sebastian."

He frowned again but didn't make another mention of the use of his given name. "Of course, this is a problem. We're going to get you an immediate guard tonight."

"Sebastian, it's not necessary." So much for drawing no attention to myself.

"Of course, it's fucking necessary. You might not use your title, but that doesn't make you any less royal."

"Look, I just want to go back in."

He shook his head. Before I knew it, he'd pulled out his phone. "Get me Ariel."

Five minutes later, a pretty redhead was barreling down the stairs. "Oh my God, is it Penny?"

Sebastian shook his head. "Ariel, I'm not sure you've met my cousin Derrick."

The woman named Ariel had bright green eyes and a warm smile. "I'm Ariel Scott, pleasure to meet you."

"It seems my cousin Derrick here needs a bodyguard."

She lifted both brows. "What happened?"

Sebastian nodded. "Derrick, why don't you tell her?"

"Look, it's fine. Some asshole escorted me out here and tried to shove me in a car. I resisted. Clearly, I'm a little rumpled, but mostly unhurt. I've had anti-kidnap training."

Sebastian shook his head. "I don't care what kind of training you've had. If something like that happens at my sister's goddamn reception, I'm not letting it lie. This family has been through too much already."

"I don't want to make this a big thing, Sebastian. It's not what I'm looking for, right now. Things are sensitive."

He nodded and leveled me a gaze. "Good thing Ariel is the picture of discretion."

♛

Zia...

WHAT A JACKASS. Next time I saw a gorgeous guy about to be shoved into a car against his will, I was going to leave him to it. Let him be kidnapped and tortured. For all I knew it was some kind of elaborate sex game. Or one of those escape room games taken too far.

Maybe he's a criminal and you thwarted some kind of heist.

If only. Most of the things I did at Royal Elite weren't *that* interesting. I still loved my job though. I got to learn from the best and put my skills to good use. There were worse jobs to have.

But you want to do more field work.

Yes, I did. I'd had a little field action when Ariel and Penny had broken into Stanstit prison. I was also shot at once while working on Neela's protection case too. That assignment had actual excitement. But most of the time I stayed home on tech duty. Which was fine, but babysitting actors and musicians didn't really come with much oomph.

Those jobs consisted of mostly following them around shopping. Being propositioned. Being told to get them something to eat. Either way, still the best gig I'd ever had. I loved being in the military. But again, I'd been relegated to tech, so mostly I sat behind a desk. Maybe one day I'd get to do something real.

My phone buzzed again.

Deedee: *Seriously. Where are you?*

Shit. Was this one of those occasions where she actually needed me? I typed out a quick message.

Me: *I'm at a wedding reception. You knew I had to do that today.*

Deedee: *I need your help. It's an emergency.*

Me: *I probably need to teach you the definition of an actual emergency.*

Deedee: *I'm trapped on the roof of Princess Tower.*

Me: *What do you mean trapped?*

Deedee: *I mean trapped. The door is locked, and I can't get back down.*

Me: *Ugh!*

My fucking sister. Why was it that I always had to run to her rescue?

Because you always run to her rescue. How is she ever going to learn?

Problem was I couldn't leave Deedee to figure it out on her own. She was my little sister. After our parents died, our aunt had taken us in, but she'd been an ineffective parent. So I'd had to raise Deedee. If there was a recital to attend, I would go. If she needed new shoes, I made sure she got them. I made sure vegetables appeared on her plate instead of pizza or burgers. I'd become her parent as soon as I realized my aunt was not much more than a token adult who had no intention of parenting.

Now there was this co-dependent shit going on. Every time I tried to teach Deedee independence, sure enough, she would get herself into some kind of mess that required me.

Zia: *I'm on my way.*

Princess Tower was located at the most southern point of the island. It overlooked the other five islands and served as sort of an unofficial lighthouse. During the day, people would go up to the top-level observation deck. But at night, it was shut down for a good reason.

A couple of years ago, some kid tried to do a prank and another kid almost fell. So for everyone's safety, the king insisted that no one go up there when it was dark. I was going to kill my fucking sister.

Unfortunately, since it was night time, the elevator was not running, which meant forty-seven goddamn flights of stairs.

I parked my Jeep at the base and stared up. God, I loved my sister. I really did. But did I love her this much?

If it's not you, who's it going to be?

That was a good point. Deedee had lots of friends. She was

that girl. Beautiful and stunning, and everyone wanted to be around her. She was gregarious and fun and outgoing. She was also that girl who thought things would magically work out for her. She would have a suitcase and just stand idly by a stairway, and inevitably, within thirty seconds, some guy would roll by and offer to carry it for her.

I did the same thing once as a test, and people just brushed past me to get to the stairs. I loved her. To death. Because there was something inherently sweet about her. And she was my sister. Who else did I have?

I turned off the lights and my engine and then ran around to my trunk. I always put a go bag back there. Just in case. Always at the ready.

Sure enough, I had a pair of tennis shoes in there. Thank God. But, no socks. Ugh. Worst. But hey, at least sneakers and not heels. I grabbed the sneaks and one by one dragged off my heels, sliding my bare feet into the sneakers and tying the laces. Then I grabbed my bolt cutters and my lock pick set. I'd only ever used it in training exercises, but I was pretty good. I even beat out Jax. A fact he still grumbled about.

Jameson likes to joke that with the skillset Ariel gave us, we were all actually going to be high-end thieves. Which we weren't. At least, I was pretty sure we weren't.

It was no secret that Lucas, the king's brother, was once a conman and a thief. But as far as I knew, he'd given that up, right?

Either way, I ran up to the main door only to find it unlatched. Jesus Christ, I didn't even want to know how she got in there. Or who she was with.

Good thing I was at least in shape. Forty-seven flights. Jesus.

After twenty, I was cursing my sister. After thirty, I had

plans to throttle her. At thirty-five, I wanted to hug her before I tossed her off of the roof. When I finally reached the top, that's where I saw her problem. The door was a key only entry. Which meant there was no way to get back in from outside. *Awesome.*

I knelt down and got to work, rolling out my tools, picking the best ones. The night was balmy, so at least my hands were warm. When Ariel had trained us the last time, it was bitter cold, but I'd still beaten Jax. With the flashlight in my mouth, I was able to get the lock mechanism turning just so, and then there was a click. I turned the handle and pulled with all my might, only to find a naked Deedee, curled up in a ball, by the center telescope. "Dee?"

She gave me a tremulous smile. "Hey, Zia. Glad to see you."

I stared at her. "Where the fuck are your clothes?"

She gave me a sheepish smile as she pushed herself to stand, using her hands to cover her boobs and crossing her legs. "Well, um, okay, don't be mad."

I crossed my arms. "Why would I be mad?"

Someone behind me cleared their throat. Like an idiot, I'd left my weapons downstairs, so when I whipped around all I had to defend us were my bare hands and my lock pick set. Still though, I had my hands up at the ready.

Then I saw the boy with the russet hair in his birthday suit. I whipped back around. "I swear to God, Deedee. Why is he naked? Why are you naked?"

My sister continued to try to cover herself with her hands. "I know you said that I couldn't join the sorority, but I just really wanted to rush or at least have the experience of rush week. And—"

I lifted a brow. "You're up here naked in the tower with

this... guy..." I called over my shoulder, "What's your name, naked dude?"

"Uh, Toby."

I rolled my eyes. "So, you're up here naked with cute Toby for a rush prank?"

My sister shifted on her feet. "Um, not a prank exactly. It's more like private initiation."

I blinked... twice. "You're being fucking hazed? You called me because you were being hazed?"

"Well, to be fair, me getting locked up here wasn't part of the hazing. I was supposed to come all the way up here and christen the top of the tower. But uh, our clothes were blown off by the wind. And the door locked, and all I had was my phone, and—"

I stared at her. I mean, what did I even say in this situation? "I don't even know what to say to you."

She tilted her chin up and met my gaze with fire like a rebellious teenager. "I'm an adult. I can have sex."

"You think this is about you banging cute Toby? I could care less. What I care about is how irresponsible you are. You came up here with no plan. Anything could have happened. And newsflash, you lost your damn clothes. You have to think Deedee."

"I'm having fun, Zia. For the love of God, you remember fun, right?"

"Nope. Because I'm too busy bailing your ass out."

She crossed her arms over her chest forgetting about her vajajay, giving me and cute Toby a show. "You're not my mother."

"Yeah you like to remind me of that. But guess what, you certainly keep calling me to bail you out like I am. Get your shit." I smacked my forehead. "Oh wait, you have no shit, because it blew away." Seriously, how was she even my sister? Another thought occurred to me. "Where the hell is your car?"

Toby spoke up. "Um, we called a car service, but then—"

I rolled my eyes hard. "Toby, cover your pseudo man bits. Let's go."

Deedee flushed. "This isn't the worst that could have happened. Look—"

I put a hand up. "Deedee, I don't know how many times I have to tell you this. I am not your damn get-out-of-jail-free card. At some point, you have to take responsibility for your life."

"I am. And you are my get-out-of-jail-free card. I mean, I called you and you came."

"I'm your sister. I'll come. But lord."

"I'm sorry, okay?" She sounded far from sorry.

"Which house is it?" I asked her.

Her eyes went round. She knew what I was going to do. She shook her head. "No, I'm not telling you."

I lifted a brow. "Are you shitting me right now?"

"No. I'm not shitting you. I'm really not going to tell you."

"Deedee Amelia Barnes—"

She shook her head. "You don't get to mom me right now. I've got to protect my people. Besides, this was my mistake. Not theirs."

"No, it's my mistake, because I came to get you... *again*. Let's go." I cast a glance over my shoulder at Toby. "You will not put your bare ass on my seats, you hear me? You will sit on a notebook or something."

He gave me a wide grin. That motherfucker wasn't remorseful either. "Yes, ma'am."

Fuck my life. My sister was an idiot and this douche-twat

just ma'amed me. Between these two and Gray Eyes with the bad attitude, my night ruination was complete. Why had I even come?

Because as long as you're needed, you will always come. Also, you are a glutton for punishment who will always try to fix things.

At some point, I was going to have to stop bailing her out, or it was going to cost me.

FIVE

THEO...

My phone buzzed and I dove for it. I'd left what I hoped was a non-alarmist message for my mother to call me after the debacle last night.

"Mom, are you okay?"

"Theo, of course I'm okay. Just a little cancer. Why? What's wrong?"

For the first time since I'd stepped out of that ballroom, I could breathe properly. Her characteristic sharp wit was intact. "Nothing. I just, I don't know, I was thinking about you." I took a deep breath and all the tension from last night ebbed through my body.

"I could tell you were anxious from your message. Is there something I need to know? Did Kyle get you into some kind of trouble? Are you calling from a sex dungeon? If you are, I'd encourage you to have fun dear."

I coughed a laugh. "Mom. Jesus." The last thing I wanted was for her to worry. She should be focused on getting better, not on potential danger. Besides she was safe for now. If things got out of hand, I'd go home. Screw the money.

Even though you need it?

"How's the job?" I could tell by her tone the question was serious. Sometimes it was hard to tell with her.

I swallowed hard. All she knew was that I'd been offered a contract position in the Winston Isles. Of course, I hadn't told her anything about it. After all, what would I say?

"It's fine. Listen, you're good with Aunt Lydia?"

"Besides her daily attempts to poison me with kale and barley and her refusal to give me rum? Fine. We're having fun. If gardening can be considered fun. I tried to get her to take me to the male review in Vegas, but she said no. Instead she's just clucking over me like a mother hen. Maybe you can help convince her naked man flesh would improve my spirits and chances of healing."

My chuckle started low in my gut before slowly erupting. "Mom, you're still impossible."

"Better believe it. I'm not dead yet. But any day now so let me have my fun."

I shook my head. "Stop saying that." There was more bite to my words than was necessary. I knew she used the humor and snark to mask her worry, but still.

She sighed. "Sorry, handsome, I will eventually go. But I'm too ornery to go just yet. I need to torture you and your aunt a little more first. You want to tell me what has your knickers in a twist?"

"It's all good. I'm fine. I was just checking in."

"Bullshit. You think I don't know my own son? What gives? Kyle set you up with male strippers again?"

I chuckled. For all her laughing, I knew she worried. When I left Base Software, she hadn't said a word, just told me to do what was best. But I knew she thought I was screwing up my life.

I was on my way to being the youngest Vice President in the history of Base Software. But I'd done what I thought was best and walked out because they screwed over my friend.

There wasn't a day I looked back on that and thought it was the wrong move. When they stole Kyle's patent, I couldn't stay. I couldn't be a part of that. But there were moments like last night when I did wonder how simple my life would have been if I hadn't walked away.

It wouldn't be simple. How would you sleep?

Kyle and I had known each other since diapers. He'd lived in the same apartment building I had. Just down the hall. Our mothers used to take us to the park at the same time every day, and when we were at home we'd run up and down the halls knocking on each other's doors to play. And then it was school and all of those things. I finally rented my mother a house when I was in college. I'd gotten a scholarship to NYU, and so did Kyle. He'd been part of a major engineering project we'd done. We won. Working together as always, the two of us couldn't fail.

Are you sure about that?

Anyway, with the scholarship, I'd been able to work while I went to school, and all the money I'd made working, I sent to her. Which got her out of the apartment in Jersey City and into a cute craftsman.

She insisted that she had a nest egg. That my absent father wanted me to have it. *She* wanted me to take it. I wanted nothing from that man. He'd never called, never sent birthday cards nothing. So, he could feel free to fuck himself.

"Look it's all good. I was just thinking about you last night and wanted to check on you."

CHAPTER 5 43

"Sometimes, it's like you're the mother."

"It's a valid question." More quietly, I asked, "You okay?"

"Some days are better than others, but today, today's good. Matter of fact, I'm having a smoothie right now."

"Good. You keep getting better. I'll be home soon."

"Uh-huh. While you're there, try and work on the dating thing, would you?"

And time to go. "Love you, Mom. Bye."

When I hung up with her, I ran my hands down my face. Jesus Christ, what the hell was I supposed to do? I could try and fool myself that everything was going to be cool but it wasn't. Last night was a prime example.

I broke rule number two. Or rather the sexy-ass brunette had broken it for me.

Rule #2: Draw zero attention.

How did that work out for you?

His Royal fucking Majesty had seen me. Thanks to little Miss Hell on Wheels and her interference, I didn't have a choice. I was getting a goddamn bodyguard whether I wanted one or not.

♛

THEO...

The Royal Elite offices weren't exactly what I had imagined. Or maybe they were. What the hell did I know? I'd never needed a bodyguard. I'd always *been* a menace, not the one who needed protection from menaces.

Well, this is what you get for signing on the dotted line without having all the information.

On the outside, the building looked like a modern art

gallery, all glass and stone and steel. Floor-to-ceiling windows lined the exterior, but I couldn't actually see inside. It was some kind of mirroring effect, possibly. *Slick.*

The car deposited me at the massive glass doors, and even though I reached for the door myself, the driver somehow beat me to it. "Is there any point during this adventure where you're actually going to let me open my own door, Tim?"

"Sorry, sir. I know you like to do it yourself, but I can't help it. It's how I've been trained."

"Fair enough," I mumbled. I had to get used to this shit.

I marched up to the front doors, and my phone buzzed. I glanced down at it and saw that Kyle was begging for an update. If at all possible, he was more interested in this whole game of charades than I was. He was the one who'd pushed me to say yes to this job. He was the one who'd insisted the PhilanthroApp could be worked on from anywhere. In the end I was glad he was here, but the last thing I needed was the added pressure. With any luck, I'd get someone I could add to my security detail and be done with it.

I wished to Christ Kyle was the one who looked like a billionaire. The stress was starting to eat at me, and there was still no word from Arlington. Where the fuck was he? And why couldn't I just get through this whole scenario unnoticed and unscathed? Nope, every time I turned around, there was always something else fucking up the whole situation.

Eyes on the prize. Pretend. You're good at that. Be what they need you to be, and everything will be fine. I could do that. I could play the part.

When I stepped inside, the stunning red head from the other night came forward with a smile. "Lord Arlington. It's nice to see you again."

I took her warm, delicate hand. She might have been slender and petite, but her handshake was firm and strong. And her gaze was direct and clear. "You can drop the title. Derrick is fine."

Her brows shot up. "Okay. If you insist, Derrick." Her lips tipped into a smirk. "Pardon me for saying so, but you're different than I was told."

"Oh yeah?" Just what I needed, Arlington's reputation to precede me. "You heard I was a prick?"

Her grin flashed. "Something like that."

I shrugged. "I'll let you be the judge." I tried to remember everything about her from the dossier I'd been given. She and the people who worked for her also worked for the king. They were appointed by Sebastian himself, so if anything went down with the king or his family, they were the ones called.

The research Kyle and I had done indicated they also took care of civilians. To be able to book them, you just needed money. *Lots and lots of money.* And thanks to my expense account, I had that in spades.

"This way. I'll get you set up. Are you feeling okay? I'm sorry, I could only assign one guard last night. It's been a bit busy. With all the dignitaries in town for the wedding, we were slightly short-staffed. But you have our undivided attention now."

Hey, if they were busy, I was more than happy to go home and forget this whole bodyguard thing. Derrick hadn't given me a damn playbook for what to do in case of attempted kidnapping. But something told me doing some shit that would get me scrutinized was not at the top of the list. "Look, Ariel, I'm sure this is a—"

She held up a hand and led me to the conference room.

"Look, I get the impression you're about to tell me this is unnecessary and that you don't need a guard, but let me tell you, I've heard it all before. For whatever reason, you want your privacy and all that. Am I correct?"

She was clairvoyant. "Something like that."

"This is the part where I tell you the king requested this. You know how Sebastian can get. He's very protective of the family, so if something happened at the wedding, then it's our job to make sure it doesn't happen again. Not to mention finding out who made the attempt and making sure they are properly dealt with. Like it or not you're a royal. It makes you a target."

"As I told the, err, Sebastian, I don't really know what happened. A guy approached me, pressed something in my back, and told me it was a gun and he wanted me to get in the car. I've been given enough anti-kidnap training to know never to get in the car." That much was true. I left out the part with the brunette. I left out the part where my attempted kidnapper knew my name. *My real name.*

When in doubt, lie.

Ariel raised a brow. "And you have no idea why someone wanted to kidnap you from the wedding?"

Lie. "None."

Her gaze narrowed. "News of the Inline Tech takeover is all over. Could this be related?"

My instinct said no. This shit felt personal. But again, I couldn't be forthcoming. "My business interests often draw unwanted attention."

"You don't need to worry, Derrick. We're very discreet. It's my duty to protect you. Sebastian made it really clear that he wants nothing that can tarnish the name of the royal family.

We've had some bumps and bruises in the last few years, so discretion is important for the family as well."

"Right. Great. So, we all want discretion. Can't we just agree this is unnecessary?"

Ariel laughed and shook her head. "I don't know what it is with you Winston men, or in your case, Arlington men. How are you guys cousins again?"

I knew the answer to this one, thankfully. "Through the queen mother. She and my father are half-siblings."

"Ah, okay. For starters I'll need an employee list as well as anyone who has been let go or fired in the last eighteen months. I'll also need security access codes for the house and office." She cleared her throat. "If you, uh, have anyone who frequents your home who is not a member of staff, I need that information, too. I don't give two shits about legality and privacy. I only care about your safety."

I frowned, not understanding for a moment. But then I remembered the article I'd seen in the news about Derrick Arlington having been drunk out of his mind with three escorts. "I'll get you what you need."

"Can you think of anyone holding a grudge?"

"Any enemies of mine would more than likely be enemies of my father. They see the blood in the water, maybe. I've only just stepped into his shoes. I haven't had time to make any business enemies yet."

"Give it time. Every day people carry around these insane blood feuds. They get passed down from generation to generation. Full on Capulets and Montagues."

"Well, there's no Romeo and Juliet here. I'm sure you're very straightforward and will probably not take that along to solve this thing. I have a company merger coming up, and I need to make sure it stays on track."

"I understand. Don't worry. All of our agents are trained in undercover work. They'll be discreet and embedded into your life seamlessly. It's our specialty. We'll do two-man shift rotations with one being your personal guard. One will live with you and act as your last line of defense. The others will be posted nearby in your building. Both home and work."

"Even off duty?"

She nodded. "We have worked out several options for your undercover person, however you want to play it. We can get you a new personal assistant, although that makes it tricky for in-home coverage. Does your staff live on the premises or off?"

I ground my teeth. I could kill Derrick for this one. "On."

She shrugged. "Okay, it's fine. That eliminates our options of having one at home and one at work as an assistant, or chef, or something, but we'll figure out a workable scenario."

I glanced at the folder. "What's your least invasive suggestion?"

She nodded, appreciating that I got to the point. "That would be to assign you a guard as your girlfriend. It's even better if she's your assistant *and* girlfriend. It'll make sense as to why she goes home with you and why she's in the office. If you prefer a male guard, we can assign one. Trace Lawson is available for that detail."

I preferred no guard at all. "You choose."

"Fair enough. We'll make this painless. Let me bring in the person who will be running point for you." She pressed a button on the desk phone. "Zia, please join us."

"I'll be right there."

My blood heated, and my brain conjured up an image of the

mouthy brunette from the reception. She was a sassy little thing, determined to harangue my assailant into submission. She wasn't half bad in terms of self-defense.

Small problem, I wanted her. What were the odds this was the same woman?

I pushed to my feet. "Let's get this over with."

Ariel flashed me a grin. "Don't sound so excited. People on my team are the best. They'll take good care of you until the threat is neutralized, and then you can go back to your life."

"The sooner we get this over with, the better." The last thing I wanted was anyone looking too closely into my life.

Zia...

HOURS OF ACTUAL SLEEP: 3.

Hours of attempted sleep, interrupted by tossing-turning dreams of the gray eyed stranger: 4.

Cranky mode: 10.

It was going to be a hell of a day.

It didn't matter how stupidly hot that idiot was. What did I care if he was shoved into someone's trunk and tortured? *There you go again, trying to fix things that don't want to be fixed... save things that don't want to be saved. Stupid loyalty.*

I should have left him alone. Let that crazy guy with the gun kidnap him.

Not that I knew what had happened after I walked away. But hey, none of my concern, right?

I parked my Jeep in my spot at Royal Elite and yawned, keeping my sunglasses in place. It was far too bright, and I'd had too little sleep. I'd woken up and gotten dressed for a workout, but it had been so brutal I'd skipped out and gotten a coffee from my favorite place on the island instead.

Trace was working out on the expansive lawn and he met me with a big grin. "Morning, sunshine."

Just the boom in his voice was enough to send a fissure of pain along my skull. "Yeah, maybe you don't need to shout that?"

He grinned. "Uh-oh, did someone overindulge at the wedding?"

"No, actually, just haven't been sleeping well."

He lifted a brow. "Are you sure you didn't overindulge?"

"When have you ever seen me overindulge.?"

He studied me closely. He couldn't see my eyes, but something must have told him something was up because his brows furrowed. "What's wrong?" He was too damn perceptive.

"Nothing. I'm fine."

"Come on, Barnes. We're a team. If you're upset about something, I should probably be upset about it too."

"Nah, it's all good."

As he followed me, he muttered, "Does it have anything to do with the ex?"

"Damn it, Tamsin." I was going to kill her and her big mouth.

"She mentioned you saw the fucker at the wedding."

"It's fine. I'm *fine*."

"I could shoot him. Nothing fatal of course, but he would know pain. He'll never even know it was me."

I considered that for just a moment too long before I turned to face him. "Just how painful could we make it?"

He gave me a predatory smile and a shrug. "Enough to put a smile on your face."

CHAPTER 5

It really would solve most of my problems. I could then go about my life without worrying that I might see him. "I appreciate the offer, but I'm good. Besides if anyone is going to shoot him, it'll be me." I turned back around and found my way into the building. Jameson met us both with a terse nod. "Unplanned client meeting. Ariel's been in with him for the last hour. From the looks of it, he's VIP. She took the intake meeting herself."

I bit back my inward groan. "Please, God, I cannot handle another movie star."

Behind me, Trace chuckled. "You still scarred from the last one?"

My jaw locked. Brighton Henry. The new 'it' movie star on the rise. And he'd been a complete nightmare. He'd mistaken bodyguard for maid, housekeeper, chef and escort for the three days I'd been assigned to him. And he kept forgetting my name, calling me Zany for the duration. "I call not it."

I marched into the office I shared with Tamsin to the right of the main conference room and tossed my backpack and keys into my drawer. I had just turned on my laptop when my intercom buzzed.

"Zia, please join us."

No. Why did I always end up with the movie star assholes? I felt like Tamsin was long overdue. But instead of complaining, I said, "I'll be right there."

I didn't even have time to take a bite of my pastry. Instead, I grabbed my laptop and phone and headed for the conference room. When my phone buzzed in my hand, one quick glance told me I didn't want to respond.

Deedee: *Where are you? Call me.*

Shit. I'd forgotten to text her back. I'd gotten distracted thinking about Gray Eyes. I'd call her after the meeting.

Through the glass walls of the conference room window, I could see there was a man sitting in the client chair. From the back, despite his relaxed appearance, something about him oozed money. Which meant I'd be minding my Ps and Qs and my mouth.

When I opened the door, the hairs at the back of my neck stood at attention and I frowned. I might not be excited about a new VIP client, but I shouldn't be anxious. I was good at my job. Maybe too good. Which was why some clients thought I should be all things to them. I held back my eye roll.

His hair was inky black, cut short above his collar. Slightly long up top but coifed perfectly. Not a hair out of place. It made me really want to mess them up. The skin on his neck was tan, like he spent time outside and not just in an office. His summer sweater looked soft and comfortable in an off white and azure blue that reminded me of the sand and water on Prince's Beach. His shoulders were broad, causing that patch of fabric between his shoulder blades to pucker ever so slightly.

Ariel gave me a warm smile. "Hey, Zia. Derrick, meet Zia Barnes. She's going to be your new bodyguard."

I gave Ariel a nod and focused my attention on the man in the chair. Strong hands held the edges as he pushed himself to his feet. That little motion. That fluidity. I knew before he turned around exactly who was in my boss's office.

Gray Eyes.

The knowledge didn't stop my breath from catching when his stormy gray eyes met mine. His jaw ticked, and when he spoke, his voice was low. So deep, it was more of a rumble than actual words. "Miss Barnes. It's nice to meet you." Something about the narrowing of his gaze said it was anything *but* nice to meet me.

What the hell was happening here? He hadn't wanted my help the night before. In fact, he'd basically little-womaned me. And now he was in my office looking for a bodyguard?

Ariel gestured for me to take a seat next to Mr. Sex on a Stick. "You'll be his new primary for the next few weeks."

No way. I couldn't do this. "I'm sure Lord Arlington would prefer someone more experienced." Ariel would be pissed. But I couldn't work for him. Day in and day out? No way.

Lady Parts: Speak for yourself.

He shook his head. "Just call me Derrick."

I blinked. Swear to God, Ariel was speaking words. Ones I *should* understand, but they were coming out like jumbled goo. Still, I somehow managed to take my seat, but I couldn't make words, though. Those were too hard.

Ariel didn't seem to notice. "Zia, you'll be the point person. Jameson has the Bouner assignment she's doing background on. Your backups will be Tamsin, Trace and Jax. This will be a three-week undercover assignment."

Undercover. Assignment. Weeks. Slowly, the bits and bobs of disjointed snippets started to make sense. This was work. I had to work. I had to get my shit together. I could do this. I was always the one with the plan. There was always a plan, and I could do this... work with the man that made my insides liquify.

"Understood," I croaked. Damn it. I needed my strong, *I'm a badass* voice right now. "What will the role be? I assume assistant."

Arial nodded, sending her bright red locks over her shoulder. "Yes. But as Mr. Arlington has live-in staff, you'll need to double as his girlfriend too."

She said it so matter of fact, as if she didn't see my underwear incinerating right before her eyes. I dragged in a shuddering breath. "Do we have any indication on the threat?"

Derrick rumbled again. "My company has a high-profile takeover acquisition going on right now. It's not exactly hostile, but it's tense." The timbre of his voice warmed my body. As he and Ariel outlined what his needs would be, I couldn't help but watch his mouth as he spoke. Full, sculpted lips. Insanely chiseled jaw. Cleft on his chin.

It was only after I noticed Ariel watching me expectantly that I realized I'd missed something. Had I been staring? "I'm sorry, what?"

Ariel lifted a brow. "I asked if you can do the background work-up. I have my hands full doing some work for the royal family."

I swallowed hard. "Yes, of course." There was one thing I couldn't figure out. Why hadn't he mentioned he already knew me from the reception? *Why haven't you mentioned it?* I was supposed to be the bodyguard to a damn billionaire playboy?

I must have really pissed someone off in another life. *Whoever you are, I'm sorry. Can we call it even?*

No way did this punishment fit the crime. I might never have seen him before, but I was aware of him. Sexiest man alive, two years running. Cousin to the king. And all-around playboy pain in the ass.

At the wedding, I hadn't known who he was. I didn't pay attention to Forbes or all the investing and tech magazines, but even I knew his name. Derrick Arlington was more than a bloody VIP billionaire. He was a VIP billionaire that someone had tried to kidnap. A billionaire that was now in our office looking for someone to protect him. But why hadn't he let me protect him before?

CHAPTER 5

Through the rest of the meeting, it was a struggle not to stare at him. I could feel the waves of tension rolling off of him. Was he pissed off too?

We covered logistics and schedules and upcoming events I'd have to attend. And we covered discretion. "Zia, you're never to break cover."

I nodded and frowned. "Won't be a problem, but if someone is after him, they'll be looking for an in, so my background story will need to be airtight."

Ariel shook her head. "Not this time. It'll be easier if we keep your life the same. We'll just backstop the last nine months with an admin gig instead of this one. That way anyone looking will find a real person. And let's give you a reason for not staying there for long. Like you're bad at your job. That way no one will be inclined to keep you busy with actual work."

I nodded. "Okay. That'll work." I had nothing to hide. And given my family situation, it would make my life much easier. Not to mention my military background wouldn't set off any alarms. Everyone had to do national service.

Derrick turned to face me, his gaze hard and impassive, his clear gray eyes framed by thick lashes. "Are you sure you can sell this? Everything hinges on you."

I lifted a brow. That was a dare. A challenge, a bait. I gave him a sweet smile then leaned closer to him. I gently a placed a hand on his cheek, crossing into his space. His eyes turned dark gray and stormy as his gaze locked with mine. The zap of electricity sent a potent charge through me. Could he feel it? "Of course I can sell this, Derrick." I made it a point to soften the way I said his name.

His gaze dipped to my lips, and his jaw twitched. His Adam's apple bobbed as he swallowed. My gaze held his as I rolled my shoulders. Then I released him and turned my attention back to Ariel as if he wasn't present.

For a long moment he stared at me.

I shouldn't have done that. I didn't need to prove a point. I knew I was good at this. Ariel didn't say anything, but she raised a brow.

Once we made the final arrangements and Derrick left, Ariel held me back. "Zia, is everything okay with you?"

I forced a smile. "Of course." I cleared my throat. "But maybe Tamsin should—I mean, if maybe I could be tech, or anything really, I can still be of service. But I don't know, the guy rubbed me the wrong way."

"Is there a reason?" Ariel eyed me.

Knowing who he was, I realized that I probably should have reported the incident at the reception. And interestingly enough, since Ariel didn't seem to know about it, that meant that Derrick hadn't reported it either. "No, I just came off assignment, and I was looking for something a little lower profile this time around."

"Sorry. Your profile is still low enough that no one will notice."

I swallowed hard. "Well, what about the guys? Trace, Jax…"

"Well, considering they're men, and neither of them has the tech expertise that might be needed, they don't make good candidates."

"Why does them being men have anything to do with this?"

Ariel pursed her lips, and I could tell she was getting annoyed with me.

"Zia, can you handle this? I didn't miss that exchange. I know he goaded you, but you weren't supposed to rise to the occasion."

I gritted my teeth. "He called my abilities into question."

She sighed then leaned back on her chair. "Derrick Arlington is Sebastian's cousin. Given his profile, this is important. Can you handle yourself and him?" When I didn't answer, she added, "Is there a problem? If there is a reason that you can't do this, I need to know now."

I swallowed hard. Ariel was pretty much everything I wanted to be in this business. I couldn't very well tell her that I'd been having sex dreams about our new client. Nope. That fell under the whole *not a good idea to reveal* kind of thing.

There's no way she would ever take me seriously for any other client again. "Sorry, I'm just a little out of it. Of course, I'll take the assignment." I forced the words past my closing throat.

Ariel studied me closely. "Look, you're not going to be on your own on this. We'll all be right there. But think of this as a personal favor to Sebastian and Penny. Derrick Arlington might not use his title, but he's still family. So we have to give our best for this. Get me?"

I nodded slowly. "Yep, I got it." This job meant everything to me. If I lost it because I let personal things get in the way, then what would I have?

Nothing. You'll have nothing. So, get over yourself and make this happen.

"Okay. Why don't you pack your things? He'll send a car for you."

"Right." Ariel dismissed me, and I headed to my room for a few moments of silence.

But I was too slow. Tamsin was already waiting for me. "Um, are we going to talk about the fact that you are now assigned to the hot fucker from the wedding?"

"Nope. I'm not going to talk about it at all. Everything is fine. Totally fine."

She stared at me. "Please tell me that you didn't run out after him and bone him senseless."

I gulped. "No, I did *not* bone him senseless."

Lady Parts: I would have.

"Because that would explain why you're white as a sheet."

"I'm fine. It's fine. Just didn't expect to see him, that's all."

"You don't want the job? Think of this as your chance to prove yourself. I mean, you keep saying how you really want to impress Ariel. I'm pretty sure if you can keep the king's cousin in one piece, then Ariel will be all kinds of impressed."

"Yeah, I hope so."

She frowned. "You're sure nothing is wrong?"

"Yeah, I'm sure." *Lies.* "It's not like he's my actual boyfriend."

Tamsin laughed. "Is this the part where I remind you that those are the famous last words our own boss basically said herself?"

"Except I know firsthand what happens when you mix business and pleasure. I won't be making that mistake again."

"Okay, listen, if you don't want to do this, I'll switch with you."

"No. I already told Ariel I could do it. It's fine. I've got this. What's the worst that could happen? It's not like there's any danger of me falling for him. He's a dick. All I have to do is make sure I cover his ass. That's easy, right?"

Something told me that it was going to be easier said than done.

SIX

THEO...

I was not watching the clock. I swear I wasn't.

You're absolutely watching the clock.

I was supposed to go pick up my shiny new bodyguard at noon before my round of afternoon meetings. And to say that I was anxious was an understatement. I didn't want this. I was already tense enough trying to be someone else. Having her around was going to be much worse. She'd be next to me the whole time, looking over my shoulder, questioning everything. It was going to be impossible.

You don't have a choice.

The king had seen me, so I had no fucking choice. I was going to kill Zia Barnes. It didn't matter that her dark eyes could see clear to my soul. I didn't want that. I didn't ask for that. I wanted to do this job and get back to my life. But oh no, there she was, interfering in things that were none of her damn business.

Not for nothing, she saved your life.

I decided I was just going to ignore that little note. She'd *probably* absolutely saved my life, because either I could have been shot right there, or I would have been shoved in the trunk, tortured somewhere else, and then shot.

At least my mother was safe. I just hoped I could convince her to stay with my aunt longer. If someone already knew who I was, I needed to get to the bottom of this as soon as possible. Who the fuck were these people and where the hell was Derrick?

I dragged my hands through my hair and forced my attention back to my monitor. But before I could focus, my assistant came in.

"Um, Mr. Arlington, what's this about a new assistant?" The hint of bite abraded the final word.

I frowned up at her. "Yes, Olivia. I have special projects I'll need some additional help with."

She pursed her lips. I wasn't sure why, but she wasn't pleased about the new development. What kind of relationship did she have with Arlington exactly?

The way she was looking at me wasn't sexual. It was more appraising but still somehow possessive. She had closed crop red hair that made her look like a pixie and she was wearing a boxy blazer and some kind of dress thing that was also boxy as if deliberately refusing to show her body. God, was Arlington that much of a fuck up?

Are you really asking that question?

"I get the feeling there is a problem, Olivia, explain."

She blinked rapidly. "It's just I'm in charge of hiring new assistants and you didn't even disclose you had special projects, or I could have picked out the perfect assistant. Honestly I don't even know her qualifica—"

I stopped her there with a raised brow. "Pardon me, Olivia, but let me get this correct. Who is the CEO of Arlington Tech?"

She pursed her lips. "You are."

"Okay, right. And who is ultimately in charge of hiring?"

The lines around her mouth only deepened. "You are, but as you know, I worked for your father before you and I know what's necessary to run—"

Again, I stopped her. "I think you're under the mistaken impression you still work for my father. Let me remind you he was ousted by the board for conduct unbecoming a CEO."

She didn't flinch as she met my gaze. "That might be but you really don't understand the inner workings of the day-to-day administration operations."

I lifted a brow. "Do I write your check so to speak?"

"I—yes."

"Do you follow my direction?"

"Well, yes, but—"

I didn't let her finish. "So in essence if I told you I wanted to hire a purple unicorn for the accounting team tomorrow, whose decision is that to make?"

Her gaze narrowed and I could tell this was going to be painful for her to admit. "You, sir. But the way your father and I worked..."

Her voice trailed off when I clenched my jaw, communicating to her exactly what I thought of my father. "So, for the last six months have you been working for him or for me?"

"You, but as you were transitioning, your father and I felt that it would be easier if I still went to him for key decisions."

Oh, did they?

"Well, lucky for you. I'm caught up. That ends now. If you

have a problem with that, let's go ahead and get you reassigned. In the meantime, Zia Barnes starts working here tomorrow. I'll be giving her direct instructions."

"I'll just bet you will," she muttered under her breath as she gave me a tight nod.

"It's funny; I couldn't hear your last comment."

She gave me a forced smile that was more a baring of teeth. "I just said I'll be of any service to you that you need with her."

I gave her a smile that told her I'd heard her message loud and clear. She was Timothy Arlington's person and she was just waiting for me to crash and burn. "Fantastic. I think we'll all get along great. We're all good here?"

Zia Barnes is going to eat her for dinner.

"Yes of course. You're the CEO, you can hire who you want."

"Thank you."

She nodded and backed out of the office. Before she even closed the door, Timothy Arlington barged in. "Just what the fuck do you think you're doing?"

I lifted my brows. "What do you mean?"

"You're off book ,boy."

I lifted my brow as I pushed to my feet. "You'll have to refresh my memory. What's your problem today?"

"You've been pulling all the financials for Inline? For what purpose? This deal has nothing to do with you. You just have to sit back and watch it happen."

I couldn't help it; I laughed. "Am I the only one who realizes I'm the CEO here? What's the problem dad?" I tried to inject unaffected disdain into my voice.

"What's the problem? You're running around here like you own the joint."

CHAPTER 6

Again, I couldn't stifle a laugh. "Um, forgive me if I'm wrong, but don't I own the joint?"

He lifted a single brow. "Don't get cocky with me, boy. You and I both know that you're not qualified to run this place. And that was our agreement. When I put you in charge, I would still be running things. You're simply not qualified."

I crossed my arms and leaned back in my seat. "Here is the thing. I've been thinking that since the Board ousted you and forced you to hire a replacement, maybe you shouldn't be running things after all. If my name is on the building, so to speak, and I'm responsible for all of it, what if I did my own thinking?"

His eyes went wide. "Are you out of your fucking mind?"

I was. I was out of my whole damn mind. There were still pieces of this company I didn't understand, areas where I probably didn't have the full lay of the land, but I was getting caught up to speed quickly. Arlington Tech was one of the best tech conglomerates in the hemisphere. Far-reaching. But there were flagships that this company was built on. And if I focused there, where the bulk of our money came from, I might be able to hold down the fort until the real Derrick came back.

"What's the problem? That I'm actually taking an interest, or that I'm not doing as I'm told?"

"Both. We would both be perfectly fine if you were the same fuck-up you've always been. What has gotten into you? You think you can run things?"

"Well, the board seems to think I can run things. They gave me a vote of confidence last week."

"That's because they don't *know* you. You haven't got the chops. Leave Inline Tech alone."

"Well, maybe you underestimate me." I spread my arms.

"Isn't this what you wanted? I'm actually trying to do what's best for the company."

"You have always been concerned about your own self-interest. And that's who you are. You've never changed. Why would you start now?"

"Well, maybe if you actually give me a shot, if you could give me an opportunity to actually learn, I could do something good."

"So what, you're going to experiment with my company? Over my dead fucking body."

"The thing is Dad, it's already a done deal. I'm already sitting in this chair, not you."

He jabbed a finger toward my chest. "I swear to God you *will* fall into line."

I knew what the right response would be, but somehow I couldn't force myself to say it. I stared up into the face that was similar enough to mine to cause someone to do a double take.

I knew this man wasn't *my* father. I'd never actually met the bum, but there were pictures of him around the house. Mom said he'd been some kind of actor or something. She never gave me his name, but we had the same kind of gray eyes, same structure of the face, even if I didn't look exactly like him. Hell, he could have been Timothy Arlington's brother, for all I knew.

As he spoke, Arlington leaned in real close. "You will fall into line. I don't want any more fucking surprises. Stop trying to derail the Inline deal. Do you understand me?"

I nodded slowly. "Sorry, Dad. I'll run everything by you. But I'm still going to poke at the deal to make sure it's air tight."

"Now is not the time to pretend to give a fuck. You can go back to your drinking and whoring. I prefer that version of you anyway."

"Why, because that version of me can be controlled? I'm

pretty sure I told you, I didn't want this. But since you insisted that I have it, I'm actually going to do my job. Now, if you'll excuse me, I have work to do."

His face flamed red, starting at his neck and spreading like an insidious virus until the tip of his ears went crimson. "Don't make me your enemy, son. It won't end well. This is my company, my legacy. I was too soft on you growing up. I won't make the same mistake twice. You fuck with this deal, and I will kill you with my bare fucking hands."

Fantastic. I'd made an enemy out of Timothy Arlington.

♛

Zia...

I SCOWLED at Derrick as I carried my bag out of Royal Elite. "So, you didn't tell Ariel why we aren't a good match?"

He smirked down at me. I hated that he was able to look down on me. "I told her what I needed. I didn't have to explain why."

"You recognize Royal Elite is an established and respected agency, right? This isn't a game."

"What game? All you need to know is that you've been assigned to me, and your whole job means me staying alive, right?"

My brows lifted. "Didn't you request me?"

"I didn't. You were assigned. Karma's cruel joke, I suppose. If you have seen the papers at all, you know I have a type. Petite. Brunette. Fit."

"You know this won't work."

"Well, it has to work. I gather from what I saw in the

meeting with Ariel that you want to impress your boss. And I get it. She returned the lost princess. She saved the exiled prince. She's a badass. You don't want to look like an idiot in front of her."

I clamped my jaw shut. "Doing a good job is important to me, regardless of who my boss is. When I was finished packing my stuff, I did my own research on you, *Lord* Arlington. Up until now you've been content to party on yachts and screw anything that moves. Now you're the big bad billionaire tech guru?"

He grinned down at me then. "Oh, come on now. I won't screw *anything* that moves. I'm pretty sure I have standards. A quick glance at the internet told you all that?"

I shrugged. "You'd be amazed what you can learn. What was your deal on Saturday? Tell me why you were about to get in that car. Surely you know that would mean certain torture."

He shook his head. "We're not talking about that." As we approached my car, he shook his head. "You're not driving."

I blinked at him. "Well, how are we going to get there?"

He inclined his head toward the black sedan at the edge of our long drive. With one nod from Derrick, the car turned in for us. As it approached, my brows lifted. It was a Maserati. Slick, black and elegant just like a panther. The driver pulled up and stepped out of the car, nodding at Derrick. "Mr. Arlington." Then he smiled down at me. "Miss Barnes."

I frowned. "How did you know my name?"

"That's Tim. It's his job to know. And while you were getting your things, I told him."

I rolled my eyes. "Look, I know you want to play fifty shades of billionaire or whatever. I'm not into that alpha bullshit. Let's

CHAPTER 6

just get this job done. I can drive my own car to wherever we'll be staying."

He exhaled deeply as if fighting exasperation. "You forget, we need to make this, *us,* look real, and this is how it will look real. My beautiful girlfriend, dressed to the nines, riding with me and not driving herself to wherever we're going."

"You realize that's sexist, right? Why can't I drive *you?*"

He shrugged. "I didn't make the rules. I'm just well aware of the optics and public perception."

Tim took my bag to the trunk, and Derrick held the door open for me. I didn't really have much choice. I knew that Ariel was counting on me. The team was counting on me. At the end of the day, my loyalty was to them. So that meant getting my butt in gear and getting this job done, whether I liked the client or not.

This wasn't a man who was concerned for his safety. Or maybe he was all about the facade. But there was something about him that didn't quite jive with the cocky billionaire I'd read about. I just didn't know what it was yet.

I pressed myself up against the door, putting as much distance between Derrick and myself as possible. I could still feel it. That intense hum of connection between us that I had noticed at the wedding. But I could ignore that. I *would* ignore it.

He was playing some kind of game, and I was a pawn. So, I had to figure out what the hell was going on and quickly. Then I'd go to my team.

Another flash of teeth made him look every bit the rogue I'd read about. "You're a handful. I think I like you."

The car slowed through traffic and pulled off to the right. I glanced up. "Is this where you live? Is this your office building?"

There weren't many skyscrapers in the Winston Isles. Honestly, just a cluster of tech and financial institutions at the heart of what was called King's City. It only really encompassed a ten-block radius. Everywhere else, there were laws protecting the views, so beyond that cluster, there was nothing else so metropolitan. And Derrick Arlington owned the one we were staring at.

"This is where I live. The Penthouse."

I stared at him. "Of course. You recognize that you're going to have to communicate with me better, right? I can't protect you if I don't know what we're doing and where we're going."

He frowned. "It's not always going to be possible."

"I hate to break it to you, but *you* hired Royal Elite, which means you need to let me do my job."

He pursed his lips. "Fine. *Lady* Zia."

I rolled my eyes. "If you're not using your title, I'm not using mine."

His brows furrowed. "How did you become a King's Knight anyway?"

"It was a package deal. The team and I came with Ariel."

When I stepped out of the car, I was sorry I'd worn my blazer over my sundress. It was so damn hot. I shrugged it off and was glad my sundress had pockets so I could avoid wearing a holster.

We went around to Derrick's side of the car, and Tim held the door for him. When Derrick stepped out, he had a brilliant smile for me. He took my hand, and I had to resist the urge to shake him off. His lips twisted into a bemused smirk as he saw what I was doing. God, the guy was such a prick.

"Oh, ease up, Lady Zia, we're only going inside to the lobby. You only have to touch me for a matter of seconds."

"Thank God. But it's easier to do my job if my hands are free."

He pressed his lips tightly together then. He nodded and then threw an arm around me instead. If it was possible, that was worse. The movement brought me closer into contact with him. His smell, something musky and intoxicating, made me want to lean in and inhale. His warmth chased away the perpetual chill in my bones.

"Let's make this quick. The sooner we get the lay of the land and we can outline the perimeters, the sooner—"

From behind us, a voice called out, "Zia?"

Garrett.

My back stiffened. *No. No, not now.* I didn't need this now. I was not prepared. I didn't have a speech. Well, at least I looked good. But still... I tried to just keep moving because, yes, I was a coward, and I was looking for a pillar to hide behind. But Derrick, the turdface, stopped, forcing me to a halt.

His gaze was inquisitive. "Sweetheart, do you know him?"

I frowned up at him. "Sweetheart? What the—" And then it occurred to me. He'd seen me hide from Garrett at the wedding. He'd been watching. Those eyes on me that I'd only noticed later... Derrick Arlington was the reason for them. He'd seen me crawl between two pillars and legitimately hide from my ex-fiancé. Oh, this was the worst kind of hell. "Uh, yes."

Garrett approached with a smile. "I thought that was you. Did I see you at the wedding too? I was going to come over and say hello, but I didn't have an opportunity. I wanted you to meet my wife."

As he approached, he frowned. As if it had only just occurred to him that I was with someone. "Oh! Uh, I'm sorry, I didn't mean to interrupt. I'm Garrett."

Derrick glanced down at his hand and glanced down at me. And then he just nodded at him. "Derrick Arlington."

Garrett's eyes went wide. "You're Derrick Arlington? The billionaire? No shit."

Well, well. Garrett kept his hand out to shake, but Derrick just lifted a brow. I might not like him. He might be a pain in the ass, but in that moment, he was giving me life.

Garrett turned his attention back to me. "I must have missed you at the wedding. I was quite busy. I just wanted to say hi. It's been a long time."

"Yeah, I guess it has." And because I could, and because he had given me the platform to do it, I leaned into Derrick's side. "Sweetheart, we really need to go. I know you wanted to get back to the flat."

Derrick knew exactly what I was doing, and he was playing along. He pulled me closer to him. He leaned down, his lips approaching mine.

Holy hell, he was going to kiss me. Heat enveloped me, and suddenly I couldn't breathe. What was I supposed to do? He gave me one of those patented killer smirks, and swear to God my pussy clenched.

He leaned close, and I held my breath. He was going to kiss me. He really was. He was going to—

Instead of kissing me, he bypassed my lips and nuzzled my neck. His lips were a gentle graze as he... holy shit, was he smelling me? His thumb grazed over my cheek as he whispered into my skin. "Try to not to look like you want to punch me, and we'll sell this better."

It's not real. It's not real. It's not real. But good luck telling my body that.

CHAPTER 6

He pulled back, and sure enough, I had forgotten how to breathe.

I. Could. Not. Move.

Meanwhile, Garrett's brows furrowed. "You two are together?"

Derrick grinned and kept his gaze on mine. "Of course. She had this whole thing in her head about how she no longer wanted to date assholes. Then along I came and got lucky."

I should have stepped in to defuse the situation, but no. This was awesome. All kinds of awesome. Also, I was pretty sure my knees didn't work anymore.

Garrett's brow really furrowed then. "Wait, how long have you two been together?"

I opened my mouth to answer but Derrick beat me to it. "Not long. But when I see what I want, I go after it. It happened so quickly. You know that spark... When something is right, you feel it. You know it in your bones. I couldn't stay away from her. Zia, love, you're right, we do need to get going."

Garrett turned bright red then. "Zia, I—" He seemed to have forgotten anything he might have had to say and shook his head. And then he started again. "Well, maybe we can catch up soon. I know you're at the palace sometimes. Maybe look me up and give me a call. We can have lunch."

I shrugged. "Well, right now Derrick is keeping me quite busy, but if I'm at the palace and I have any time, I'll let you know."

Derrick grinned then. A grin that I'd started to associate with being his evil grin.

You've known the guy for like five minutes, and you can already tell which smiles he's using.

"Oh, you know my cousin Sebastian?"

Garrett blinked again and then he bowed low. "My Lord, I didn't know."

Derrick waved his hand. "No, it's fine. I don't really use my title, ever. Too pretentious. And in the world of business, you can't stand on ceremony. Well, anyway, it was good to meet you."

And with that, Derrick led me inside, leaving my ex staring after us.

Theo...

IN THE CAR, Zia had sat as far away as she could from me without physically being outside.

But now she was close... so close. Her hair smelled like coconut and hibiscus. The skin on her bare neck was satiny soft. I couldn't help but run my thumb over the softness of her cheek. Just that little motion was enough to make my head spin. Inhaling had been a big mistake.

Sniffing her was like getting a hit of my drug of choice.

Newsflash, asshole, stop touching her. She can bring the house of cards down around you.

I swallowed hard and released her, despite every nerve ending telling me to keep holding her tight.

I didn't know what the hell I was doing. It was okay to admit that, right? I couldn't have her. After all, there was that little matter of me impersonating a local celebrity. Oh, and I'd taken over his life. Not a problem at all.

Get it together.

I had to get my mind right and *never* touch her again.

When I backed away from temptation, she narrowed her gaze at me. "You didn't have to do that."

Oh, she thought I'd done that for that asshole's benefit? Sure, we'd go with that. I shrugged. "Well, he was being an asshole. I'd have done it for anyone. But it helps the narrative that you've moved on."

She didn't look like she quite believed me. "You are different than I expected."

"How's that?" Another reminder that I was failing at rule number three.

"I don't know. There's something off about you. You're nicer than I thought."

I chose to ignore that and led her to the private elevator that would take us to the penthouse. "Come on, let's go."

"So, where exactly will I be staying?" she asked me.

"In the penthouse with me. Where else?"

"And is there a bedroom close by yours? I need to know the lay of the land, how accessible your room is, those kinds of things."

I wasn't sure why I was annoyed that she wasn't worried about *me* but rather about my safety. "Yes, there's a bedroom right next to mine. But you'll be staying with me."

She stopped short, forcing poor Tim to practically run into her back. "Excuse me? Exactly how did you think this was going to work?"

I stopped in the middle of the lobby. "You stay with me, cover my ass, and make sure I don't get dead. How hard is that?"

Zia crossed her arms over her chest and stared at me. I swear to God it took all my efforts to not look down. I nearly congratulated myself that I was so strong.

"I'm not sleeping with you."

I frowned down at her. "What?" As much as I wished touching her was in the cards, I wasn't an idiot. I wasn't going there. She thought I was someone else.

"Your reputation precedes you."

"Let me make it real clear for you, I prefer my women willing and less harpy-like, so you're safe. I have zero intention of sleeping with you."

"But you still expect me to actually share your bedroom?"

I rolled my shoulders. "Look, I have staff. Lots of staff, and I'm not sure which of them I can trust. The last thing I need is for one of them to make a comment to the press or to anyone on the board before our acquisition of Inline. I need utmost secrecy. Either you can do this, or you can't. I won't put a hand on you. If you can't see this through, I'll call Ariel and get someone who can."

She pursed her lips. I could see it. She didn't like not meeting a challenge. But she was suspicious. And I'd have to watch her, because if I wasn't careful, then she would unravel this whole thing. "Are you satisfied? Can we get this show on the road?"

"You expect me to sleep in your bed?"

I rolled my eyes. "You're a real a pain in the ass, you know that? I'll take the couch; you can have the bed."

"Oh, be still my heart. Chivalry isn't dead."

I couldn't help it. A smile tugged at my lips. But I battened down the hatches because I didn't think Derrick would be the kind to laugh at that. I had seen him as the broody, asshole billionaire. I could pull that off, sort of. I just had to think about doing the exact opposite of what I would do and do that instead.

"Now if you're done being a brat, can we go upstairs?"

I led the way to the private elevator and showed her the key lock, fingerprint scanner, and her badge. She would need all three to get in. I didn't think it would be a problem.

"Do you have a gun safe?" She asked as we stepped into the elevator.

I blinked down at her. "A what?"

"A gun safe. If you have staff that lives there, I'm going to need to keep things secure but accessible."

"No, I don't have a gun safe, but I do have a regular safe in the office."

"Do you have one in the bedroom?"

I had no idea. I hadn't gone exploring. I had access to the safe in the office because Derrick told me there was cash in there, but I wasn't sure about the bedroom. And I certainly couldn't go looking now with her there. "How about I have one installed? Will that suffice?"

She gave me a brisk nod, and then the elevator rocketed us up to the penthouse. When we stepped out, she gasped at the view from the glass walls that surrounded us, taking in the magnificent vistas of the island. "Jesus Christ, you can see Princess Island from here."

I nodded. "Yeah. It stunned me the first time I saw it too."

She lifted a brow. "I'm sorry, but didn't you grow up in the big mansion on Knob Hill? This view must be nothing to you."

I nodded. Derrick had grown up there. She was right.

She took it all in, and I let her know that Tim would bring up her bag later. I wanted to get her settled as quickly as possible. As we stepped out onto the marble floor, I could tell that she was taking it all in. The expensive glass, chrome, steel, the artwork on the walls...

Take it all in, none of it is mine.

"This is... wow."

I shrugged. "Yeah, I guess."

"You're so cavalier. God, I feel like if I lived here, I would be staring at my artwork every day."

"You get to a point where you sometimes don't notice the things that matter."

"Isn't that a shame," she muttered.

I led the way down to the master bedroom, so she would at least know where she'd be staying. When I opened the door, she coughed. "Jesus. This is bigger than my old flat."

It was huge. The bed was massive. There were two bathrooms too.

"Okay, bed's yours. I'll take the couch."

She marched over and put her shoulder bag down next to it. "The bed is wasted on me." She eyed me up and down. "You're huge. You need the bed."

I rolled my eyes. I took the bag and planted it near the bed.

She shook her head. "No, I'll take the couch."

"I'm not so much of a dick that I'm willing to take the bed while you tuck yourself on that couch."

She narrowed her gaze and cocked her head. The move sent a shot straight to my dick. "I do dig the chivalry, I really do. That's cute. But I'm rational, and you're being ridiculous." She laughed. "And seriously, you want me between you and the door, so it's really the best place for me to be."

"Are you always this stubborn?"

"Yes. You should know that. Though, you're even more stubborn than I am."

"Oh boy, I get the feeling this is going to be a very long couple of weeks."

'Probably. Hope you're ready."

CHAPTER 6

"At this point, I don't really have a choice. We're stuck with each other."

"When you say it like that, it sounds like you're not looking forward to it."

My body, despite my mind overruling it, wanted to scream out, 'Oh, we're looking forward to this all right.'

SEVEN

ZIA...

I honestly didn't think I'd be able to sleep. But the moment my head hit the pillow it was lights out. It wasn't until morning that I realized Derrick was deadly serious about his live-in staff.

My ears registered movements in the hallway first. Subconsciously, I palmed my gun under my pillow without even thinking about it. I would need to get used to this new arrangement because I couldn't have myself caught off guard and accidentally shoot the man I was meant to protect.

When I realized that the footsteps were coming closer and accompanied by a whirling hum, I launched myself out of bed.

I dragged the pillow, sheets, and blanket with me to the empty side of the bed. I tossed them in a closet and dove into the bed. Derrick woke the moment I landed, and he rolled me until I was under him.

His eyes were sleepy. "What's wrong?" he croaked, his voice still heavy with sleep.

"Someone's coming," I whispered back.

His rock-hard muscle surrounded me, trapping me. His

scent hit me first, and I breathed deep. A delicious musky, woodsy scent. God, why did he smell so damn good? And not for nothing, Mr. Billionaire, wasn't soft. He was no paper pusher. He was all firm muscle and quick reflexes.

A low growl registered from deep in his chest, and I sucked in a sharp breath. The spike of heat pierced me low in my belly. I didn't have time to react. I didn't have time to ring all the what-the-fuck alarms. I had nanoseconds.

Like it or not someone was coming through the door at any moment, so I had to sell it. I looped my arms around his neck, pulled him down close.

For a moment, he held himself perfectly still.

Frozen.

But then he his gaze narrowed and dipped to my lips. Then with a low growl, he slanted his lips over mine, giving me the kind of kiss I'd read about in books.

Derrick shoved his hand in my hair and angled my head, his lips claiming me with each tongue stroke. And I. Was. Lost.

I arched into his chest, unfortunately bringing my hips in direct contact with his early morning wood.

We both hissed. He groaned a curse. Mine was more of a whimpering moan. I knew what words were, I just couldn't find any in the moment.

God, get yourself together, Barnes.

With a muffled groan, he slid a hand under me, cupped my ass, then shifted me just right so that his dick nestled against my cleft. Electric heat lit me up from the inside. Each roll of his hips delicious and forbidden in a way that made dry humping so fun as a teenager.

I didn't mean to arch into him. I really didn't. But the man was pure sin with his mouth. And I didn't mean to tug his hair.

Because if I'd known about the intense heat that would pulse at my core once I did that, I'd have never considered it. If I'd known his hips would rock into mine, teasing me enough to give me vivid dreams for weeks about his skill in the sack, I would have stayed on the couch.

But it was too late for such things. Because now I knew. And knowing wasn't even half the battle. It was only the beginning of the war I'd have to wage with myself for the rest of the time I'd guard him.

In that moment, time stood still. It could have been hours I spent kissing him or seconds. However long it was, we were eventually interrupted.

Someone walked in and tut-tutted around, speaking in a language I didn't understand. It sounded Eastern European. She went to the blackout window control and pushed it.

Derrick groaned as he ripped his lips from mine. "Elena. A little privacy, please."

She wasn't even phased. "Oh, you're still in bed? At this hour?"

Derrick's voice was deep. Growly. "I'm not *alone*."

She glanced over to the bed but didn't pause her movements.

"Zia, Elena. Elena, this is Zia. She's my girlfriend."

Elena eyed me up and down. I could tell from her silence that she found me lacking. "Tsk. You did not tell me we'd have a guest. I'm not prepared. I don't have enough breakfast."

Derrick sighed. "Elena, there's more than enough food. Just tell Chef—"

"You tell Chef. You wake up and go and tell him."

"Christ, do I work for you, or do you work for me?"

She pointed a finger at him. "You watch your tone with me. I raised you."

He rolled off me with a grumble. "Yes, a fact of which you remind me dozens of times a day, it seems."

I'd expected him to go full billionaire-crazy at her lack of respect, but he didn't. He almost... indulged her?

"Elena, please do me the favor and tell Chef we have an additional person for breakfast and she'll be staying awhile."

Elena's brows drew up as she eyed me again. And this time it was like she was really seeing me, not just as the flavor of the night like she'd thought a moment ago. But as a prospect? A threat?

Even as I clutched the sheet to myself, she tsked. "You know you'll hold on to a man better with lingerie, not flannel."

My jaw unhinged. I slid my gaze over to Derrick who rolled over and laughed into the pillow. "She's not wrong," he chortled.

"If I were you, I would shut up," I sniffed. My flannel bottoms had kept me cozy. He could suck it.

He can suck other things too.

No. Hell no. Never mind the tingle in my lips. Or the heat still pulsing in pinpoints over my clit. Those things were just chemistry magnified because no one had kissed me in a while. *Oh yeah, what about the nuzzling downstairs?*

Whatever the fuck that was. Okay fine, that had momentarily stunned me, but he was a good kisser. So what? That changed nothing.

He shrugged, but his shoulders kept shaking because he was laughing at me.

Elena stood in front of us. "Bring your things. I'll iron and hang them." She had zero qualms that I was in bed with her boss. She was like somebody's mom with no filter and who had never had any fucks to give to begin with.

"Oh, that's not necessary. I can iron and hang my own things."

She lifted a brow. "Bring your things, I said."

No way was I letting her shuffle through my things. I gave her a sweet smile. At least that's the smile I was going for. "Okay, let me guess, you're used to doing everything around here?"

She gave me a brisk nod. "Yes. Your things I hang and clean. If you're staying and you're good for my boy, then I'll be good for you."

Her boy? Derrick was a full-grown man. Why did he need looking after? And this woman was intrusive. We could have been having sex in here for God's sake.

You wish.

No, I don't.

Oh yes, you do.

"Look, I, uh, don't need looking after. Honestly, I can take care of myself. I'll handle my own things."

She crossed her arms and stood there as if waiting for something. For Christ's sake, I could be naked from the waist down, and Derrick was in just boxers. And she was pulling a battle axe routine? "Okay, how about we compromise? I will lay out the things that I might need laundered, dry cleaned, or ironed. Does that work? I'll do it after I officially wake up."

She gave me another brisk nod and marched out the door. Derrick, the moron, was still laughing when the door clicked behind her. "I did try to warn you about the staff."

"I feel like you could have been more forthcoming with that information. She isn't just a live-in staff member. She's a full-time mommy."

"She has devised all manner of ways to get me the hell out of bed."

I glanced at the clock. A quarter to six. "Jesus Christ, the ocean isn't even awake yet."

"Tell me about it," he grumbled.

"And what if you were busy in here?"

He pulled the pillow down and slid his sleepy, hooded gaze over my body. The warmth crept in through the center of my chest and spread out, making my extremities tingle. "Well, then I would have locked the door with a deadbolt. Since that would have been a fire hazard when we were sleeping, I didn't want to do that. But if I really want her kept out, I can do that."

"Oh, okay. Well, that's good to know. You obviously won't be needing a deadbolt."

A smirk tilted his lips. "Of course not. Like I said, willing and not prickly. You fit none of those criteria."

She rolled her eyes. "Whatever. I'm going to get ready."

"Oh, and Zia, next time you want a kiss, all you have to do is ask nicely."

Arrogant ass. I gave him a barking laugh and sweet, sweet dimples. I knew the effects of my dimples. "You are so full of yourself. It's never going to happen. We can put money on that."

He shrugged. "Okay. We'll see. See you in a few, sweet cheeks."

"If you call me sweet cheeks again, I'll shoot you."

Very deliberately, he gave me a smirk. "Sweet cheeks!" And then I turned and walked away. I could practically feel his glare on my back.

God, why was this the most fun I'd had in months?

Theo...

THIS WAS A MISTAKE. All of this was a huge bloody mistake. My first mistake had been taking the gig, but hey, where the hell else was I going to get two million dollars?

The next mistake had been leaving the wedding reception. If I'd stayed put, and hadn't been so concerned with exposure, nothing would have happened.

They might have hurt your mother.

That had been the real risk. They'd played on my fear. Which meant they knew enough about me to be dangerous. Just thinking about that threat made my hands curl into fists. But I'd talked to her, and she wasn't even home.

If I'd stayed put, I never would have run into Zia or the king, and I wouldn't currently have the sexiest woman I'd ever seen sleeping mere feet from me and posing as my girlfriend. She wouldn't be driving me mad or making me conjure fantasies about that little moaning sound she made. I wouldn't have grabbed her ass and instantly become obsessed with squeezing it, biting it, spanking it, licking it. Worse, I wouldn't have been forced to ride into the office with her this morning while she primly sat with her tan trench coat knotted tight, concealing the deceptively prim white dress she was wearing.

The thing came to her knees and had sleeves, but it was the way it draped and shifted when she moved that made it so incredibly sexy. She'd come out of the bathroom wearing it this morning, and I'd just about swallowed my tongue. Then she'd covered my wet dream come to life with her coat and hadn't removed it right away when we'd come in.

Not that I gave a shit. It was her dress, and she could wear what she wanted.

Except if she brushes against you one more time, you're going to take your ass fantasy a step further.

Fuuuck. I needed to stop. Just stop. Should be easy. I didn't even know her, and she sure as shit wasn't a fan of me.

Oh yeah, those sounds this morning were her protestations.

My dick swelled in tacit agreement with my ticked-off libido. She'd jumped into bed, and I'd simply responded. I couldn't be held responsible for the monster erection that refused to go away. This was all her fault.

Uh-huh.

There was a knock at my door, and I barked out, "What?"

Zia appeared in the doorway, hand on her hip, framing her lithe form, and I nearly growled with the feral need to tear that fucking dress off. It hugged her curves, and the white color kissed her bronze skin. The material skimmed everywhere it should. Enticing. Teasing. All I knew was I wanted to rip that thing off with my teeth.

"Kyle Winters is here."

I nodded. "Send him in."

She stepped aside, allowing Kyle passage into my office. My idiot best friend gave her an appreciative gaze from head to toe. And then his gaze snapped to mine. The motherfucker had committed her image to his spank bank, I could tell. And I wanted to rip his throat out for it.

"Mr. Arlington, would you like me to take notes for your meeting?"

I scowled at her. Zia was still standing there as if she was waiting for some kind of introduction. So Kyle could stare at her some more? *Not going to happen sweetheart.*

"No. This meeting is private."

I expected a snappy come back or something to indicate

how she planned to make me pay for it later. But instead, she rolled her eyes and closed the door behind her.

Kyle whistled low. "Jesus. She's...Wow."

I growled at him. "Yeah, that's her."

He held up his hands as if in peace, but then added, "Just so you know, she can cuff me anytime."

I glowered at him and angled my head toward my balcony. Since my secret was already out, I wanted to take all the precautions possible. With the sounds of the city below us, it would be more difficult to listen in on our conversation.

Kyle followed me, shaking his head as he walked. "If I didn't know better, man... You are him."

I knew what he meant. I forced my scowl to loosen. "Don't get caught up in it. None of this shit is real."

"I know, but it's like that movie *Sliding Doors*. This is what you would have looked like if I hadn't fucked up your life."

I clenched my jaw. My choices to follow him had been my own. We were a package deal. I'd never regretted walking away.

Are you sure about that?

"I have the life I'm supposed to have." I quickly changed the subject. I didn't expect Zia to be content staying in her office for long. "Did you get my text earlier? I'm clearly missing something between Derrick and the old man."

Kyle nodded. "I'm still looking. But it's not a secret there's no love lost. The rumor mill says that the elder thought he'd be able to control his son." He lifted a hand in my direction. "Clearly that plan went tits-up. You think he's behind the kidnap attempt?"

I rubbed my jaw. "It's possible, but it didn't feel that way. It felt like he hated me. Me as in Derrick. Not like he knew I was an imposter. But I'm not sure. Keep digging. Something is up with this merger with Inline. He's angrier than a grizzly that I'm asking questions."

"I will. But listen, anytime you think it's getting too hot, we gotta bail, okay?" He glanced around. "This isn't one of those noble times and causes things. These people don't need you to save them. They don't need any version of you. For once, if shit goes bad, think of yourself. Your mom will be okay. *We* will be okay."

I hated that he knew me so well. "I'm fine. It's under control for the time being."

He sighed. "And you're not going to listen to me. Fine. But watch your back. In the meantime, have you heard from your benefactor?"

I shook my head. "Radio silence, and it's got me worried."

Kyle jammed his hands in his pockets and glanced out over the cityscape. "It's not too late to back out. We could be gone tomorrow."

He's right. You could be.

"Nope, I'm going to find out who put a gun to my back first."

He sighed then pinched the bridge of his nose. "Okay. In that case, get another ally. We're in the abyss here, and it's only going to get more dangerous. I think the safest bet is Brian Cohen. He seems to hate Derrick's father almost as much as Derrick does."

Brian had been more than forthcoming and seemed to be in Derrick's corner. But it was too risky. Someone out there already knew our secret and had been ready to kidnap me for it. "No, let's keep it between us for the time being. Just see what you can find on your own."

My best friend gave me the same smile that he'd been giving me since we were kids. Full of hope. His sidekick smile, he called it. "Okay, then you need to perfect your act. Until we have more information, or I talk you into leaving, you just have to *be* him. You can't afford to fuck up. You need to *be* him. Including how you act with her. You're not Theo, you're Derrick. How would Derrick treat her?"

"I'm working on it." He was totally right. I had to respond to her how Derrick would. Not how *I* wanted to.

"Well, work harder. If you want to stay, you better be going for that Oscar."

When Kyle left, Zia popped in. "Who is that guy again?"

I watched her warily. "That's Kyle Winters. I'm having him do an audit of the company we're acquiring." The lie rolled smoothly off my tongue.

"Wait, if you're already acquiring it, shouldn't you have already done your research?"

"Yeah, we should have. But lately, I've gotten the feeling people are sloppy. So, Kyle is just going to double check their work."

She narrowed her gaze at me. "Is there something you're not telling me?"

A smile tugged at my lips. "A lot actually."

She rolled her eyes. "Listen, if you want this to be discreet, I really do need to be in these meetings. What if he was behind your kidnapping?"

I almost laughed. "He would never."

"Yeah, so says you. But people do anything for power and money. *Anything*. Everyone is a suspect."

I lifted a brow. "Are you always this intense?"

"Oh, you know just when I'm trying to save your life."

"One time you saved my life. *One*. And I'm getting the impression you're not going to let me forget it."

"Nope. Especially if you keep fighting the arrangement. There is no Kyle Winters on the employee roster. If you're hiring outside consultants, we'll need to vet them."

I met her gaze. Beautiful or not, she was going to be a giant pain in the ass. But Christ, I liked her spark. "I'll give you the contract file I have for him." We'd backstopped his ID. I just prayed it would hold.

"See, this is what team work looks like," she said as she sashayed out.

When she was gone, I scrubbed a hand over my face. Kyle's ID had better hold.

Or she's going to find out who you really are.

EIGHT

ZIA...

As it turned out, pretending to be a shitty assistant wasn't that hard.

In the end, I just had to remember my sister in every temp job she'd ever had and just do that. I was supposed to stay as close to Derrick as possible while not actually letting daily drudgery of the work interfere. It was one hell of a balance.

It was easy enough to suck at this job. And in hindsight I could see why Deedee had been so frustrated.

I wasn't exactly the *go get coffee* girl. I was the *hack into someone's bank account and see where the infusions of cash came from* girl. I was self-taught when it came to hacking and coding and software programming. It was what had made me so useful to the military.

I was good in the field too but give me a computer any day. I had never really learned the benefits of fetching someone coffee or filing things. I always assumed there was a program for that.

And usually, there was.

Derrick's permanent assistant, Olivia, was a nightmare. She hadn't gotten the *Zia isn't here to work for you* memo. She kept routing all phone calls to me and asking me to file things, which would have been fine if their filing system made any sense. Or rather, *her* filing system. But I went in there and nothing made sense. At all. Nothing was organized by date or client. She had her own way of doing things, which meant it was a nearly impossible task for me to sift through. Luckily, I'd written a program and uploaded it to the servers that would let me take a look at the more sensitive files. If she was going to pretend I worked for her, I might as well take advantage.

A call came in from a woman named Miranda who wanted to speak to Derrick. The moment she said her name, I recognized it from his never-put-through list. There was a list with four women's names on them. "Who was that? Did you mess with Derrick's calendar?"

I blinked up at Olivia, trying for an innocent doe-eyed look.

Good luck with that.

"Of course not. Some woman wanted to talk to him, but she was being vague. Miranda something or other." I played dumb.

She had her laptop in her arms, and she gave an exaggerated eye roll. "That woman will never give up. I don't know how many times she calls a week. I'm going to Derrick's next meeting with him. You're on phone duty."

I made a mental note to look into Miranda and gave Olivia a bright smile as I stood and reached for my laptop. "Are you sure? I feel like I can do it. Derrick really wants me as his right hand." I added extra syrupy sweetness to Derrick's name.

She abruptly stepped into my space. "*I* am his right hand. You think because you're in his bed that he'll keep you? What the hell do you think happened to Miranda?" She tried that slight lean thing into my personal space trying to intimidate me.

Little did she know I'd learned from my aunt long ago that you never backed down from a bully.

I stood my ground and didn't budge. Her motion only put her off kilter, throwing her off balance and forcing her to teeter then fall on her ass.

I bit the inside of my cheek to keep from laughing.

"For the love of God. What does he even see in you?" she muttered as she pushed to her feet.

Derrick yanked the door open then. His voice was like a cold winter wind. "What the hell is going on here?" His voice was tense, cold. Had something happened? Where was the guy from this morning? The one who had rolled me over, slammed his lips over mine, and made my toes fucking curl from one slide of his tongue? Where was that guy?

That guy is a mirage. Focus on your job.

This guy was a brooding pain in the ass who was on his way to my shit list.

Olivia dusted herself off. "Nothing, I was just getting ready to accompany you to the meeting."

He glowered down at her. "Not necessary. I'll take Miss Barnes."

Olivia gawked at him.

He didn't slow down, leaving me to run after him and Olivia to stare at my retreating back. When I caught up to him at the elevator, I frowned. "I'm supposed to go ahead of you, remember? Ward off any danger," I ground through my teeth. "That's how this whole thing works."

The elevator dinged and we both stepped in.

His gaze narrowed, as it raked over me from head to toe. I wasn't ashamed to admit that I flushed hot under the prolonged gaze. "You should probably keep up then."

It was an effort not to roll my eyes right out of my head. Instead, I muttered under my breath. "Jackass."

From behind me in the elevator, his chuckle was low. "What was that, Miss Barnes?"

"I said, as you wish, Mr. Arlington."

The humor in his low tone was like silk fluttering over my skin. "I could get used to how you say that."

And there went my panties. Get your shit together, Zia. What the hell was wrong with me and my lady parts?

In hand, my phone buzzed. Annoyed and grateful to be dragged out of my Arlington fantasies, I glanced down.

Jax: *I'm downstairs. All you have to do is walk by me and I'll be on him.*

"Are you coming to the meeting?" Derrick's voice was low.

I shook my head. "No. Jax is going with you. I'll be checking in with the team on any leads we might have."

"What am I supposed to say about Jax?"

I smiled at him over my shoulder. "Nothing. The guy is basically a ghost. He'll be there, but you'll never see him. I'm meant to be conspicuous and benign for those times everyone thinks you have your guard down. He and Trace are more in your face, but you'll never see them unless you need them."

I replied to Jax.

Me: *Thanks. He's supposed to be headed straight to the restaurant then to the Penthouse, but on the schedule, I see there's a new meeting that popped up, so you'll have to follow him. You might want backup.*

Jax: *Already on it. Trace is backup in case he makes another stop.*

Me: *Great. Thanks.*

Jax: *Anything suspicious?*

Me: *No, everything is as normal as can be.*

Liar. Okay maybe, but I couldn't tell Jax that the thing out of the ordinary was how good the billionaire looked in his suit and how it was unfair to my lady parts.

Jax: *Great. See you in a few.*

"Do you need back up?"

The elevator stopped and I turned to face him. His usual stormy gray eyes had a warmth to them like the sky before a summer rain. Was he worried about me? "No. I'm just going into to Royal Elite. But it's sweet of you to worry."

I would have sworn his lips twitched and he was fighting a smile. Why was he being nice to me?

"I have to say, I like this look better on you than flannel," he added with a hint of a smirk.

Before I could snap back with a response, be brushed past me and climbed into the waiting car.

Zia...

I WALKED SWIFTLY into Royal Elite after parking my car. Derrick had had someone bring it over last night since he knew I'd be needing it occasionally. Ahh, that billionaire service.

The sun glinting on the glass and the sounds of the waves crashing on the shore made me feel like I was back home. Gave me some grounding.

I knew I only had a limited amount of time as there was

another client assignment happening this evening period. When I walked in, the women on my team were already waiting.

Tamsin gave me a wide grin. "Ah, there she is! The woman who is shacking up with a billionaire and basically living my best life."

Jameson, who normally didn't say much, chortled

I rolled my eyes. "You guys know I'm on assignment, right? And he's kind of annoying?"

Ariel strolled out from the kitchen, coffee mug in hand. This one said, *Good morning, I see the assassins have failed.* I knew it was a gift from Princess Jessa. She had the best mug collection I'd ever seen.

"Oh, give her a rest. I mean billionaires can be so difficult what with their spa bathrooms, private chefs on staff."

I lifted a brow at my boss and crossed my arms. "*Et tu*, Ariel?"

She chuckled. "Okay sorry. I've got to tell you, even I'm jealous of your assignment."

"Yeah well, don't be. He's a pain in the ass."

She did nod as she took her seat. "Yeah, Sebastian already warned me. You surviving?"

"You mean how close am I to killing him myself?"

She smirked as she flicked her bright auburn hair over her shoulder. "Yeah you know, whatever."

"Pretty damn close."

She laughed as she pulled up laptop screens putting them on the giant monitor in our conference room. "Okay, what do we have? Any leads?"

I settled back opening my own laptop with my notes. "Okay we've got a possibility in Miranda Lincoln. She's an ex of his.

The longest relationship he's ever had on record. Nine months. Then all of a sudden three months ago, she was just gone."

Tamsin sat forward, a deep frown knotted between her brows. "Do you have any reason?"

I shook my head. "No, he is taciturn at best when it comes to anything that would actually be helpful. I've got a couple of software spider programs that are snooping around Arlington Tech's databases to see if there's anything out of the ordinary with any of their current mergers and acquisitions or any products they're putting out, but because he's the client and not someone I'm investigating I'm minding my Ps and Qs before you yell at me, Ariel."

Ariel threw up her hands. "I don't yell. I give resting judgment face."

"So you're not going to give me grief about the legality of what I've got going on?"

Her brows lifted. "What? Somebody's trying to kill the mother fucker, so right now legality schmegality."

I laughed. "Says the hacker."

"*Former* hacker. God, I always get a bad rap."

Tamsin interrupted. "Um, enough about who's trying to kill him and more about what his abs look like."

Sometimes I wasn't sure why she was my best friend. "You know, I'm not sure I like you."

"So you keep saying. But be real with us. Is he as delectable shirtless as he looks in pics?"

Ariel shook her head for me. "No one is boning anyone. Or ogling billionaire abs. Do I have to remind you guys this is a sensitive case? He's a cousin to the king. So Ps and Qs and all that."

This made Tamsin laugh. "Does that mean you're giving her

instructions *not* to bone him? Because I seem to recall you boning the Prince."

Ariel's face went beet red, the color creeping up her neck, flushing her cheeks to the tips of her ears. "What I did with Prince Tristan is none of your business. And I'm sure Zia knows how to comport herself in a professional manner."

"Yeah, professional."

Now was not the time to mention that I'd already kissed the guy. Or been kissed by him. And enjoyed every damn minute of it.

"Not going to sleep with him, Tams."

She shrugged. "If you say so. But honestly, I feel like you're missing out, because the way he fills out a tux is just... wow."

"Oh my God, can we get back to the task at hand?"

Ariel laughed. "I feel like that's my line. But she's right. Let's get back to it. Any other possible leads?"

I shrugged. "He's got this guy working for him as a consultant. He's not on the books, and I can't find him. I have done a background workup, and he's there. But he's *not* there. It feels like a cover. I don't know."

This had Ariel sitting forward. "What's his name?"

"Kyle Winters. I mean his background looks real. Went to Columbia, computer science. Worked in various tech companies. He looks legit. But his connection to Derrick... I can't really find one. I don't know where he hired him from or how he found him. It's like he's a pseudo ghost?"

That had Ariel tapping away on her keyboard. "Kyle Winters. Graduation year?"

"I don't know."

She nodded. "Okay, I'll see what I can find on him. Any other leads?"

I frowned when I remembered Derrick saying something about his father. "Yeah, he's got a tense relationship with his father. I doubt the older Arlington would attempt to kidnap his own son, but he was ousted from the company he built and Derek was named his successor. There's bad blood there. I don't have enough information yet. But those are our three main targets."

Ariel nodded. "Okay, I'll take the Winters guy personally. I want you and Tamsin to pick a day to do a good tail work-up on Miranda again. If she sneezes, we should know about it."

I nodded. "I agree considering the fact that they parted so abruptly and no one seems to know why. The rumor was that they were already engaged. She's exactly the type of woman he would want. Socialite, wealthy in her own right. Active in charities and all those kind of rich people things."

Ariel nodded. "Yeah. If he's not giving you a reason, I'd like to know it. I hate when clients withhold things because that means we have to go digging. As if we have time for that."

"Yeah. I understand."

She nodded at Jameson. "J, dig for dirt on the father and the history of the company."

"On it."

I checked my watch. "Okay, thanks. I better get back."

Ariel gave me a soft smile. "You're sure you're okay? His reputation precedes him. He's a dick. If Lucas doesn't even like him, the guy's a dick for real."

"He's a pain in the ass. Dick is the wrong word, at least to me right now." I wasn't surprised to find out that was true. He was a pain yes, argumentative, stubborn. But he didn't have that cruel streak I'd heard about, at least not one I'd seen yet. "I've got this. I can handle him."

If only that was the truth.

***

THEO...

As first days went, it went well as could be expected. I still didn't like having someone in my shit, but maybe I could do this? I could do it; I could pull this off.

No, you probably can't.

Christ. I took a glance over at her and her nose was buried in her tablet. "Let me guess, Royal Elite is on the case?"

She lifted her head and blinked at me rapidly. "Sorry what?"

I shook my head. "Never mind."

"Sorry, I just—when I get into work, I get into work. I get absorbed."

"It's cute." What the hell? I was telling her she was cute now?

Her eyes went wide. "Uh, says the workaholic."

I grinned at her. "I know how to have fun."

Her laugh was light. "Oh, I've heard about your wild debauched ways. Funny thing is I haven't seen anything even remotely resembling party behavior."

"Yeah well, everything changed when I became CEO. I needed to grow up."

She studied me closely, her dark eyes threatening to poke around my soul. "I keep looking for the party kid. I don't see it."

"Well, I like to think people are capable of chan—" Something caught my attention in an alley as we drove by. "Stop the car."

Tim's gaze met mine in the rearview mirror and pulled over and came to a screeching halt out of traffic.

Zia wasted no time. She palmed her gun. "What? What's the matter?"

I shook my head. "No, it's not life or death. At least not mine." But still, I was out of the car in seconds. Behind me I could hear Zia shouting, telling me to get back where I was and asking me what the hell was I doing. And yes, there were a lot of expletives and I was pretty sure she called me a dumbass idiot. But I was single-mindedly focused.

In the stupid loafers I was wearing, I slipped as I sprinted down the street and headed toward the alley we'd just passed. Yep, there was a kid getting his ass kicked. "Hey. What the hell do you think you're doing?"

The kid on the ground was holding on tight to something. The other kid who was wailing on him was trying to grab it from him.

"Hey, I said stop it." As I ran toward them, the bigger kid glanced up at me. Dark beady eyes, sandy brown hair. His gaze swept over me quickly as if trying to make an assessment on whether or not I could be a threat.

With one final tug, he took whatever it was out of the other kid's hand and took off running.

Behind me I could hear Zia's feet on pavement. The clips of her heels as they hit pavement and splashed in water, but she was surprisingly quick in them.

And behind her was Tim.

The kid on the ground was breathing hard, and he slung an arm over his face, sobbing. "Hey kid, Are you okay?" I knelt down in the puddle, taking no notice at the dirt, grime, and oil, or whatever the hell that sticky substance was that was on the bottom of my shoe, was doing to Derrick's wardrobe. I didn't give a shit about that. "Talk to me. Are you hurt?"

CHAPTER 8

The smaller kid pushed to a sitting position. "I'm fine."

He didn't sound fine though. He sounded like he was crying. "Tell me if you're hurt. We can get you medical attention."

"You think I can go to a doctor? My parents can't afford that."

I shook my head. "Don't you worry about that. If you're hurt, we'll get you seen and your mom doesn't have to worry about it."

His gaze puckered up at me. He had soft brown eyes and tawny skin. His coloring reminded me of Penny, but his hair was bone straight, not the wild corkscrew curls of our queen. The kid looked more like he was of East Indian decent.

"Who are you?"

That was a good question. "Someone who's had his ass kicked before."

I extended a hand and he placed his scrawny one in mine. Zia caught up to us. "Jesus Christ. Are you out of you goddamn m—" Quickly, she shut her mouth when she saw I had someone with me. Then her voice went soft. "Oh, is everything okay?"

I shook my head. "No, my friend here," I paused and waited for him to inject his name.

"Peter," he mumbled.

"My friend Peter here just ran into an asshole. And I'm hoping Peter can describe him."

"He's a kid from school. Big, asshole. Name's Jackson Trist. Been giving me shit since I started here."

I nodded solemnly, as if I knew anything about the schools. "Where are you from?"

"I just moved here from Miami. Dad got a job on one of the boats. Schools are supposed to be great, but that doesn't stop assholes."

"Yeah. Assholes are going to do what they're going to do. Why wouldn't you let go of what he was trying to take? Was it worth getting your ass kicked?"

He didn't answer me. "Look, I'm fine. You don't have to do this nice guy thing."

"Trust me, I'm not a nice guy. Just ask her."

Zia offered hopefully. "Uh-huh, I guarantee he's not."

"Yep, thanks for that. I've just been there."

The kid narrowed his eyes at me as his gaze flickered from my quaffed hair to my stupidly expensive suit, and then to my shoes. All of which cost more than most yearly school fees on the island. "Yeah, right."

"Well, I may not look it now, but I know the feeling. Trust me. Peter you've got a shiner there. You should get some ice on it. You live around here? I could take you home."

He shrugged me off. "You don't have to do this. I don't need anything."

"Well, I was here. I saw something. I stopped it. But if you don't want my help, you don't want my help." I made the turn around hoping the reverse psychology was going to work on him. When I was a kid, it would have worked on me. As I turned, he stopped me. "Fine, I live around the corner."

"Great, then I hope your mother won't mind visitors."

He chuckled softly. "My mother. She works at the palace. She's a maid. She won't be home until late tonight. Dad will be home after seven when his boat docks."

I sighed. "Right." He led us through the alley and turned the corner. It led up to one of the row houses on the street. "This is me."

"Well, let's at least make sure you get inside and get some ice on that."

"Look, I don't know who you are. And thanks for helping me not get my ass kicked so bad that I didn't actually need a hospital visit, but you don't need to do this. I'm sure you have to be somewhere rich people go."

"I'm helping you get settled. She's coming too, so you know I'm not some kind of crazy."

Zia waved. "Well, he might be crazy. But I know how to handle him."

It was the first smile I'd seen out of the kid, and I completely understood. Zia Barnes had a way about her.

When the kid led us into the basement apartment of the row house, I noted that the entry way, though small and dark, was clean, neat and had plants that were bright and cheerful. He led us in, and considering it was a basement unit, it still had a decent amount of light streaming in. "Uh, if you're coming in, you gotta take off your shoes." I did as I was told as Zia appeared.

He led us into the kitchen and pulled a bag of peas out of the freezer. "See, ice. Happy?"

I glanced around. There were photos on the wall of him and his family. Smiling, happy pictures. It reminded me of me and my mom. They didn't have a lot, but they were making it work and they were happy.

"Okay, Peter. What's your last name?"

He shrugged. "Pento."

"Peter Pento. Okay. Uh, I'm Derrick. This is Zia."

He nodded at her and gave her a lop-sided grin. "'Sup."

She gave him a beaming smile, complete with dimples. "'Sup."

"Right, now that we've made acquaintances, why don't you tell me what that kid stole and where I can find him?"

Peter's eyes got wide. "No, no, no, no. Look, I appreciate what you did, making sure I got home okay. That was dope. But you don't need to do anything else."

I narrowly gazed at him. "Okay. Peter, what are you? Sixteen? Fifteen?"

He rolled his shoulders. "Fourteen. I'm tall for my age."

I nodded. "Well, that'll come in handy. But assholes like that kid today, they're gonna come back. They are going to keep doing those things unless you deal with them appropriately."

"You're not gonna, like, put a hit out on him, are you?"

I grinned. "Is that what you want?"

He shook his head violently. "He's a turd, but I don't want anyone to die."

I chuckled. "I'm not going to kill anyone. But I'm going to talk to his parents or the principal. He stole something from you. What was it?"

"My tablet. I saved for it myself from my job and stuff, and my parents chipped in on my birthday. I use it for school stuff, so I don't know what the hell I'm going to do."

I nodded and pulled out my phone and typed a quick message to Tim.

Derrick Arlington: *Hey, can you go back to the car, grab my tablet, and bring it here?*

Tim: *Yep, be right there.*

As we chatted with Peter for a minute, I could tell the kid was well adjusted and smart. There were lots of books in the tiny apartment. He was just a kid trying to do well in school. That bully was going to regret touching him.

There was a knock at the door, and I went to answer it. There was Tim with my tablet.

Quickly I made a few taps, secured everything to the cloud, wiped all the apps, and then hit reset.

Then, I turned to Peter. "Here you go. You'll need to find a charger for it. I have one at home, but maybe I can drop it off here for you, if you want. I took all my stuff off and did a factory reset, so it's basically brand new."

His eyes went wide. "What? I can't take this."

"Yes, you can. You were just saying you need it for school and you didn't know how you were going to replace it. I've just replaced it."

His mouth hung open, and then he blinked up at me. "What's the catch? What do I have to do for it? No one's this nice."

I shrugged. "I'm not this nice. I'm dead serious, and you have to kick ass at school. Think you can manage that?"

He touched the tablet in awe. "Why?"

I shrugged. "Because I see something of myself in you. Now, do you have a phone number or something? I'll check on you later."

Then I turned and left him there. I'd have Olivia check on him and then get me some information about that other kid. I wasn't going to do anything to him, but I was going to scare the bejesus out of him. He needed to learn a lesson quickly, otherwise, he was going to continue to be a bully and a thief.

I could hear Zia jogging in her heels to keep up with me. When we reached the car, she slid a glance at me. "That was unbelievable."

I shrugged. "It was nothing."

"You have a heart in there."

"You tell anyone, and I'll have to kill you."

She laughed then. "You forget, I can kick your ass."

"So you think."

Once we were buckled back in our seats, her gaze softened. "That was actually a really nice thing you did."

"What thing?" I shut down all emotional centers in my brain. I wasn't going to let her give me that look, the one that went all mushy and soft. I couldn't have her seeing me as mushy and soft. Because if she started looking at me like that, I was going to crack. So, I put up the cold shell and left it there.

Zia Barnes was dangerous. If I got all soft with her, it was going to get me exposed. And that was not something I could afford.

NINE

ZIA...

"Correct me if I'm wrong but shouldn't you be with your billionaire right now?" Tamsin asked.

With Derrick in a board meeting and Trace as my back up, I took the opportunity to help Tamsin set up the tail on Miranda Lincoln. "He's not going anywhere, and Trace has him covered. After this, I'm taking a little field trip."

"So, any new developments since last night?"

I shook my head. "No. No developments. I know you think I should bang him, but it's not going to happen. I prefer uncomplicated."

Tamsin leaned forward, snapping more pictures of Miranda Lincoln as she jogged into her apartment building. I lifted the sound mic, pointing it in the direction of Miranda's apartment. "God, you know, I hate these things. They're never that accurate."

Tamsin shrugged. "Until we get a judge to actually sign off on listening devices, the only listening we can do is from the outside."

"Those pesky little laws."

She laughed. "Yeah, right? But seriously though, I know Ariel already asked and we gave you shit yesterday, but are you okay?"

I shrugged. Why did they keep asking? "I guess so. It's just a job."

She gave me a narrow-eyed gaze. "Uh-huh, if you say so."

My phone buzzed.

Ariel: *Do you have time this afternoon. I need you to head to Republic Prison.*

Zia: *Sure. Why?*

Ariel called then, and I answered on the first ring.

There was no preamble. "It was faster to call. I found something."

Adrenaline spiked my blood. If she was calling me because she found something, that meant she had a mission for me. "What do you need?"

"It seems that Derrick Arlington was kidnapped when he was nine years old."

I blinked. "What?"

"Yeah. There was a ransom request, but his father refused to pay it."

"Jesus." No wonder he hated his father.

"Yeah. My sentiments exactly. He found a way to escape and made it home. He was bruised and malnourished, but still alive. He'd been gone for ten days. At the time, he gave details to the police about what he could remember, but as far as I can tell, he never spoke about it to the public after his return."

"Jesus, did they have any leads?"

"I'll do you one better. They convicted a man named Alistair Cummings for the crime. He's currently serving a twenty-year stint in Republic. I want you go and talk to him. See if the current kidnapping attempt has anything to do with the past."

"Okay, I'm on it."

"Be careful."

When she hung up, I gave Tamsin the run down, and she was just as surprised as I was. "Holy hell."

"Tell me about it. It certainly explains a lot." I couldn't help but feel for that lost little boy.

Tamsin shook her head at me. "Don't go getting that soft look for him. He's a grown man now. He doesn't need you to take care of him."

"I know. I'm just experiencing empathy."

She shook her head. "I already told you that shit is bad for your health. Just as long as this empathy bullshit doesn't catch you a case of feelings. I say sleep with him, but you need to kick it like Elsa and conceal, don't feel."

I snorted a laugh. "Look, I've already told you. I won't mix business and pleasure again. Never again. Besides, I certainly wouldn't date someone like Derrick."

"What, you have an objection to the rich?"

"No. Of course not. I mean, I'm pretty sure I would love an endless closet as much as the next girl. But being an accessory, being looked over, for someone's ambition, I don't want that. And I really, really, *really* don't want a playboy. At all. I want someone grounded, nice. Someone who helps me and my sister."

Tamsin shook her head. "Make sure you shoot me in the eyeball the moment I think having a nice normal life is *fun*."

I laughed. "That's a good point. We don't do this job for a nice normal life."

"We sure don't."

Miranda had entered her apartment, and the mic started picking up conversation. "Oh, you're still here?" she asked.

"Of course, I'm still here. Where else would I go? You cuffed me to the bed."

Tamsin and I jerked glances at each other and then stared back at the apartment. *Holy shit.* This was the motherload. We could hear everything. We'd parked at the northwest corner of the building, so we were mere feet from her bedroom and getting great sound.

"You know how to get the key," Miranda said.

"Yeah, to get the key, I had to break out of this."

"And you know you can."

"I'd rather not tear up my wrist, if you don't mind."

There was a low throaty laugh. *Hers?*

"Oh, I'm sorry. What's the magic word?"

"I don't feel like playing right now, Miranda."

"Well then, I guess you're staying."

There was a growl. "I'm not playing with you, Miranda. Uncuff me."

"Uncuff yourself, or say the magic word."

"God, you're such a pain in the ass."

"Um, if I'm recalling it correctly, I'm the one with the pain in the ass. It's as if you like me using our magic word."

"I'm not playing with you right now." The man's voice was tense.

"What's the word?" She asked, teasing.

There was a sigh, then a man's voice said, "Baby, you know how much I love it when you call me Derrick."

Tamsin slapped a hand over her mouth, and my mouth hung open. What kind of fuckery was this? Some kind of role-playing game?

"You see? That wasn't so hard. Now I'll unlock you."

There was a clinking and clanking sound and then a squeal. And then "Oh—"

A series of moans and groans continued, and Tamsin asked, "How many inches do you think she's working with?"

I coughed a laugh. "Oh my God, you are so terrible. Can we turn this off? I really don't want to hear them doing it."

"Hey, we gotta hear everything. And right now, we know that she has a man that she insists on calling Derrick. Do you think she's over him?"

"Hell, I don't know. People are crazy. As of yesterday, she was still calling him. I don't know what for, but we really get nothing out of listening to this."

There was more groaning, and then the guy said in an ethereal, low tone, "What's my name?"

And then Miranda moaned, "Derrick. Oh my God, Derrick, yes. Yes. Right there. Right there." And then there was... well... a long groan and then silence.

Tamsin sat back and stared at me. "It looks like you have some competition. Someone who's pleased at simply saying his name over and over again."

I laughed and slapped my hands over my face. "Oh my God, what am I supposed to say to him now?"

"I don't know. Ask him, 'Hey, was your ex a freak? Does she like to rename guys that came after you?'"

"He likely wouldn't know."

"Hey, maybe he would, and that's why they broke up. She has a Derrick name fetish or something."

"Jesus Christ, she's certainly not over him," I said.

Tamsin coughed. "Girl, if you broke up with a billionaire, you'd be pissed off about it too. We all would. She's definitely a viable suspect. I'll have Ariel work on getting the listening permit. We need ears inside. Just in case we missed hearing anything."

"No, I agree. In the meantime, I think I need to get back."

Tamsin gave me a cheeky smirk. "Make sure you ask him about Miranda. I'm dying to hear what it is about him that she just can't let go of."

"No. I'm not giving you juicy details. I will ask about Miranda, but that's it."

She shrugged. "Don't worry, I'll help Ariel do all the digging, so I'll find out on my own. But it's so much more fun when your best friend tells you."

"No, we're not having this conversation. I'm gonna go. Call me if there are any developments. I'll check in after I make my visit to Republic."

As I started to climb out of the car, Tamsin started to moan. "Oh Derrick, right there. Right there, Derrick. Derrick! Oh my God, Derrick. Your dick is so thick Derrick. Oh my God." And then she broke out into a fit of giggles. "Mark my words, you're going to make that man your bed buddy."

"Not at all what I want. Let me know if there's anything else from Miranda." Then I slammed the door behind me.

I didn't need to hear any more. And not because I was jealous Miranda knew exactly what Derrick felt like.

Whatever you need to tell yourself.

♛

Zia...

THERE WAS a certain scent associated with a prison.

CHAPTER 9

It smelled like despair. Like complete and utter hopelessness.

Republic Prison was the main prison for violent crimes. Only the truly special were sent to Stanstit. Stanstit prison was reserved for traitors and treasoners. By and large, the prison sat empty. Although it did contain the king's own cousin and Prince Tristan's brother, Ashton.

Republic held run of the mill violent criminals. And Alistair Cummings was one of them.

Ariel had arranged with the warden for me to have a private audience with him. He would still be in his chains, and the guard would be close by. But like it or not, I was talking to him.

When I was led to the private room, I couldn't help but notice all the gray. The place was completely devoid of sunlight. Oh, sure, there were windows that allowed diffused light to come through, but it wasn't the bright blue of the outside. It was like all the hope had been sucked out of the place.

There was really no point in feeling sorry for a man like Alistair Cummings. He deserved to be in there. But still, he was a human being. And to never see the sunlight again? That was something I couldn't fathom.

Except, he kidnapped a little boy.

Yeah, there was that.

When I was shown into the room, the guard gave me instructions; no touching, stay on my side of the table, and he would, of course, be right behind me.

When Cummings was let in, he frowned when he saw me. "Who the hell are you?"

"Mr. Cummings, my name is Zia Barnes. I work for Royal Elite. I'm one of the King's Knights."

"Well, la di da, aren't you fancy?"

He didn't look the part. Yes, he had on a gray jumpsuit that made his pallor look sallow. But he was clean and well fed. Average looking. "Mr. Cummings, look, I won't waste a lot of your time, but I came to ask you about the reason you're in here."

He rolled his eyes and sat back. "What, you wanna ask me about a kidnapping I committed over twenty years ago?"

"Yeah, I do. From what I understand, your partner was killed when you were arrested."

"Not killed. He was murdered. I'm telling you right now, that's the real travesty. The fact that I'm not up for parole after all these years and that he was shot in cold blood. It must be nice to be a billionaire and related to the king."

"Are you saying Timothy Arlington is keeping you here?"

"What I'm saying is that the justice system is stacked against me. I made a mistake."

"I hardly classify the kidnapping of a young child a *mistake*. That's a crime."

"Fuck. It was a simple K&R. All Arlington had to do was pay the fucking ransom, and we'd have returned the kid."

"Except, you didn't return him."

"He *escaped*. The plan was always to send him home. But Timothy Arlington wouldn't pay the ransom. It was clear we either had to get rid of the kid or let him go. And I don't care what they told you. I'm *not* a killer."

"Right, just a kidnapper."

He scowled. "What do you want, lady?"

"Your partner, Gus Vincent. When your warehouse was raided, he was shot and killed, correct?"

"Look, between the time the kid ran off and the police showing up, it wasn't that long. It was four miles to the nearest civilization. A kid that young, running four miles would have

CHAPTER 9

taken him at least an hour. We knew the second the kid slipped his ties. We checked the video timestamp, and he'd only been gone twenty minutes. But seconds later, a tactical team bursts in and shoots Gus. Arlington knew where his kid was the whole time."

My brows lifted. "Are you serious?"

He nodded. "I'm telling you. I wouldn't have put it past Arlington to have arranged the kidnapping with Gus himself. He knew insurance would pay. It's the only thing that explains why he didn't come and get his kid."

It was my turn to sit back. That was a depth of cruelty even I hadn't imagined. "So, Derrick Arlington ran away?"

"God, it wasn't my first round of K&R—"he slid his gaze to the guard—"hypothetically speaking. "I'm just saying that perhaps, someone like me, had never seen anything like it. The kid had slipped his ties three times. Three separate times he tried to run off. He was whining and a pain in the ass. God, it was terrible. I wanted to send him home immediately, but Gus wanted to kill him."

"Well, lucky for Derrick Arlington he was good at escaping."

"Yeah, whatever. Now, I'm stuck in here. Did you get what you wanted?"

"Just one more question, Mr. Cummings, who hired you to kidnap him?"

He shook his head. "That was Gus's deal. He came to me and said, 'Hey, I have this K&R job to pick up a billionaire's kid.' The guy who hired him said we'd split it fifty-fifty. I supposed the guy had some kind of beef with Timothy Arlington over a business deal or something. That's all I ever knew."

"Any chance you have a name?"

Cummings sat back again and lifted up his hands, chains

jingling. "Nope. I don't remember a thing. I mean, granted, you could maybe sweeten the pot a little for me and see if you can jog my memory." He winked.

"Here's the thing, guys like you never seem to remember exactly what's needed. You want me to keep coming back here over and over again until you remember something, all the while promising the moon. I don't really have time to waste like that. You've already given me quite a bit. Thank you for your time, Mr. Cummings."

He scowled at me. "Where do you think you're going?"

"I'm leaving. Again, thank you. You were more helpful than you know."

I couldn't wait to get the hell out of there.

In the end, I didn't really have that much information. But I did have something. The one thing I did get was information on Derrick's determination. Three times he'd tried to run, and his own father had supposedly known where he was. Not to mention, he'd refused to pay the ransom.

Derrick had to know. Why hadn't he mentioned it himself? I was going to find out.

As I left, I sent a text to Ariel.

Zia: *Just met with Cummings. Not much information. But he suggested that Timothy Arlington knew where Derrick was being held the whole time. He suggested that maybe it was Arlington, himself, who arranged his son's kidnapping.*

Ariel: *Why would he hate his own son that much?*

Zia: *I have no idea. He also said that a business associate of Timothy Arlington's was supposedly behind it, but I don't know how much of that is true.*

Ariel: *I'll look into it. Maybe it's nothing, but if something's there, we'll dig it up.*

I practically ran to the doors. It wasn't until I was out in the sunlight that I dragged in several breaths of clean fresh air, glad I would never have to return there.

TEN

ZIA...

I was still reeling from my conversation with Cummings when I returned to the office. How determined did Derrick have to be to escape kidnappers? At age nine?

And what kind of parent left their child in the hands of kidnappers, especially when they had the means of getting them back. Christ, and I'd thought my family was fucked up.

The key now was to get Derrick to talk to me. My instincts told me not to show my hand yet. But he was the client, not a suspect, so I had to ask him about what I'd found out. Maybe it would jog a memory of who else might be after him.

Yeah, good luck with that.

When I walked in, Olivia came stomping over to my desk on her staggering heels, tipping slightly. "Do you think you can handle things for a bit? I know you're just here to look pretty, but it's my lunch break and I've covered for you all morning. You just have to answer the phones and take messages. Can you do that?"

I narrowed my gaze at her, willing my temper not to spill over. I wanted to deliver an elbow to her temple and knock her ass off her feet, but I didn't, because violence was not the way to solve my problems. Instead, I smiled sweetly and vowed to feed her plant coffee. "Yup, I got it."

"And for the love of God, don't file anything until I get back. Your filing system makes no sense."

"Are you sure you don't want me to color code anything? Because I feel like that could really improve the *feng shui* of the files..." My voice trailed, and she stomped off, shaking her head. That was almost too easy.

Derrick barked from his office. "Olivia, Come in here."

Since Olivia was gone, I grabbed my notes and went on in, making sure to smooth my skirt as I walked. It was probably wrinkled to all hell. I likely smelled of prison.

"No need to yell. Olivia's not here. She went to lunch."

Derrick groaned. "Christ, I would swear she's deliberately trying to sabotage me. She's pissed I didn't take her to the meeting the other day."

"Why don't you replace her?"

He sighed. "I have been asking myself the same damn question." His gaze slid over me. "Productive morning? Any leads on who's trying to kill me?"

I lifted a brow. "Trying to get rid of me already?"

"The sooner you find out who's after me, the sooner you can admit how sexy you think I am."

I bit back my smile. "It's nice to have hopes and dreams."

"Trust me, it's something we both want."

When he said that, his gaze flickered to my lips, and I could still feel his lips on mine. There was the phantom pressure of his length against my core, and I throbbed. I narrowed my gaze at him. He couldn't tell I was throbbing, could he?

That would be decidedly unfair.

It was already unfair that he was as good-looking as he was, and he knew it. Everything was so perfect and in its place. I was desperate to mess him up, run my hands through his hair and make it stick up.

Lady Parts: Hell yes, we can get behind that plan.

Brain: No. No, we cannot get behind that plan. Focus. Find who's trying to kill him and get out unscathed.

Easier said than done.

"I don't date clients."

His grin was broad. "Who said anything about dating?"

God, the grin was damned contagious. But I could not give in. "Does that line ever work for you?"

"You'd be surprised how often," he said with a chuckle. Then he asked, "Did you find anything?"

Here went nothing. "Well, it seems someone tried to kidnap you when you were nine years old." I watched him closely. My gaze pinned on his. Something flickered in his eyes, and I couldn't tell what it was. But before I could study him further, he shut it down quickly. Was that surprise? Did he think we wouldn't find out?

He cleared his throat. "That was a long time ago. I'm thirty now. I don't think whoever was after me then is after me now. That would be ridiculous."

"Not ridiculous. It's pertinent information we should have had directly from you. Do you remember anything from that time? Do you know how you escaped?"

His voice was more tense now. "Enlighten me as to why you think that has any relevance now."

"Look, I get that it must have been horrible. And I'm so sorry you went through that. I'm so sorry your father has a rat-sized dick and didn't come get you, but this is absolutely pertinent."

His lips twitched when I said rat-sized dick. "Zia, I don't want to revisit the past."

"I'm sorry, but we can't let it go. I went to see Alistair Cummings this morning." His gaze remained impassive. Like he didn't care. "He's in prison with no possibility of parole." Again, no reaction, so I barreled on. "He claimed that he and his partner were hired for a simple K&R job but that he didn't know who his employer was. He was *hired* to take you. Doesn't that seem the least bit odd to you considering someone else is trying to take you in your adult life?"

"Zia, you recognize that kidnap and ransom is a lucrative business, right? He's probably not the first to take a swipe at my family."

"Why do you seem entirely uninterested in this? This is your life, so why do I care more about it more than you do?"

He frowned. "So you care about me?"

I glowered at him. "I don't. I care about my job. My boss and my king have made you my priority, so I need you to get on board and give me all the help that you can."

"You have full access. Office. Home. You're *everywhere* I turn. I have given you access."

"No, you've made it *look* like you've given me access. You're going to have to be open with me, Derrick, or this won't work."

He frowned just a little bit when I called him Derrick.

"If you don't want me to call you Derrick, what do you want me to call you?"

Through clenched teeth, he muttered. "Derrick is fine."

"Okay, then. Look, I'm doing you a favor. Right now, I see a couple of different avenues as to why someone is after you. The one that makes the most sense is a disgruntled ex. Can you tell me more about Miranda Lincoln? Like why you broke up?"

He nodded slowly. "It had run its course. She was dissatisfied with how the relationship ended."

"Would you care to elaborate?"

"I broke up with her. She wanted us to keep seeing each other. She became obsessive and then threatened me twice, publicly. Loudly."

"Do you know she's not over you?"

He frowned. "No. But how do you know that? And what does that have to do with my kidnapping? She's a socialite. I sincerely doubt she even knows how to kidnap someone."

I leaned forward. "Do you know she has a new boyfriend?"

He shrugged. "Is there a reason I should care?"

"Only that they role play by her calling him Derrick. That strikes me as a tad bit obsessive."

His eyes went wide. "I'm not sure I want to know how you know that."

"You probably don't."

"Why would she have called someone else my name? That makes no sense."

He really didn't get it? "Well, you must have never been in love, have you? That all-consuming kind of love?"

His gaze was intent on me then. As if he could see the truth behind what I was saying. "Have you?"

I swallowed hard. *Focus, Barnes. Focus.* "Look, I believe people can lose their minds over someone that they think they love. They can lose all reason and refuse to do things that are good for them instead of doing the thing that feels good. It's crazy, but true. And Miranda is not over you. She's a threat. She still calls here looking for you."

He ignored what I said about Miranda. "I watched you at the wedding. You ran into the crowd and hid between two pillars just to avoid someone. Was that love?"

Heat burned my skin, scorching it, most definitely turning it to ash. "You don't know why I was running. You have no idea."

"Sure, I do."

"So, you've never done anything crazy for love?"

He shook his head. "Nope."

"Then you, my friend, have *never* been in love."

"You're right. And God save me from that affliction."

I wasn't sure why, but that hurt.

Why would it hurt? He's not yours.

"Can we just get on the same page and agree that you won't keep us I the dark? In the meantime, I'm going to keep chasing down this Alistair Cummings link. Maybe there is a connection."

"I'm an open book. All you have to do is flip the pages, Miss Barnes."

I didn't believe him for a minute. The problem was... I wanted to.

ELEVEN

THEO...

It was official. Zia was trying to drive me insane. That was it. It was the only logical answer. Not even a full seventy-two hours with her and I was losing it. Not to mention she was starting to dig in all the places I didn't want her digging.

Or, you want her.

I hadn't really thought it through. The proximity, needing her in my orbit, how impossible it had been to sleep. How did she not feel it too?

Just because you look like the billionaire, doesn't mean you have the same appeal.

That was bullshit. She could feel it. I knew she could feel it. The way she'd arched under me when I kissed her. That had been a mistake.

But Elena had been in there about to see her and well, I reacted.

Also, you wanted to kiss her.

Yeah, I had. And then I kissed her. Now all day had been like this gnawing, clawing need. When I had gone out to ask about the file, I had expected to see Olivia. And I had been pissed off when it was Zia, because, of course... instant fucking erection. The need made me edgy, and I'd bitten her head off. Of course, she wasn't going to know where the goddamn files were. I'd gone looking for the files myself, and they weren't in any logical location. I didn't know what the fuck Olivia and Arlington had been doing the whole time, but their shit was a mess. It was like they wanted Arlington Tech to fail. I had spent a good amount of time rearranging some files myself so that I could at least stay on top of the things I was supposed to cover, but shit, it was a fucking disaster.

And yet you expected her to be able to find it?

Okay, I'd been a dick. Because I wanted her.

News flash asshole, you more than want her.

The problem was I had already heard that little needy sound she'd made at the back of her throat when she was aroused, and I wanted to fucking hear it again. But that wasn't going to happen, because I wasn't me. She'd made that little needy sound for Derrick Arlington. And well, I'm pretty sure she didn't like me... or him. Her body liked me, but she didn't *actually* like me, so I suppose that feeling was mutual.

When six thirty rolled around, I grabbed my laptop and the file I'd been working on for the merger, and I opened the door. I didn't know where the fuck Arlington was, but I'd keep acting as if I was him until Kyle and I could fucking find him. When he'd said I would have everything I needed and I'd signed on the dotted line, I didn't think I'd be left alone in a pool of sharks, all circling around trying to decide which angle had the tastiest bits.

Zia was ready when I dragged open the door. I had to work to not swallow my own tongue. White was killer on her. Just fucking dynamite. She slipped her coat over her arm and laid her laptop on the crook of her elbow. "Are you ready? Jax is downstairs."

I frowned. "Jax?"

She shook her head. "You won't see him. He'll follow you until you're back to the penthouse."

"And where are you going to be?"

"It's the rotation. I'm off tonight."

"You're supposed to be staying with me though."

"Relax, buttercup. Is there something you need tonight? Perhaps someone should fetch your coffee? A pastry?"

"More like I need you guarding my body." *Fuuuck.* That sounded so cheesy.

It might have been cheesy, but her gaze flickered away from mine and she swallowed hard at that. "You'll be fine. No one is getting into that penthouse without us knowing. It's armed with cameras, and Jax will be nearby.

"What do you mean nearby?"

"He'll be posted at the elevator. He will be in your vestibule. It's fine. No one is going to know."

"My staff..."

"This is how it goes. Rotations. The only ways into that penthouse are the elevator and the stairs. The vestibule on the stairs, he'll be there. And once I take care of a few things, I'll be back."

My gaze narrowed at her. The lines around her mouth were tight and she kept checking her watch. "Am I boring you? Do you have a hot date tonight?"

What I wanted to do was tear apart anybody she was seeing. Was someone else going to have his hands on her? Yes, I recognized that was irrational. Why the hell I thought I had any right to know about her personal life was beyond me. But still, there it was, my inner caveman, thumping his chest and looking for his club.

"The best part about this is that it's none of your business."

I ground my teeth together. "Whatever, just remember to be discreet, because you're my girlfriend, so I can't have you running around on a date."

She rolled her eyes. "Girlfriend for show."

By the time I reached the main lobby, she was marching a step ahead of me, and I reached out, took her hand, and pulled her back.

Her gaze snapped down to our joined hands and then up to my face. "What the fuck do you think you're doing?"

I grinned at her. "You're my girlfriend, remember? I'm keeping up appearances."

She opened her mouth. Closed it. Opened it again and closed it. It was hilarious watching her do the copy routine.

"Fine." She started marching again, but I stopped her.

"Where is Jax?" I asked as I tucked her body close to mine. Her back was rigid and stiff, but the moment I curved my arm around her waist, she relaxed. Unfortunately, that just made the caveman thump his chest harder.

"First car at the curb, right behind yours."

"Where's your car? I should walk you to it."

"I'm taking a cab."

"Fine." If she thought I was going to let her just climb in the cab, she had another think coming.

At my car, she tried to slip past me with a wave.

I lifted a brow. "Aren't you forgetting something?"

She shook her head. "Nope."

I grinned at her. "And here I thought you were the best in the business."

With an eye roll, she gave me a dimpled grin. I knew I was supposed to be able to form coherent thought and shit, but dimples. I was a fucking goner for her dimples. Then she kissed me on the cheek. And before I even had a moment to respond, she was slipping out of my grasp again.

Hey dumbass, remember that thing where you were gonna push her away? How's that going?

I needed to get with the program. Zia Barnes was dangerous in so many ways.

Zia...

TAMSIN NEVER HAD KNOWN where to find her chill. Less than twenty minutes into our run that evening, she started on me. "How was the prison visit?"

I pursed my lips. "Mostly a dead end, I think. Cummings was a hired K&R guy. Never met with his employer face to face. He couldn't really give much. He did say that Derrick had been determined to escape and had tried more than once. The second time they caught him and threatened to kill him, but he was defiant."

She shook her head. "No. don't do that. You're getting that but-he-needs-saving face on me. He's not a puppy. And that was a long time ago."

"I know I know. I'm not getting soft I swear." I left out Derrick's good Samaritan antics the first night I was guarding him. I knew it would sound like I was starting to care about him.

And it was hard not to. He was nothing like the man I'd read about.

CHAPTER 11

"How is that tasty bit of man-cake anyway? Is he still looking like he wants to take a bite out of your ass?"

"Nothing is happening with man-cake. And he does not look at me like that."

"Liar. I saw you guys when you were leaving Royal Elite. I could feel the tension all the way inside. The way he looks at you, the little touches when he thinks no one is noticing. He looked like he wanted to eat you. Can you do this and not get emotionally attached?"

"Oh my God. I *have* to touch him. I'm his bodyguard." Had I touched him? *You did a whole lot more than touch him yesterday morning.* "And I'm super clear on what's happening here. No emotions. Just picture me singing 'Let it Go.'"

"I love you and I'm your best friend, so I'll help you stay in denial all day long, but even you have to see that man is fine with a capital Fuck Me.

I laughed. "Tamsin, since when do you use the word fine?"

"Well, I'm just saying. He is gorgeous. *Bangable. Shag City.*"

"Look, I hear you, and while it would be flattering if it were true, I really don't like the guy. It seemed like we might be able to work together, but in the office he's less than charming."

"Now you're getting the picture. You need to hit that. Then quit that."

"What?"

"He can get your cobwebs out." She gave me a wide grin as we headed toward the pier.

I choked a laugh. "Oh my God, you're terrible."

"Yes, I know. And one of us should be getting some."

I was more than willing to change the subject. "What are your dating prospects?"

She shook her head. "None."

"Come on, you're not even trying. You say I'm not trying, but you aren't putting yourself out there."

"Look, there might have been someone, but he's got like a whole situation going. Besides, we made out once, and now it's awkward."

"Oh, you didn't get to bang him?"

"No, which is also disappointing, because from the equipment I checked out, he is blessed. Very, very blessed."

"Ugh, so what's the situation? Is he married? Tell me he's not married Tams."

She rolled her eyes. "No. I don't do married dudes."

"Okay, well, what's so complicated? Does he have lots of kids or something?"

"No, not him personally, but he looks after someone. So, it's complicated."

I narrowed my gaze at her as our feet hit the concrete. "Oh my God, Trace?"

I'd never seen Tamsin blush before. She was far too outrageous and said too many wild things to ever be bothered with blushing. But she went boiled-lobster red.

"Oh my God, you and Trace hooked up?" I stopped running and stared at her. "Holy fucking shit. *Holy fucking shit.* Trace? Talk about smoking hot. He and Derrick could be brothers he's so hot."

She shook her head. "Last I checked, Trace wasn't a billionaire."

"Who cares? He's hot."

"Yes, hot and packing, apparently. But his sister..."

"His sister is fifteen. What are you even talking about?"

"Well, he stopped me. He said it was too complicated. He had to look after Kate. You know how that goes."

Oh my God, I did know how that went. I'd used that same excuse lots of times about Deedee when I couldn't stand to get emotionally tied to someone or I didn't like them. I didn't open that up though. "Look, you guys could work around that situation. I think this could be good for you."

"Well, you need to tell him that because he's currently not about it."

"Well that's his loss, because you are awesome."

"Thank you. But we are not talking about me and Trace. We are talking about you and that absolutely fuckable billionaire."

"Billionaire client. *Client* being the keyword."

"Fine. Okay. Client. I mean, God, live a little. You've always followed the rules."

"No, I don't, remember? The one time I didn't follow the rule, love kicked my heart right in the middle. I'm not so eager to repeat the experience."

"I know. It sucks. But I've never known you to be a quitter."

"I'm not a quitter. Besides, it's not like that."

"Uh-huh. Sure, it's not. So you're telling me that you're locked up in that bedroom with him and you're not looking over at him across the room while you're nestled up on that couch thinking 'God, let me just climb into bed with that fine piece of man-cake?'"

I grimaced.

She frowned. "What's wrong?"

"Um, is now a good time to mention that we've kissed... twice?"

Tamsin's eyes went wide, and her mouth opened to form an O. "Holy shit. I told you. Man-cake. How did that happen?"

I quickly explained while we grabbed our water bottles.

"Well, that makes perfect sense. You were undercover. Then

you were under him. And he totally covered for you with Garrett, so I like him already."

"But then he was a total dick to me in the office today, so there's that."

"Uh-huh. Whatever you say. I stopped listening when you said you were on the same bed and he grabbed your ass." She whooped. "There was ASS grabbage!"

"Jesus Christ, Tams. I need you to give me *good* advice. Good, sound, actionable advice."

"I am. Bang the new billionaire. How is that for advice?"

"Sometimes I swear you hate me."

"Oh no. I love you. I just want one of us to have an orgasm sometime this century. You seem the more likely candidate. Besides, he is a temporary assignment. It's not like you're gonna fall for the guy."

She did have a point there. There was zero chance of me falling for Derrick Arlington.

TWELVE

THEO...

Kyle and I had taken to meeting out on the balcony of my office. I was certainly going to miss this view when I left.

Is that all you'll miss?

He set his laptop on the table I'd had set with coffee and pastries. "You all right?"

I shrugged. "Well, still alive so that's a plus."

He chuckled softly. "No one's tried to kill you lately, so that's good."

"We're setting a real low bar, dude."

"Hey, sometimes, it's the small things."

"What are we looking at? You said you had something."

Kyle nodded. "I don't know what to tell you, but that merger you've been working so hard on, something fishy this way comes. They've got accounts I can't track. They're dealing with shell companies of shell companies of shell companies of shell companies. Offshore accounts. On the surface, sure, all the money looks legit. Coming from places it should be coming from. But when you dig into those companies, they don't exist.

Or they exist in name only, or they don't have products or ways sell to them."

I cursed under my breath.

Kyle continued. "Look, this is the part where you get to say, 'I told you so.' This is my idea. I thought it'd be easy. We'd come hang out in the islands, meet some cute island girls, go home. Intact. But right now, we got a billionaire we can't find. A merger that's built on quicksand. And someone trying to kill you. So maybe now we throw in the towel?"

I shook my head. "No. We both put our lives on hold for this. We can do it. We just have to hang in there. Besides, you basically just confirmed what I already knew. I already had a hunch about Inline. The question now is who stands to gain from this merger? Obviously, Arlington. The board members. But who would have the most to lose? The investors are the ones who will lose if we're right about this. Rocco Stains, the founder of Inline... I can't pin him down. On paper, he looks good, right?"

Kyle nodded. "Oh, yeah, on paper he looks legit. Cornell graduate. On par with the likes of Zuckerberg. Brilliant. To him, data is king. Simple, but unhackable. Uncrackable. And I should know. I tried. Granted, hacking isn't one of my super skills, but I'm not bad. And if you want a peek at anything they're holding, you're going to need a server farm and about 100 friends because there's no getting to it. So yeah, as a business model it looks great. 'Come to us, we'll protect your data.' The problem is money. Where's it fucking coming from? Not to mention, I was looking at the paperwork they sent over. For the last 10 years, they've had money going to some kind of slush fund that's unaccounted for."

I frowned. "They're not paying taxes on it?"

"No, that's just it, they *are* paying taxes on it. More than they should maybe. The account is labeled... Hold on a second, let me see if I can find it."

He pulled open his laptop, tapped quickly, and then said, "THDA Enterprises. I don't know what the acronym is for, but that's what it's labeled, THDA. That account has been pulling .01% of profits for the last 10 years. The company's twelve years old. Now, I've just told you I don't exactly know where the money's coming from, shell companies of shell companies of shell companies, but they've got millions of after-tax money in that account. .So you're not going to get them on some tax evasion bullshit. But I want to know what they are doing with the money."

I ran a hand through my hair. "Jesus Christ. What am I even doing here?"

"My sentiments exactly. Time to go. This shit has gotten out of hand. This shit is too crazy."

I turned to stare at him. "Wait, so it wasn't too crazy when a guy who looked *just* like me with my exact face strolled into our office and made us an offer we couldn't refuse?"

"Come on, dude, he was your freaking doppelgänger. You know how I'm obsessed with that shit."

I rolled my eyes. "Your fascination with having a twin got us here, so we have to make the best of it."

"Jesus Christ, this is going to get us both killed." He shook his head. "This is just like that time with Carla Suvy when I suggested, that you ask her to prom."

"Yeah, you knew full well her brother had threatened anyone who tried to date his sister. I didn't know this. But you were convinced it was going to be just fine because I could wing it. And then, when you realized he was dead serious about murdering anyone who dated his sister, you wanted to throw in the towel."

Kyle chuckled. "Yeah, but you were insistent that you'd made a commitment. Had to stick it out."

"Yep, ended up with a broken nose for my efforts."

Kyle groaned. "God, we've gotten in a lot of trouble together."

I laughed. "Yeah. Usually because I'm following your dumb ass."

"No one told you to follow me."

"Oh, yeah? Then who would bail you out of trouble?"

Kyle's smile was warm and affable, like always. But I knew behind that, he was the guy you called at four in the morning because tragedy had struck. He was that friend that you called when you thought you might have found your birth father. The one who drove with you the nine hours to Buffalo just to meet a guy who could be your father and collect a DNA sample, only to then discover he was not, in fact, your father.

He might get me in a lot of trouble, but he was still my best friend. And I would walk through fire for him. "Kyle, you know I can't just give up."

"You have nothing to prove here, not a thing. Your whole life, you have thought you are somehow unworthy, so you're always trying to prove that you are. You don't have to do stupid shit to prove anything to anyone."

"I hear you. But we're already here. We're committed. Let's just finish this out."

Kyle sounded resigned when he sighed. "All right, fair enough. What are you going to do about the merger?"

"I have to just delay it at the very least until we can get more information."

"The board members are going to hate that."

"Yeah, I know. And Arlington's going to lose his shit. But it can't be helped."

"Let's just pray that you're doing the right thing."

"Yeah, I certainly fucking hope so."

♛

THEO...

We didn't speak much when Zia came back to the penthouse. We made the show of kissed cheeks and how was your run for the chef and Elena, but then I went to the office and she headed to bed, with Elena calling out to tell her not to wear flannel.

When I went to bed, she was curled up on the couch, snoring. She was cute when she slept. Hair wild, mouth open. But as wild as she slept, she was fully alert the moment I stepped in the room.

She palmed her gun and only relaxed when I announced myself.

I was just as aware of her as she was of me though. Because I knew the second she was awake. Her phone buzzed and illuminated the room, then she got up and wasted no time rushing to her closet. When she came out, she was dressed for expedience. Tight black leggings, black top, hoodie, baseball hat.

What the hell was she doing, robbing a bank?

I stayed as still as possible as I watched her gather her things and tiptoe out of the room. I pulled open my phone to check the security app. In the living room, she scribbled a note and left it on the table. The moment she hit the front door, I was up and out of bed. I grabbed a T-shirt on the way and shoved my feet into my tennis shoes. In the living room, I found the note she'd left me.

Family emergency. Jax is still on duty. Don't go anywhere. I'll be back as soon as I can.

Where the hell was she going? She'd put a tracker app on my phone so she could find me if we got separated. She probably didn't think that it worked both ways, but I knew it did. I ran to my room and changed out the pajama bottoms for jeans, and then I was out the door. If Jax was watching me, he'd know I was following her. So wherever she was going, we were going together.

It's none of your business.

As if that mattered. Something was up with her. Something she wasn't telling me. After she'd given me that long speech about being able to trust me. This was getting out of hand. Not that I was obsessed with her or anything.

Sure, you're not.

Well, very likely, she needed help, and knowing her, there was no way she was going to ask. But if she wasn't going to ask, I was going to give it whether she wanted it or not.

That's exactly what a stalker would say.

Fine. So, I was a stalker. Sue me. But she needed help, clearly. Where was she sneaking off to in the middle of the night?

It was one in the morning.

She was easy to find in a matter of minutes. She drove through downtown and up into the Knob Hill area. Where the hell was she going? Did she have another billionaire client I didn't know about?

What does it matter? You're not really a billionaire client.

Still, though, it irked me. Did she have a boyfriend? The

idea that she rushed out of the flat for a booty call irked me. Her car turned on Highland, continued a short distance, and then stopped. "What the in the world are you doing?" I muttered to myself.

I parked right next to her black company SUV and then climbed out of the Maserati. I glanced around, but I couldn't find her. When I heard loud whispering a bit further down the road, I squinted my eyes trying to figure out just what she was doing in the dark.

I knew the moment Jax caught up to me because he rolled by in a black SUV similar to Zia's and he cocked his head. I shrugged and indicated her car, then I followed the sounds I'd heard and recognized the building right away. Or at least the emblem.

Thrones House. Technically, it was part of the university. They were supposedly one of those secret campus societies. Derrick had been one. *Crowns.* There were three universities on campus, each with their own secret society. They were the rich ones who thought they could further differentiate themselves from their fellow students. *Fantastic.*

To my left someone whispered, "Come on, just give me a shove."

Then Zia's voice. "I swear to God. how did you even get stuck in here?"`

"It was one of the pledge pranks. I had to come in and steal a scepter."

"Do you understand what happens to you if you get caught in here?"

"That's why I needed you. I'm stuck."

"I swear to God, Deedee, I'm putting an end to this. You cannot keep doing this."

"I'm sorry but I really need this to work."

"You needed help last time. Who bailed you out?"

"You did. But this is different."

"How? How is this different?"

"At least this time I have my clothes on."

My brows lifted as I eavesdropped and followed the sound.

Zia was already in ass-chewing mode. "Barely. Your dress is up over your ass. Your ass is flapping in the wind. Literally flapping."

I couldn't help it; I coughed a laugh. A girl was apparently stuck in what looked to be a portal of some kind. And then there was Zia, attempting to shove her through. She had her hand on the girl's ass, but I wasn't sure if she was pulling or pushing.

"Ah, looks like you guys could use a hand."

Zia whirled. "Oh my God, what the hell are you doing here?"

"Well, your note was inadequate. 'Family emergency' Was a little vague. It's one in the morning, so I followed you."

Her eyes went wide. "You recognize someone is trying to hurt you, right?"

"Yeah. And you're my bodyguard, but you left me. So how are you doing your job?"

"I left you a goddamn bodyguard. All you had to do was stay in the house."

Behind me, there was a little rumble that sounded an awful lot like a laugh. And then Jax spoke. "Oi, what the fuck is going on here?"

From inside the building, there was another feminine voice calling out, "Excuse me, can you guys argue about this later? I need help here."

CHAPTER 12

Zia scowled. "Since you two are here, can you get my sister out of the goddamn window?"

I lifted my brows. "This is your sister?"

She gave me the, don't-get-me-started face. Which by now I knew well.

From inside, the girl complained. "Seriously, can someone help me?"

I stepped forward, trying to assess the best way to do that without actually touching her ass. It wasn't going to be possible. Jax stepped forward too. He frowned. "I'll rock, paper, scissors you for it."

"No, it's okay. You're an actual bodyguard. You should do it."

"You think you should leave me to do the work?"

We were evenly matched in height. He was slightly bigger than I was though.

He spoke softly to Zia's sister. "Deedee, it's Jax. I'm here to help."

Deedee, as it were, groaned from inside. "Oh my God, you cannot touch my bare ass."

Jax coughed. "It's fine. We're just going to get you out of here and get you sorted."

"No, you can't touch my ass. I know your wife."

"Trust me, I know my wife too. She wouldn't want me to leave you like this. Because sooner or later, someone is going to notice and call the police. You certainly don't want to be arrested."

I groaned. "Ugh, for the love of God, I'll do it."

Zia glowered at me. "Do not touch my sister's ass."

I sighed. "Okay, fine. We can leave her like this if you prefer."

Zia groaned. "Fine, just... don't touch it too much."

I lifted a brow. "Jealous?"

"Screw you."

I grinned. "I know you'd like to." The way she narrowed her eyes, I could tell she wanted to spit fire at me. But that was going to have to wait because Jax was here. She'd wanted people to notice she was good at her job. It was important to her. She might think I was a giant pain in her ass, but she would essentially comply.

"Just get her out."

"Hey, Deedee. My name is Th—" I stopped myself. Damn, I'd almost used my real name. "I'm Derrick. I'm a friend of your sister's. I'm here to help you out."

"Oh my God, you sound hot. Are you hot? Zia, I told you. Your life is too good to be true."

Zia's gaze flickered over me. "He's not hot, but he thinks he is."

I grinned. "Deedee, don't worry about anything. I'm going to rotate you first so I can pull you out."

"No! Push me in. I still need the scepter."

My gaze darted to Zia. "Scepter?"

"She's rushing a fucking sorority. This is the second time in a week I've had to come and rescue her."

I lifted a brow. "Seriously? This is for some sorority nonsense?"

From inside, Deedee groaned. "It's not nonsense. It's really important, okay?"

I could hear the tremble in her voice, and I was not prepared for that shit.

"Okay, okay. I hear you. It's important. I'll give you a hand, okay? So you want to go in, is that right?"

"Yes. For the love of God, yes."

"Jesus, okay. Do you have something to grab on to in there? I don't want to drop you on your ass. Looks like you're a little bit off the ground."

"Yeah, there's a chair. If I could just... got it."

"Okay." I inclined my head to Jax to give me a hand. Lifting her and pushing her through the portal was a lot more difficult than just pulling her out, because I had to be careful of her. She was Zia's sister, after all. The two of us lifted and hoisted, and finally, she was through the portal. We heard a clutter inside. "Damn it. Aww."

Zia ran to the portal. "Oh my God, are you okay?"

"Yeah, I'm fine. It's just... The chair wasn't as steady as I thought."

"I swear to God, get your ass back out here."

"Wait, I need to find the scepter."

Down the path, I saw a flashlight gleaming. Jax saw the same thing at the same time. I grabbed Zia and dove for the thickest bush to the side of the guest house. I wrapped my body around hers, cocooning her. Her face in my chest as I used the bush for cover.

"You realize I'm supposed to be the bodyguard, right?"

"I doubt whoever is coming up here is trying to shoot me. At least this way, if someone catches us, we could pretend we're just making out."

"As if."

Okay yeah, it might not have been a good idea to goad her, but I couldn't help it, because while I was dying for her, she was acting like she was completely unaffected by this. "Oh, we've already made out, remember? I seem to recall that you liked it."

"Shut up, you pompous—"

I clamped my hand over her lips and shook my head while I gave her a wide grin. "Shh. Someone will hear us."

Her eyes narrowed, and I could tell she wanted to murder me. It didn't matter whether she'd been sworn to protect me or not, I was a dead man if she got her hands on me. The people with the flashlight passed. There were two of them walking and talking about some vacation that they were going to take. When they passed, I breathed a sigh of relief. Jax came up behind us. "It's clear. Let's get Deedee and go."

We all head back around to the portal on the outside of the house, but there was no sign of Deedee.

Zia broke free of my hold. "Deedee, where are you?"

"Over here."

Her voice came from the darkness behind me. "Shit," I muttered.

She held the scepter in her hand. "Backdoor. It's much easier than the portal. I don't know why I didn't think to pick it or something. I guess I should have picked up your skills, Zia."

Before, I might have been holding Zia to protect her from whoever was coming on the path, and then I might have held on to her shoulders as comfort. At least that's what I told myself. But now, I held on to her to keep her from killing her sister. I was sure of that. She launched, but I held her tight. "I swear to God, Deedee, I will kill you myself."

Deedee rolled her eyes. "Oh my God, you're such a drama queen."

"You are the one who texted me a 911."

"And I thought you weren't coming for me anymore."

Zia's brows rose. "You're kidding me, right? After all the shit I've bailed you out of? This is what you're telling me?"

Deedee rolled her eyes. "Look, I was just stuck, okay? So, of course, you're my sister. But if you're going to give me a lecture every time you come running, I won't even text you anymore."

"You know what? Next time you can get arrested." Zia charged down the worn path.

I glanced between Zia and Deedee. I knew Zia was pissed, but I didn't think she wanted her sister to be left alone in the dark, so I stayed put. Jax groaned. "Jesus Christ, family drama. Deedee, come on, cut your sister a break, would you? You're really taking the piss here."

Deedee grinned up at him. "Can you say that again? British speak is so sexy."

Jax rolled his eyes. "You know what, move, or I will physically move you."

She lifted a brow. "You can't do that. I don't work for you."

"No, you don't. But I am a King's Knight. And since your sister is also a Knight, your protection is under our purview. I'm authorized to make you comply, whatever it takes."

Deedee took a step back. "You wouldn't."

"I would. I guarantee you."

I crossed my arms and stood behind Jax. "And if he doesn't, I will. You really are spoiled, you know that?"

Her eyes went wide. "Who the fuck *are* you?"

"Nobody. Just a friend of your sister's. But you're a brat, and you're acting like one. Next time, if you want to be treated like an adult, don't get yourself in a twist. Because one day, Zia is really not going to show up."

Deedee's face fell. "You don't know anything about my sister."

"I know enough to know that she's pretty badass. She doesn't need to be chasing after you."

"You act like you know her."

"I do know her." With that, I turned my back on Jax and Deedee, leaving her to follow behind.

Theo...

I COULD fucking hear her moving. I could hear her breathing. Every moment, every breath triggered my memory of how she felt underneath me, how she moved, the low-key sound at the back of her throat... But the squeaking with every turn of hers on the leather couch was driving me batshit.

Jesus, there was no way in hell I was going to survive the night. The previous night had been bad enough, but fuck me, now I knew what she felt like. I knew what she tasted like. I knew what she sounded like. And I wanted more of that. I wanted her to melt on my tongue. Kyle was right. She was exactly my type, which was why she was so fucking dangerous to me. I was screwed.

It was only going to be a matter of time before she knew it too. During our meeting today, I couldn't take my damn eyes off of her. Luckily, it had been a straightforward investigation of another product. Another company to acquire, but Jesus Christ, every shift of her body, the crossing and uncrossing of her legs, it was as if she was trying to deliberately drive me insane. And then she told me that she didn't know where to buy any fucks. And instant hard-on. What the fuck was wrong with me? The more she argued, the more I wanted her. The more dirty looks she gave me, the more I wanted to make her moan. There had to be something wrong with me. It was the only answer. She tossed again and I was done. I snatched the covers off and marched over.

"Get up. Take the bed."

She slid her eye mask up and glowered up at me. "I told you, I'm sleeping on the couch."

"And I told you, this is ridiculous. Yes, you have a gun, a big bad gun. But I also happen to know by now that you'll do anything to protect me. So if you don't get up and climb into that bed by yourself, I will drag you there, kicking and screaming."

"You recognize that's assault, right?"

My brows snapped down. "I'm not fucking with you. Get up. Get in the bed."

She crossed her arms and raised a brow. "What? Are you going to bone me senseless? I gotta tell you, your foreplay needs work."

Was it me, or did she clamp her legs tight together? The muscles in her thighs tensed slightly. All I knew for sure was that my dick turned to steel.

"I don't want to fight with you anymore. I'm tired. Just get in the goddamn bed."

"I will put you down. I am not getting in that bed. Not *with* you."

I sighed. "Look, I won't fucking touch you, okay? If you're scared, or whatever, you don't have to be. Not of me. I might talk about tanning your ass, but I would never put my hands on somebody who didn't want them there. I already told you. Until you ask, I'm not touching you."

"And I'm not asking."

And...what do you know, my dick wanted her just the same, but he relinquished control to my brain. "Awesome. Now that we have established that, get in the bed. I can't stand to hear you toss and turn anymore."

She blinked in surprise. "You can hear me?"

"Yes, I can hear you. Every damn creak."

"Well, it's not my fault your couch is leather and noisy."

"Just get in the bed. I'll take the couch, okay? I just—I don't want you to be uncomfortable."

Her brows lowered, finally settling into their frowning grooves. "Why do you care?"

I gave her the only answer I could. "Because while you are protecting me, you're also in my house. It's my job to make you comfortable. So just do it."

"No. I'm staying on the couch."

She gave me no choice. I was going to have to touch her.

Oh yeah, let's see how well this goes.

I closed the final distance between us and bent down.

She pulled out her Taser from under her pillow. "I swear to God, I will Tase you."

"Well, sometimes you've just got to do what you've got to do." Watching her warily, I easily lifted her. Jesus Christ, she weighed nothing. Was she eating enough?

"Put me down, you overgrown oaf."

"In case you've forgotten, I live with staff. If someone hears you screaming, they're going to come in, and then we're going to have to explain why I'm dragging you into the bed."

"I happen to know that these walls are insulated. They can't hear a thing. Which is evidenced by the fact that you can't hear me singing in the shower. Trust me, I'm doing you a favor."

"Why are you so stubborn?"

"Why are you so determined?" She added with a huff, "And while we're at it, I just want to point out that when a man digs in, the world thinks he's determined. When a woman does, she's stubborn."

"You can fight me about the semantics and patriarchy tomorrow. Right now, I just want to know that you're comfortable, okay?"

"I'm not kicking you out of your bed. You're too big for the couch. You'll be uncomfortable."

I couldn't help it. The smile tugged at my lips, and I might have been leering at her a little bit. "Are you saying you care?"

"You know what? You're the kind of guy that can just ruin a moment."

"See, right? We were totally having a moment."

She rolled her eyes. "Oh my God, you're impossible."

"Yeah, I've heard that before. Come on." I hoisted her tighter against my chest and she flushed. But what she didn't get was that she was softness and light and smelled fucking incredible, and I could not let her go.

I went to the other side of the bed that I didn't sleep on. I wanted to lay her down, make sure she was comfortable, and ask her all the questions, but instead I tossed her in a desperate need to get her away from me before I did or said something stupid.

I couldn't get sentimental. I couldn't care about her. Caring about her was going to get me into trouble. And I didn't have time for that. "Next time I tell you to do something, listen."

She sat up looking ready to argue or fight. And my dick was all-in on that action.

Oh yes, tell me off. Give daddy what he needs.

Brain: You, dick, are a sick bastard.

Dick: I know. But I might just be the one to get us laid.

No. No one was getting laid, but at least I knew she was safe and comfortable. "Now get to bed. We both have a long day tomorrow."

"You're a muleheaded, obstinate—"

"Yes, I know." I marched to the other side of the bed, shoved in ear plugs and murmured, "Have a good night, Lady Zia."

THIRTEEN

THEO...

AFTER OUR MIDNIGHT RENDEZVOUS FOR THE GOOD OF sorority life, Zia and I had slipped into a pattern. At night, I'd listen to her breathe and toss and turn, then during the day, I'd try to pretend I wasn't sporting a massive hard-on while she did her level best to drive me batshit.

One good note was I'd managed to convince my mother to stay with my aunt for the rest of the month and commute for her treatments.

The bad news, unfortunately, had compounded. There was still no word from Arlington. And like Kyle, I started to wonder if something had happened to him. Maybe he'd been the first one kidnapped and tortured.

And to make matters worse, Royal Elite was poking through Derrick's past. I just prayed to God I wouldn't have any more surprises. The Cummings bombshell had rocked me. And Zia had noticed it for sure. I had to tread carefully.

Besides Arlington, the more I dug into the Inline merger the worse I felt. My job was to make the acquisition happen, but the numbers didn't make sense. Everything I'd seen thus far said it was a poor investment. On that morning's call I'd suggested to the board that we postpone the merger until we could do more due diligence. That had gone over as expected...like a rave in the royal ballroom.

How the fuck did I end up here?

Arlington had exactly the life I'd once thought I wanted. He had the life I'd walked away from to do the right thing for a friend. But somehow, I'd ended up right here at the pinnacle, and my choices were going to once again define me.

After several tense days and nights of working with Zia, I was ready for a break. Jax was on duty that night, so maybe Zia would go out, give me a moment to breathe, to not think about how soft her skin looked every goddamn second of the day.

Not that I was thinking about that, but just saying that soft is soft. And she smelled good, like lemon and something sweet. Every time I caught a whiff of her hair, I had to hold my breath, lest I'd have to walk around with a hard-on for the rest of the day.

As if that wasn't already happening.

It was a problem. I fully admitted it. I might have to get Kyle to take me out. The problem was, anywhere I went, Zia went. Or maybe I could go out a night she had off. Blow off some steam, find someone else to relieve the pressure.

Or you could fuck her and get it out of your system.

Yes.

No. No. No. No. I wasn't going to do that. My life was already complicated enough. Something told me touching her wasn't going to make it any better.

I knew she was waiting on me to leave, but I still had a few things to do. I still couldn't get over the fact that her sole job was to wait for me to be done and follow me so she could make sure

CHAPTER 13

no one killed me. Honestly, I wasn't sure anyone would try again after what she did the last time. But still, a directive was a directive, so I was stuck with her.

Or, you could get her reassigned.

I'd considered that, honestly. Walking back into Royal Elite and asking for someone else. *Anyone* else. But she'd take that personally. And for all I knew her boss might too. Ariel Scott seemed reasonable and understanding, but I didn't know how badly that would reflect on Zia.

Zia was the kind of person who wanted to do something right the first time. She said there was always a solution to every problem. So if there was a solution, I should see it staring at me. My only concern was that the solution would mean both of us naked, sweating, panting, and...

Not helping.

I looked over the files Kyle sent me. He's found evidence of a small start-up acquired by Arlington Technologies fifteen years ago. When my gaze scanned to the original developer, my eyes went wide.

Derrick had tried to break off with a software company of his own when he was fifteen. He'd actually had some traction, been touted as a wunderkind. But before he'd been able to really get moving, that company had been acquired by Arlington.

My initial hunch said that Arlington didn't seem to know I wasn't his son, But I couldn't ignore the level of animosity.

So far Royal Elite was digging into Derrick's past and history. It would only be a matter of time until they found out about the start-up. To get in front of that I'd have to tell them about this.

The danger in that was they might start looking at Arlington too closely and ignore the likely culprit. Kyle was right. I was in over my damn head. And if I wasn't careful, I was going to get dead.

I'd tried several times to reach Derrick, but he had not answered or returned my calls. I left him several messages, but nothing.

If they'd come after me once, had they come after him before? It certainly would explain why he hadn't been answering my calls. I wondered what the hell was I doing there. I needed to go home and take care of business. What would happen when I walked away? Would I be able to leave it all behind with no word from Arlington?

There was a commotion at the door, and it swung open. Timothy Arlington barged in with Zia on his heels. "Just what the hell do you think you're doing?"

I leaned back in my chair, letting the leather take my full weight. "What have I done now?"

"What, are you dumb now? Why are you poking your nose where it doesn't belong? You don't have access to the files you're trying to obtain. Are you trying to stop this merger?"

I sat back, slouching in my chair slightly, examining him. "Now, why is it that the CEO of the company has files he can't access? I'm doing my due diligence."

Timothy slammed his hands on my desk. The sound had Zia running in. I put up a hand to stop her. "You don't know what you're playing with, son. Leave it alone."

"No, I will not leave it alone. You recognize that there are discrepancies in the records, right? Earnings... there's a very small percentage on that file alone that is unaccounted for. I'm no forensic accountant, but if I'm doing the numbers right, that's a fuck ton of money. What is the THDA account? And what are they covering up?"

CHAPTER 13

"If you go near those files, there's going to be trouble."

"Yeah, you keep telling me that, but I don't know why I should listen to you. You're a disgraced former CEO, which means if there's something you don't want me to touch, that's exactly the thing I need to look into. Makes sense, doesn't it?"

"God, you're the bane of my existence. There are some days when I wished I'd picked—"

He cut himself off, and I frowned. "You wish you picked what? Go ahead and finish your thought, Dad."

He ground his teeth. "Stop digging, boy."

"I'm not going to stop digging, so you might as well tell me. Are we in some kind of trouble? Do they have something on you? With the payoff and acquiring their company, is there something you don't want to come out?"

"I told you to stop. If you keep digging, I won't protect you. What happens will happen."

"All right, have it your way. I will keep digging. And if I find something I don't like, this acquisition will not go through. Do you understand me?"

His eyes flared wide. "You wouldn't dare."

"I would. I have to do what I can do to make sure that the board knows that there are major discrepancies, that we don't know what they're hiding. I'll do what I need to do."

"You're insane. It will be the end of this company. Do you know how much money we've got tied up in this deal?"

"Hundreds of millions of dollars. I know. I'm well aware."

"And you would toss that away for nothing?"

"I know you assume this company is yours. But currently, I'm sitting at the head of the table, so I'm going to do what's needed to be certain I'm making the best decision."

At least that much was true. While I was faking being

Derrick Arlington, I was actually turning into Derrick Arlington. This wasn't a company I had a personal stake in, but I wanted to do a good job.

It was a compulsion. I couldn't not do a job to the best of my ability. I had to make this right. I had to be the perfect CEO, because that's what they needed. That was what the job entailed. And at the moment, the face I had was Derrick Arlington's, which meant I had to protect Arlington Tech with everything I had. And if there was something Timothy Arlington didn't want me to look at, that was exactly where I needed to look. "If you're done old man, I have work to do."

"Somehow the drugged-out party boy has turned into someone who gives two shits. I remember when you couldn't find a fuck to give."

"Well, I guess things change."

He jabbed a finger in the air, directed at me. "I will ruin you."

"You're welcome to try, old man. You're welcome to try."

Maybe you shouldn't goad the one person who could actually ruin everything.

I didn't give a shit. Something was wrong, and I was going to prove it all.

♛

Zia...

I DIDN'T KNOW why I was bothering.

Because that ass chewing sounded like something Aunt Edna would have said.

And having lived with my aunt for enough years to know

that nothing I did was ever going to be right, I felt bad for him. The delivery I'd ordered had finally come in. I'd ordered for myself because he'd said he wasn't hungry, but I could offer an olive branch. Or in this case, chicken curry.

When Timothy Arlington stormed out, I made a note to mentally check what they'd been shouting about and then I knocked on Derrick's open door. "I come in peace." And I held up the bag.

"I'm not hungry."

His gaze was glued to the computer, but I wasn't going to be deterred. Because in those kinds of moments, sometimes you needed someone to make you feel better. I marched over and took out the take out, took out the forks, the chicken, and the rice. I let the scent waft through the room.

He groaned, low and throaty, and God, everything inside me clenched. "Ugh, now you're trying to torture me?"

"Nope. Enough work. Eat."

He frowned. "But isn't this your dinner?"

"I can't eat all of it. And after what I just heard, I figured you could use some comfort food."

"So how much did you hear?"

"Ah, all of it." I shrugged. "Sorry."

He shrugged. "What are you sorry for?"

"Sounds like your dad is a dick. You came by it, honestly."

He broke into a laugh then. "You know what, that's probably fair."

I shrugged. "See? You're already smiling."

He took a bite of the chicken curry and groaned around a mouthful. "Oh my God woman, what are you doing to me?"

"Feeding you, because left to your own devices, you would stubbornly sit here the rest of the night staring at the computer, trying to find the missing piece, and you wouldn't eat. *I* need to eat, and I feel bad eating without knowing that you're eating too."

"Are you always like this?"

"Always like what?" I took a bite and then groaned as my stomach growled, begging me to shove more inside.

Derrick gazed at me earnestly. "You know, selfless. Always thinking about other people."

I wiped my mouth and tried to chew before I spoke. "Oh, I'm not selfless. I'm just as selfish as the next person. It's just been ingrained in me to take care of other people, I guess. Also, I need things a certain way to feel okay, you know? After my parents died, we went to live with my aunt. She was fine, but she wasn't exactly parent material. She was never prepared, always left us hanging, so I started doing that stuff for my sister, more out of necessity, I guess. Even though sometimes I don't want to do things for my sister, it became a habit. Now I carry around stuff like first aid kits and all those things just in case someone needs something. But I promise you, I'm just as selfish as the next person. Sometimes I just want to do what *I* want to do, and I don't want to bend over backward giving to anyone else. Selfish."

He shook his head. "You're missing the point. The point is you always *choose* to do the right thing. I've never been someone who's compelled to do the right thing. That makes you a better person."

"That's bullshit. I'm not a better person. I just know what it's like to not have someone in your corner. So... whatever."

He took another mouthful, and his lids fluttered closed as he moaned. "I didn't realize how hungry I was until I started eating."

CHAPTER 13

"See? Aren't you glad I thought of everything?"

"Well, as bodyguards go, you're the best I've ever had."

I laughed. "I'm the *hottest* bodyguard you've ever had."

"Yeah, that's a good point. None of the others when I was a kid were anything like you. Not as pretty and certainly never catering to my needs."

I choked a laugh. "Please don't say catering to my needs. The last client I had seemed to think that I was there to act as his mom and his personal escort. That man would have me up at four in the morning trying to order him eggs and pancakes. Can you imagine?"

Derrick frowned. "What?"

"Yeah, right? Four in the morning for eggs and pancakes?"

He shook his head. "No. The personal escort part."

"Yeah, there are a lot of men who think that when I'm there to guard their body, I am there to, you know, *guard their body*."

He started to laugh. "That's awful. But that was really funny how you said it."

I laughed. "Well, I had some backup with me, otherwise I would probably have possibly murdered someone, which is counter-intuitive to my job description."

"Sorry, blokes are wankers."

"Does that mean you're going to stop being a wanker yourself?"

"Hey, I have never assumed that you're an escort. Nor have I requested food from you at four-thirty in the morning."

"And you know what? That is appreciated."

He sat back and ran a hand through his hair. "Look, I know I'm a pain in the ass."

"Yes, something we both agree on."

"It's just this merger, I guess."

"Right. Well, you're a billionaire, after all. I'm pretty sure you being a dick comes with the territory. I won't take it personally."

"You know you give as good as you get?"

I grinned then. "Oh, yeah. You want to talk about what you and your dad were fighting about?"

He shook his head. "Just the takeover. It's a bad deal so I'm suggesting we pause. He doesn't like that tactic. He originated the deal and stands to make a killing. I'm not sure if it's a good old-fashioned pissing contest over me being the new CEO, or if he's hiding something. I don't know. I just get the impression he hates me, you know?"

"He's your dad. He can't hate you. Now I know parents try sometimes, but they're just not capable, really. Most parents anyway."

"You really think Timothy Arlington is like most parents?"

He had a point there. "Okay, maybe not. But I'm sure there's a lot of history to unpack between the two of you. It sucks, I know. But you have to know that whatever is going on, it's not really about you. It's about him and how he can't control his reactions to you. So, look at it that way and you'll sleep easier."

His gaze met mine then, the gray irises as clear as raindrops. "You know years ago, I tried to break out on my own with a start-up. Of course, he found out about it and acquired me quickly. It was as if he couldn't let me have something of my own."

Damn. I sighed. "If it's so bad, why do you stay?"

"You know that's a good question. Sometimes I think I can be what everyone needs all the time. Like if I can just adapt everything will be good. It serves me well most of the time. But this," he shook his head. "This is something else." With a sigh,

CHAPTER 13

he added, "You're right. We need to work together. I think it's the only way to find out what the hell is really going on."

"Wow, is this a truce?"

He gave me that lopsided grin that tended to make my panties spontaneously combust. "Yeah, I guess it is."

"There's no reason that we can't be civil."

"Ah, I knew it. You *do* like me."

"And just like that you ruined our beautiful moment. I'll just take my chicken curry and go."

He pulled the Styrofoam dish closer to him. "No, you don't."

"I swear to God I'll fight you for it."

His gaze narrowed on me, and he smirked with his full lips, and God, I wanted to kiss him, and lick him, and yeah... more clenching of the lady parts.

"I guarantee you I'd win."

"I wouldn't be so sure about that, princess."

FOURTEEN

ZIA...

IT SEEMED DERRICK WAS SERIOUS ABOUT THE TRUCE.

When he wasn't actively fighting me protecting him, he wasn't too bad. He still got a bit grouchy and growly at me on occasion, but for the most part, we learned to co-exist. He was still insisting I sleep in the bed. And we'd come up with a compromise and put a pillow in between us. He stayed on his side, and for the life of me, I couldn't understand why the hell I was disappointed by that.

Sure you can't.

That particular morning, I had my hand on his bare chest. And God, it was like touching carved granite. We both woke up, neither one of us particularly acknowledging that 'hey, there had been touching' or that I was so hyper-aware of everything that he did, every move he made.

It was Saturday, so we weren't going into the office. He didn't go through his usual morning routine, so he had the sexiest scruff I had ever seen in my life. It made me want to bite his chin. He had his laptop open and he was staring at it like usual, muttering to himself as he tapped. It was an endearing little habit. Like he was silently talking to himself. Not words I could understand, but still, I could tell he was irritated by it.

"You want to go somewhere?"

He blinked as his gaze flickered to mine. "What?"

"Just... I don't know. Do you want to go somewhere? We've been cooped up between here and the office. I thought maybe we could go out, get some fresh air. You can bring the laptop. You can work. But just in another location, I guess."

His brow furrowed. "See? I told you. You like me."

"I don't like you. I'm just saying I'm going stir crazy. I'm on duty today, and Tamsin is on duty too. We can go sit somewhere as like, friends or something."

His grin flashed, and God, I was sure I was pregnant. That was how you got pregnant, right?

"You do like me."

"No, you're still a pompous jackass."

"Yeah, but I'm a pompous jackass that you like."

"Oh my God, never mind. We'll stay here. Cooped up."

"Cooped up in about four thousand square feet."

"Whatever. Still cooped up."

His stormy eyes fixed on mine. "No, you're right. Let's go out."

"I don't want to go out if you're still being pompous," I huffed.

"I'm always pompous. You like me anyway."

He didn't shave, and he went totally casual. And God, he was possibly even more delicious to look at.

I went and changed into a summer dress. One with pockets so I could conceal my weapons easily. His gaze flickered over my body briefly. "You clean up nice."

"I always clean up nice. I look nice at the office too."

He swallowed hard. "At the office is different."

I studied him as we marched out to the foyer. "Why is it different in the office?"

"In the office, you've got that hot-librarian thing going. It's very distracting."

I blinked. "So you're saying that I'm not hot now?"

His gaze flickered toward me again, settling on my breasts. "I think we both know you're hot. But it's a completely different vibe. Now you look like a real person. Approachable. The hot librarian might smack your knuckles if you talk to her wrong."

"Here's a clue, billionaire bad boy, I'll smack your knuckles anyway, but in your case, you might like that."

His brows lifted and he grinned. "Oh, is that so? See now, you've gone ahead and twisted all the fantasies around."

"Oh my God, you are such a guy."

"Yup, I'm a guy." He had his laptop bag and his sunglasses. "I am in your capable hands. Where are we going?"

"You'll see."

"Give me a clue."

I shook my head. "Nope."

We went down the elevator and Tamsin rushed out of the security tower. "I don't have anything on schedule today. What's wrong?"

I shook my head. "Nothing is wrong. This is Derrick. Derrick this is Tamsin. She's one of your guards and also my best friend."

She gave him a nod. "Lord Arlington."

He shook his head. "Call me Derrick."

A flash of warmth spread through me. I had this under control. I wasn't falling for him. Just because he'd been vulnerable and nice to me once didn't mean I couldn't recognize a jackass when I saw one.

"Okay, so where are we going?"

I nodded at Tamsin. "We're headed to Lola's."

Her brows lifted. "He's going to Lola's?"

Derrick frowned then. "What's Lola's?"

"It's just this place in some old part of town. Not the fancy Old Town where all the tourists go. It's where the real people live. It's on the north end of the island. It's where I grew up. And Lola's is an institution. We'll get some lunch. Sit on the observation deck. You can get some work done. I can get some work done. You can feel the ocean air on your face."

"Somewhere where the air blows on my hair or something?"

I nodded. "Exactly."

Tamsin headed to the Royal Elite SUV. Standard protocol was having someone in the follow car, in case our vehicle was disabled for some reason. "So, why are we going to Lola's?"

I shrugged. "I don't know. I haven't been in a while. The drinks are good, the food is outstanding, and you look like you need some messing up."

He scratched his jaw. "I think I'm pretty messed up right now."

"I know, and I like it. You're less foreboding with the scruff, I guess. And if you were any other guy, that would be really sexy."

He grinned again. "Oh, so now you think I'm sexy too. I'm telling you our relationship is growing by leaps and bounds."

"Oh my God, you are incorrigible."

"And sexy. Don't forget sexy."

I rolled my eyes and kept my jaw shut, because the moment I opened it, I'd have to agree with him.

Lola's was just how I remembered it. Loud and bustling.

The locals running in to get lunch and fresh catches of the day. We picked a table outside, resting our feet on the sandy boards of the deck. "This is amazing. What smells so good?"

"Lola's cooking. Lola is local. Her husband is from Ghana, West Africa. When they got married, he started helping out in the kitchens too. So, he infuses a lot of the island food he makes with things from his West African roots. Which obviously influenced island cuisine anyway, so it all goes really well together."

He picked up a menu. "What is red-red?"

"It's a plantain with bean stew. I guess they make it in Ghana. If all the food there tastes like that, I'd move to Ghana, immediately."

He grinned. "I've had plantain before. There is this ramshackle restaurant in New York I used to go to all the time."

I frowned. "You spent a lot of time in New York?"

Something flickered in his gaze. "Yeah, you know, for business. I like to try different things when I travel."

"I never would have guessed it. Aren't you full of surprises, Derrick Arlington?"

He winced.

I studied him carefully. "Okay. This is not the first time I've noticed. You wince when I say your full name."

He watched me for a moment. "No, I don't. There is this connotation when you say Derrick Arlington. I want to shake it off sometimes."

"I guess I get that. You're never just Derrick. You're always Derrick Arlington."

He nodded. "Something like that." His attention diverted again. "Okay. This is ridiculous."

Tamsin was sitting at another table. He signaled for her and

CHAPTER 14

then called her over. Ear-piece in, she glanced over. "Everything okay?"

He pulled out a seat. "Sit. No need for you to sit at another table. That's silly. You both can watch me just as well from here."

Tamsin's gaze flickered to me. "Protocol."

I shrugged. "Don't look at me. He breaks protocol all the time. Did he tell you? He followed me without a guard when I went to go rescue Deedee."

Tamsin rolled her eyes. "Oh my God, your fucking sister."

"This time it was a pledge prank."

Tamsin laughed at that. "Ugh, college students. Remember that one heiress we had to guard? She was rushing some sorority. God, her father was so pissed when she ran across the campus naked."

I snorted a laugh. "Hey, that's what you get."

Tamsin rolled her eyes. "That's what I got trying to run after her with a blanket to cover her up."

Derrick laughed. "You guys must have the strangest clients."

I nodded. "Yeah. Some of them are okay. Some of them are assholes."

He grinned. "Like me?"

"Oh, no." I shook my head. "You are a baby asshole in comparison. You actually might have a heart. Some of these assholes? Nope, no hearts."

Tamsin grabbed a handful of peanuts and started peeling off the skin in the palm of her hand. "And poor Zia seems to always get assigned to them."

I shrugged. "That's because I have no fucks to give. And I'm generally not going to be intimidated."

Tamsin laughed. "No, it's because you know how to deal with difficult people and you always have a solution."

Derrick watched me. "So, Tamsin, tell me all of Zia's secrets."

My eyes went wide. Was that why he'd invited Tamsin to sit with us? "Tamsin, chick code."

Tamsin laughed. "Oh, chick code is real, but there are innocuous things I could tell him. Like how badass you are with a computer. Only Ariel is better, honestly. Jax tries, but he's not as good."

I couldn't help but preen under her compliment.

Derrick nodded. "Okay, that's good to know. Next time I have a problem, you can help me with it."

"You mean those files you're looking for?" I asked.

He nodded. "Yeah. If you're that good."

"Oh, I am."

The rest of the lunch went off without a hitch. When we went up on the observation deck, Tamsin headed back down the stairs to cover the exit. She wanted to at least act like we followed some kind of protocol.

"I like her. She's fun."

I laughed. "Yeah, that's why I like her. And she's a great friend. She's always there when I need her."

"Did you guys meet when you guys started at Royal Elite, or...?"

"We actually met before in the military. Tamsin was a class ahead of me, so she went off after her service to get another job. We were excited when we met back up at Royal Elite, so everything worked out in the end."

"That's cool." He watched me closely. His gaze tracked my every move.

CHAPTER 14

"Why do you do that?"

"Do what?" His voice was low and husky. And dear God, I had to shift in my seat to ward off the pressure between my thighs.

"That. You're staring at me. It's like you're trying to examine me or something."

"No, I'm just trying to figure you out."

"There's nothing to figure out. What you see is what you get."

"Okay. Then why would someone like you, someone who's clearly strong and fun and who thinks she's funny—"

I interrupted him. "I am funny."

"Whatever. You clearly are amazing. Why would you ever hide from someone?"

"I'm not hiding from anyone." He lifted a brow and waited. "Oh, you mean at the wedding." I inhaled a deep breath. "I don't know. It seems silly now in retrospect, I guess. But I just panicked, you know?"

"So it ended really badly?"

"Just the whole thing was bad. I wasn't at all like myself. I completely lost myself. Seeing him again was going to trigger the old me."

"What? Was it a classic case of *we're just friends who became secret fuck friends* kind of thing?"

"Not exactly. He was my commanding officer, so a personal relationship was not allowed. In the beginning, it was great. He wanted to take care of me, you know? And it was the first time since my parents had died that someone had wanted to take care of me. I don't know. Like I already told you, I'm not selfless by nature. The idea of someone else looking after things for once was nice. Someone picking the restaurant and making sure that we had a reservation and we got there. Those little things. In the beginning, he even tried to help with Deedee. You know, he would shuttle her to class or whatever when I needed help. But then it became more about him telling me what to do. Not really in the controlling kind of way, but all of a sudden, his suggestions were the default, you know? Then I became less and less like myself, and when that started happening, I couldn't count on him anymore. The guy who wanted to take care of me vanished all of a sudden."

"And there went your security."

Why did he get me? I nodded slowly. "I'd gotten secure in him, thinking I had a partner, someone to help, and then *that* guy was gone without any explanation, and *I* had to take care of *him*. Not just for little dating things, but every bill he hadn't paid or just... his car would break down and he'd call me to take care of it. Suddenly, it seemed like I was taking care of him and Deedee and my aunt and *everything* all over again. And it just messed with my head. Then I discovered why he'd stopped being there for me."

Derrick sighed. "He had someone else."

"Bingo. Apparently, he'd been sleeping with her the whole time he was sleeping with me, and she wasn't his subordinate, so they could be out in the open. And God, when I say this out loud, I sound like an idiot."

"You don't sound like an idiot to me."

"Well, I sound like an idiot to me. God, I mean, yes, sneaking around was hot at first, but man, that shit got old real quick. It's my own fault. I really should have known better. I can only count on myself. Things go much better that way."

"No, I'm sure one day you'll find somebody you can count on."

"But you know even if I did, I wouldn't want to because I know what it's like when it's swept away. It's terrible. I won't be that person."

"We all need someone sometimes, Zia."

"Yeah, well, I don't want to be the one who needs anyone."

"I know you don't."

"Come on, let's head on down to the beach."

"Ah, this is why you were so concerned about my footwear."

"Well, you were wearing your fancy Nikes. I just didn't want you to get sand all over them."

"Come on."

He grabbed his laptop bag, and we headed down to the beach. As we went through the doorway, his hands trailed on my back, guiding me out. The flutter low in my belly warned me that it wasn't just about arousal. I could fall for him.

Theo...

THIS IS A DATE.

No. This wasn't date. I just wanted to say thank you. Arlington wasn't my father, but I'd still been a little rattled by our conversation yesterday, and she'd been surprisingly helpful. Arlington really hated Derrick. It was palpable.

He was where I needed to watch my step. He hated his son enough to notice any missteps I made.

"What are we doing here? Do you have a meeting here?"

I rubbed the back of my neck as I gave her a sheepish smile. "Actually, I figured you've been on me a little over a week and I barely know you, but this isn't a date."

Zia barked out a laugh as she glanced around. "I dunno, Arlington, crystal chandeliers, dim lighting, smells so good my mouth is watering. I'm starting to think this is a date. I feel like I told you already that I don't date playboys."

I stifled my laugh. "Not a date. Two colleagues having dinner. One of them is trying to be nice because he's been a bit of a prick."

"You have been. That's true, so I will let you make it up to me with food. And dessert. And wine. Let's not forget the wine."

I laughed. "Understood. Wine. Coming right up."

I led her through the restaurant. I'd managed to get us a private seating, so the restaurant was cleared, and we were the only diners for the evening. And it was chef's choice, so it was going to be an adventure. As we were led to our table, Zia took everything in. Occasionally her fingers reached out to trace over the furnishings.

"Did you know I have wanted to eat here forever? I used to tell myself that when I hit a big milestone I'd make myself a reservation. That I would celebrate it here."

"Why didn't you ever have that dinner?"

She shrugged as the maître d pulled out her seat. "Deedee needed stuff. Then, well, it was really expensive. Then I figured Garrett would propose here." Her voice softened. "Turns out he did. Just not to me."

Hell. "His bloody loss then, wasn't it? And you're here now. We can make this a fuck-him dinner if you want to."

Her smile was soft. No hint of those killer dimples, but I'd take it.

"Look, I owe you. You've been watching my ass, and I wanted to say thank you."

CHAPTER 14

Her brows popped. "What?"

"Look, I know I've been a bit of a handful. It comes with the territory, but you didn't do anything to deserve that, so I'm sorry. And I'd like to start fresh."

Her brows furrowed then. "You know, it's like I get two versions of you."

Shit.

My brain scrambled to find purchase as she studied me. Where had I gone wrong?

"In the office, especially, you're this hard-assed kind of a boss. Even Olivia jumps when you say jump. No one questions you. They're afraid. And maybe they should be."

"This is illuminating."

She shook her head. "What I mean is there are these other moments when you seem different. More normal. Still an asshole, but I don't know... a lesser one?"

I watched her warily. She saw too much. She watched too much. I definitely underestimated her suspicious nature. "That's just work me, I guess. I know it probably seems dumb to you, but I do need people to fear me. I don't necessarily want that, but I need it. I have to show strength, that I'm a capable leader, or they'll eat me alive."

Easy does it. Getting a little close to home, aren't you?

It was a little closer to home than I wanted. Those were all the things Derrick and I had discussed. But it was true. I wasn't Derrick, but stepping into his shoes and into his life, there was a part of me that wanted to prove myself. Prove that I could do it if I ever had the inclination to be an incorporator. Prove it to myself. Prove it to Derrick. The way he'd walked into my office that day and called me a loser and told me I was wasting my God-given talent had irked. I wanted to be successful. And Kyle and I had been on the cusp of that. But then everything had gone tits-up. So, now that I was stepping into Derrick's life, I wanted to be good at it. But there was also a part of me that just wasn't that cruel. Maybe that was a weakness. Maybe not. The point was she'd noticed.

"When I can let my guard down for a little bit, I can let the real me out. But I learned early that it's not a good idea to let the real me out."

She nodded slowly. "So, who is the real you? The real Derrick Arlington?"

I pursed my lips and then just blurted out the words. "Call me Theo."

Her brows lifted. "Theo?"

Well you really screwed the pooch this time. And without benefit of lube. Rule #2. Christ. "It was the name my mother preferred for me. I, uhm," I cleared my throat. "I prefer it."

Heads up. This still qualifies as a lie.

I'd already told so many...

She nodded then. "Actually, you know what? I did see that on one of your youthful indiscretions when you were sixteen or something. I think there is some record of where you were out in some club and your friends kept calling you Theo."

I frowned then. "What are you talking about?"

Theo? Why would Derrick ever use the name Theo?

"Um, I can't remember the details. It was in Ibiza or someplace like that. You and your friends were on some yacht, living it up as you do. It was on YouTube or something. You were wasted, the lot of you. They keep chanting, 'Theo, Theo,' and you were dancing and yukking it up. You don't remember?"

I ran a hand through my hair. "No, I don't remember."

CHAPTER 14

"Look, sorry, no judgment. It's just that I saw it when doing some research on you. I assumed you'd remember."

"I think it's safe to say that there's a lot from my years of indiscretion that I don't remember. Let's just leave it at that."

"Oh, well, if you want me to call you Theo, I can call you Theo."

"Thanks."

"Do you want to make that note to Ariel too?"

I shook my head. *Hellll, no.* That name was for her only. "No. It's just—I guess it's what my friends call me." Heat crept up my neck.

Zia's lips tipped into a brilliant smile. "So what, we're friends now?"

"Something like that."

For once you have the money and the wealth to have anyone when you want. And of course, you want the one who thinks you're someone else.

"Let's order drinks."

Once the drinks arrived, things relaxed a little bit. I'd seen it on our day out, but when it was just the two of us, I could see that Zia was fun. Really fun. She talked about her sister. Deedee, it seemed, was more than a handful. When Zia talked about her, she laughed and spoke animatedly. Her eyes brightened and her hands articulated wildly. She was running a hand through her hair in a non-practiced fashion because she was simply telling a story, and I couldn't take my eyes off her. I took a long sip of water.

I needed to focus on anything other than her lips while she talked. As I drank, I coughed a little. My throat itched.

Zia's brows snapped down. "Are you sure you're okay? What's going on with your face?"

I tried to swallow the itching, but it only worsened. "What do you mean what's wrong with my face?" My voice was raspy as I spoke. Crap. I reached into the neck of my shirt to attempt to loosen my tie, but that didn't help.

"Well, you've gone bright red."

I frowned at her. I knew she was saying words, but I was having a bitch of a time processing them.

"Are you allergic to something?"

I shook my head. "No, I'm not. Well, mushrooms, but I never order them. As long as I don't eat one, I'm fine—" I glanced down at my steak and the vegetables underneath them. I didn't see a single mushroom anywhere. I waved over the waiter. By the time he got there, I couldn't even talk to him.

Zia took over, jumping out of her chair. "He's not supposed to have mushrooms. The dinner, did it include mushrooms?"

Oh God, my throat. I could feel my tongue swelling. *Shit.* I had ingested mushrooms, and I knew for a fact Derrick didn't have the same allergy. He was only allergic to strawberries, which I was clear on. Good thing I had an EpiPen on me. I stood, wanting to ask for my coat, but I couldn't talk at that point. My tongue was too thick in my mouth, taking too much room.

Zia was shouting orders to the waitstaff, calling the chef in.

When the chef came over, she glowered up at him. "Does your meal include mushrooms?"

He shook his head. "No, not in the steak. And the vegetables were done in a lovely vinaigrette. No mushrooms."

She didn't waste time yelling at him. I started to weave, and she caught me. She eased me gently down onto the ground. "Do you have an EpiPen?"

I nodded and tried to talk. All I could do was mutely point in the direction of where they'd taken our coats.

"In your coat?"

I nodded frantically as the edges of my vision began to gray. The fear rode the back of the adrenaline in my blood. Christ I was scared. So fucking scared.

I understood the danger of what was going on here. One, I could die. Absolutely. But two, exposure. Exposure would be bad. Exposure would be trouble.

"No press." Was all I could force past my throat as Zia leaned over me.

Standing up, she ran over to the coat check and grabbed mine, searching the pockets as she brought it over. As she moved, she had to bunch up her dress at the slit. Even as my vision was graying, the light going dim, and everything going blurry, I could still see the expansive thigh with every step forward. Fuck, she was beautiful.

"Here we go, EpiPen, where do I jab it?"

I couldn't talk. Hell, I could barely breathe. I just indicated a spot on my leg, and she nodded.

Before I knew what was going on, pain... immediate and instant on my leg. I wanted to howl with the sting of it. But then the panic rose in my chest and my vision was going.

Going.

Gone.

Theo...

I WOKE WITH A DRY MOUTH, and my head was pounding. My throat was scratchy. It felt like someone had stuffed sawdust-covered cotton into my mouth. I cleared my throat, and oh yeah, not a good idea. It felt like I had swallowed a fire poker. I pushed myself into a sitting position and blinked. I was in my room. How the hell? There was rustling to my left, and I felt around looking for the light switch. When it flickered on, I was surprised to find Zia there.

"Theo, hey. You gave me a mighty scare. I'm pretty pissed off about that, by the way."

I frowned and tried to swallow again.

"It seems to be a constant complaint with you." She pushed herself out of the chair she had apparently dragged over and poured me a glass of water, handing it to me. "Yeah well, that's the nature of our relationship. You keep things from me, like a random mushroom allergy. That's not anywhere in your medical records. And then I don't know how to mitigate those things. Then you almost died on my goddamn watch. So yeah, I'm a little pissed off."

I ignored that for a moment. "How did we get back here?"

"Well, considering you wouldn't let me take you to the hospital or call a doctor, I had no choice. I got your driver to bring us back. I called Royal Elite. We have a scenario for such things."

I let my head drop back on the pillow after taking several sips of the water. "Fuck. I feel like death."

"Well, lucky for both of us, you're not dead. Seriously, you have to stop making my job so damn hard. We had an arrangement. You don't die on my watch, remember?"

"Yeah, I remember."

Her gaze searched mine, brows knitted in worry. "Seriously though, are you okay?"

CHAPTER 14

"Don't tell me you were worried about me."

She sniffed. "Nope. You're still a pain in the ass who likes to keep too many secrets for my liking."

"I'm not keeping secrets. I just don't like broadcasting my weaknesses."

"Even for those meant to protect you?"

"Look, it's a later in life allergy. I learned about it on a trip. And now I mostly just avoid eating mushrooms. It's never a problem. If you noticed, I did ask if the dish had mushrooms, didn't I?"

"Yeah, but I thought that was more of a preference than anything."

"Nope."

"Which makes me wonder, how the hell did someone know to put mushrooms in your food? I had Trace and Jax talk to the chef and anyone on staff. The chef insisted the dish is not meant to be made with mushrooms, not even in the sauce he uses. He, like everyone else, has no idea how it happened."

"Shit."

"Yep. So, this makes me circle back. That guy from the wedding... How did he know you were going there?"

"I mean, it's not like I was hiding it. I was a guest." At least Derrick was.

She shrugged. "I know. But I have to go through it methodically. Where was he trying to take you?"

This much was true. "I don't know."

"Derrick, you recognize I'm trying to help you, right? So, anything you could tell me, any direction you can point me, it makes covering your ass a whole lot easier. I get it. There are things you don't want me knowing. Fine, okay. But at some point, you're going to have to trust me. You scared the shit out of me tonight."

I couldn't help but smile. "See, I'm growing on you."

She rolled her eyes. "Don't get used to it. Please tell me, is there anything else you're allergic to? Any other way that someone could hurt you? Just how sensitive is your allergy?"

"Usually, I have to eat one. I hadn't even gotten that far into the meal. It has never been that bad before."

"Okay look, the safest course of action is to have someone prepare all of your food. Someone you trust. Or we'll have someone on Royal Elite staff make it."

I laughed. "This is ridiculous, you know that."

"Well, someone tried to kill you, so it's not ridiculous."

"I get that. But this is an overcorrection. Just find out who knew we'd be going to the restaurant today and who had access to the food."

She sighed, a small pout lighting her lips. "Okay that's a question for you. Who made the reservation?"

"I made it myself." Why would I have someone else make my reservations?

Because that's what Derrick would do.

"Did anyone know?"

I shrugged. "I did put it on the calendar so Olivia wouldn't book a call for tonight."

My eyes went wide. "Olivia has access to your calendar?"

I frowned. "Yes, she's been my assistant for six months, but she's worked for my father for years. And that calendar is public."

"Look, I know she's your assistant, but she had access to your schedule. Knew where you were."

I shook my head. I racked my brain as I tried to follow what reason she'd have to try to poison Derrick. The problem was Derrick was only allergic to strawberries. And my mushroom allergy was not a standard one. Someone who knew me well would have had to provide that information. And my arrangement with Derrick was more about me learning about him than him learning about me.

"It's not Olivia. I'm sure she doesn't know about my allergy. No one does."

"Well clearly someone does, Derrick. You were almost poisoned tonight."

As she paced, I reached out and took her hand. "I told you, call me Theo."

She breathed in deep. "Theo, I need my team. We have to protect you. We should maybe move you to Royal Elite."

When I laughed, my throat hurt. "No. I told you I need discretion. That's not going to work. How's this. I'll take the food precautions, okay? In the meantime, we try to find out who wants me dead."

"Why are you being so stubborn about this?"

"It could have been an accident. My point is we know nothing."

"And my point is that it's my job to protect you as much as possible."

"And you are okay. This wasn't on you."

"Oh, yeah?" She asked, her eyes wide. "Then who is it on? I feel like it's my fault. It was on my watch."

I struggled with how much to tell her. "I don't know anyone who wants me dead this badly."

"I think it has to do with the deal, so when you're feeling up to it, we need to go over it. Every aspect of this acquisition and who wouldn't want it to go through. Lucky for you, we've got some excellent hackers on the staff. We can find the right kind of information. Just point us in the right direction, because I don't ever want to have to look at you like that again."

"I knew it. You do like me."

She narrowed her dark eyes at me. "I don't like you. But what I like less is someone trying to make it look like I'm bad at my job."

She might pretend that she didn't like me, but she looked worried. Really worried.

"I'm wearing you down. Sooner or later you're going to see how awesome I am."

"Yeah, whatever. Get some rest. When you wake up, we have some work to do."

My eyes were feeling heavy again. I was exhausted. And I might not want to comply, but I needed to because she was right. Only a few people knew about my allergy. One of those people was my mother. Derrick and I had discussed it, but he had an allergy to strawberries, not mushrooms. So, whoever had tried to kill me, knew I was an impostor.

FIFTEEN

ZIA...

WHAT THE FUCK HAD JUST HAPPENED?

One moment we were having fun, talking, and I was getting to know him. The *real* him. Not the billionaire suit he put on every morning. That shell was a full body suit, meant to protect the man inside.

I liked the man inside.

And honestly you really should know better. You can't like him.

No. I couldn't. It was a bad idea in all the ways. And I'd learned my lesson and was all into self-preservation.

But someone had tried to hurt the man I liked. Or maybe they'd gone after the billionaire.

They're the same person, sweet cheeks.

I paced as I watched him in bed. This wasn't supposed to happen. No one was supposed to get past me to get to him. I'd messed up. How had I fucking missed an allergy?

I was worried about him. I'd studied his file, and there had been nothing about an allergy to mushrooms. Was it something he kept secret on purpose? And how had someone known? Or was it just an accident?

His dark hair flopped over his brow as I paced the bedroom. He was fine now. With Jax's help, I'd managed to get him upstairs into his own bed. I was on duty, so all I had to do was watch over him and not let him die, which was possibly going to be harder than it looked.

He groaned from his bed, and I whirled around. "You're not worried about me, are you, bright eyes?"

I wrinkled my nose at the stupid nickname for me. "Well, I was waiting for you to wake up so I could kill you myself. You recognize that I've never lost a client, right? Stop trying to give me a bad mark."

He coughed and then he tried to sit up. "You've had many solo clients, have you?"

"It's usually a team effort, but I've handled about eight solo clients."

"All of them as resilient as me?"

I shrugged. "I usually get boy bands and diplomats. None of whom were as much trouble as you."

"Oh yeah, because I tried to get poisoned."

I frowned. He looked okay. His lips had stopped swelling. His tongue too. When he talked, he sounded more like himself. Although his accent was flatter, and weirdly, more American? Maybe he was trying to get his tongue to work properly.

"Relax, I'm not going to bloody die on you."

"Well, it was touch and go there for a second."

He rolled his eyes and laid back on the pillow. "Jesus Christ, if you're going to hover, can you do it from the bed? Trying to track you is making my eyes hurt."

"Are you in pain? We should call a doctor."

He shook his head. "Jesus, just sit down. We don't need a doctor. You used my EpiPen, which I might add, you seemed to take an awful lot of glee in."

"Excuse me for saving your life."

His voice softened. "Thanks, by the way."

Was that a genuine thank you out of his mouth? I couldn't even believe it. It seemed that Dr. Jekyll was back.

"Are you thirsty? Do you want water? Something... give me something to do."

His lips broke into a wry smile. "You can't sit, can you?"

"No, I'm not the one with solutions to problems, but I'm the kind of person who does things. I always have been, so I need to do something. I don't sit well."

"Well, I'm asking you to sit, please."

I sat on the edge of the bed, his feet within range. Jax and I had removed his socks and shoes, but we left his clothes on and mostly hoped he'd be able to get himself right on the bed when he was at least feeling better enough to do that.

"How did you get me out of there?"

"Jax was backup. So between the two of us we managed." I took a deep breath. "That was a close one. I think we need to be more careful and while we're on the topic of your safety, I think the Arts Gala is out of the question. You take one sip of champagne and someone could poison you."

He coughed. "It will be fine."

I blinked at him. "Are you serious right now? Someone literally just poisoned you. I had to jam an EpiPen into your leg. I mean, I took pleasure in it, but still..."

"Look, it's important, okay? I've got to walk through the steps. All of them."

"I don't know what you mean by that. All I know is that it's my job to protect you and you're making it difficult."

"And all I know is that you're supposed to make my job possible. Whether it's easy on you or not."

"Jesus Christ, you are such a stubborn pain in the ass, you know that?"

His lips tipped in that sexy smirk I'd noticed at the wedding. His dark lashes fluttered on his cheeks, and then he lifted his gaze to meet mine. My stupid heart ticked up several beats faster, I could have sworn he heard it. Those clear gray eyes blinked at me as if he knew exactly what was going on in my body. "'Talk to me, bright eyes. Who are you anyway?"

"No one interesting. I'm just someone trying to do a job."

He chuckled then. "Oh, right. Just a robot?"

I shook my head. "Yep."

He was silent, as if waiting for me to elaborate more. When I didn't, he shook his head. "Come on, I'm trying to get the grogginess out of my head. I still have some work I need to do. You might as well talk to me while we wait."

"Fine, what do you want to know?"

His smile was slow. "So, it's just you and your sister?"

I nodded. "Yeah, she's in Uni now and changing her major every two minutes."

He chuckled. "Okay, what is it now?"

"Oh my God, right now it's photography, with super expensive equipment, and she has never shown an aptitude or an interest in photography before. But of course, she has to have everything required for the course."

"Just how many majors has she had?"

"Uh, four?"

He shrugged. "Maybe she's just having a hard time finding her thing."

"I don't really understand her. I knew exactly what I wanted to do and what I needed to do to make it happen, you know? I had a lot more responsibility, and I deliberately made it so that she could focus on being a kid? I wonder if I did the wrong thing, because right now, she can't make decisions to save her life."

"What were some of her majors?"

"Well, she wanted to be a linguistics major despite never having taken any languages before. She speaks French, but she doesn't even practice it. And then she changed to psychology, but she didn't enjoy that. Then there was philosophy. Apparently, there were too many dense books in that one. And now it's photography."

"She's a kid, right? She's supposed to change her mind."

"Well, she's twenty. She has a little time, I guess, but at the end of the day, she's got to figure it out. I won't always be there with a safety net."

"You're her sister. Something tells me, you'll always be there."

I shrugged. "Yeah, but just once I wonder what it would be like to be completely free of responsibilities, you know?"

Why was I talking to him? When he was like this, it was too easy to let my guard down a little bit. Too easy to relax into it. Too easy to talk to him. When he wasn't being a dick, I actually liked the guy.

"What about a boyfriend? You're reasonably attractive. I assume with the assignment you have now, that means you're not with anyone."

"I could have a boyfriend."

"Wouldn't that make it awkward for him? You being assigned to me?"

"This is like an acting job. None of this is real."

His gaze lifted again and held. The stormy gray of his eyes measuring mine. "You're right, none of this is real."

I couldn't help but wonder if I'd somehow cracked our very thin lines of truce by pointing it out.

"I don't have a boyfriend."

I don't know why I said it. But a part of me wanted to soothe his concern. That was dumb. All of this was dumb. I should stop talking to him, immediately.

"What about you Mr. Billionaire? From all the magazine articles I've seen, it seems that you've never had relationships. Nobody special. Except Miranda."

He shrugged. "You shouldn't believe everything you read."

"Well, what's the truth?"

"Relationships are tricky. You never know people's intentions or motivations. You never know what's real and what you can trust."

And wasn't that the truth? In the silence of the penthouse, the late-night lights of the Winston Isles twinkling on the horizon somewhere, he seemed real. He seemed like someone I could talk to. But I should know better because he was just like Garrett. Garrett had seemed great, but I knew that player type. The ones who gave you their undivided attention for a limited period of time.

"So, no one special, huh? Ever?"

He frowned then. "Ah, once, but it didn't last."

I shrugged. "I wonder why."

"Like I said, it's hard to hold on to people."

"Yes, it's always hard."

"Maybe, maybe not."

I almost wished he would go back to the brooding, irritating, barking asshole he was before. That was easier to deal with. I didn't know how to reconcile these two versions of him.

"So your sister... Is she doing okay?"

"Oh my gosh, don't tell me, you, Derrick Arlington, care about someone other than yourself?"

He lifted a brow. "That's not an answer."

"It's fine. She just wants more money, which I'm determined not to give her."

"What if she needs it?"

"Well, I've got to teach her responsibility. I'm not a bank account. I'm not an atm. If she wants to switch to this new major, she's going to have to figure it out. I gave her some money for equipment, but I told her that was it. If she wants to do it, she'll find a way. That's how I did it."

"Well, she's different."

"I know, so I'm worried. But she's my sister and I probably spoiled her too much, so I'm paying the piper now."

"Are you sure you're doing the right thing?"

I shrugged. "I have no way of knowing."

"Something tells me you'll handle it just fine."

"And you know me so well?"

"You might be surprised, you might not be her mom, but you're the closest thing she's got now, right?"

I shrugged. "Yeah."

"Well, I know all about good moms. You seem like the type."

"Oh shit, Mr. Billionaire, don't tell me you're starting to actually like me."

He gave me a wolfish grin then. "Oh, I like you."

"Really? Hard to tell with all your barking."

"I just want to see if you can handle my bite."

Oh boy, several problems with that statement.

One, I absolutely wanted him to bite me. Secondly, he actually could not bite me. And third, I wouldn't allow myself to be bitten. Not by someone like him. Never again.

SIXTEEN

ZIA...

My feet hurt. And then the stupid spanks were making it so I couldn't breathe. But on the plus side, I looked amazing.

When I stepped out into the living room, Theo did a double take. "Wow."

I spun around, showcasing my dress's pockets. "See? Pockets. I can hide my weapons."

"Why do I get the impression that every single thing you own has pockets for this exact reason? To conceal your weapons."

"Because they do. It makes it easier, especially if I'm not wearing a blazer or something. The guys have it easy. They just put on a jacket and then bam! Weapon concealed."

He shook his head. "You know, I've never met anyone quite like you."

"That's because I'm an original. Accept no substitutes."

He laughed. "You really do look amazing."

"Is that a compliment?"

His eyes went wide in mock surprise. "I'm always complimenting you."

"Except when you're not. I believe when you first met me you called me obstinate and out of my mind."

"To be fair, you did try and goad the kidnapper. How was I supposed to know you were a badass?"

"You know, in the future, you should just assume I'm a badass."

"That's not how I built a business."

"Yeah, I know. But still, I'm awesome."

He smiled and laughed, and when he did that, he was stunning. He'd left some of the scruff from the weekend and wasn't completely clean shaven. "Why do I get the impression that if you didn't have to be an industry tycoon you would just wear a beard?"

"Well, maybe. There was a time that I had a beard."

I blinked up at him. "Really?"

"Yeah, for a while."

"I feel like I've never seen a single picture of you with a beard."

He frowned at me. "Yeah well, I guess it didn't last long."

"I want to see pictures."

"One day."

"Are you ready?"

"Ladies first."

The Arts and Education Gala was Sebastian and Penny's baby. Before she'd been a badass Royal Guard, she'd been an artist. And Sebastian, before he'd finally become king, had been a photographer. With their duties now, neither one of them got to use their skills very much, but they'd set up a whole trust to help kids like them who never would have a

CHAPTER 16

chance to go to art school or have careers in the arts. Derrick, *Theo*, was a sponsor.

The event, for once, wasn't being held at the palace, but instead at Neela's gallery. Her former best friend had been an art gallery dealer who turned out to be a criminal who'd faked her own death. But before that, she willed all of her estate to her baby, whom Neela and Jax adopted. So the event would be held there with the sparkling vistas of the Islands as our backdrop. When we arrived, the party was in full swing. The entire Royal Elite team was in attendance. Everyone had their jobs. The Royal Guard were mostly guarding the king and Penny. I was on Theo duty. Trace was my backup. Tamsin was on Prince Tristan as backup for Ariel.

It got a little complicated. We had the new trainees act as double protection for the king and queen, if necessary.

When we walked in, Sebastian and Penny greeted us. Penny looked splendid. She was wearing jade green, which highlighted her tawny-colored skin, and her baby bump was showing. She'd been bumpless for so long we were all teasing her that she wasn't really pregnant but was just using a fake baby to get Sebastian to be at her beck and call. But she was showing now, and her hands rested protectively on her belly. I loved how pregnant women automatically did that. When we approached, I curtsied low. "Your Majesties."

Both of them waved me off as if they weren't interested in formality. Despite me having kicked both their asses at the last family game night, I stopped to show respect.

Penny gave me a warm hug, as did Sebastian.

Sebastian and Theo shook hands. Their exchange was downright friendly. Why was it that I didn't know that they were close?

Penny was as surprised as I was. "Well, that's new," she leaned in and muttered.

I glanced at her. "What? They didn't get along before?"

She shook her head. "Nope. Derrick has always been around, but Sebastian never liked him. He was always a full-on pompous prick, so I wonder what's going on here?"

"Maybe it's like his housekeeper said; he's had a personality transplant."

She laughed. "Body snatched. Either way, this is better."

"Don't worry, sometimes he can still be a pompous ass."

She laughed. "Well, he's still a man, right? Can't they all?"

We left them to greet the rest of the guests, and Theo's hand slid down my back to gently guide me through the crowd. It was meant to be an impersonal touch, but somehow, it was oddly intimate. The zing that chased up my spine had lust pulling low in my belly as he led me toward a tray of every delectable treat I could possibly want in the world. "Go on. Pick one. I know you want to."

"How did you know I have a sweet tooth?"

He laughed. "You think I haven't noticed that Elena has been serving you Madeleines, chocolates, and baking fresh croissants for you?" He shrugged. "I figured she knew something I didn't know. Have a treat."

God, I was desperate for the chocolate ganash. "You've been noticing what I've been doing?"

His gaze narrowed on mine. "You know I have."

What was that supposed to mean?

This was already too tense and weird for me. Was Tamsin right? Was he paying special attention to me?

Yes girl, yes. Now jump on it.

CHAPTER 16

No. I was not going to jump on it. I'd learned my lesson after all.

Theo was Sebastian's cousin, a billionaire, and a client. There were a million reasons why this was a really bad idea.

My libido did not agree, but thank God she wasn't in-charge. After we helped ourselves to treats and snagged glasses of champagne, Theo led me outside.

"I'm pretty sure you're supposed to be inside mingling."

He shrugged. "Nah, maybe in a bit. I'd rather just stay out here and talk to you."

I studied him again. "Why do I get the impression you don't want to do this? That you're not really down for the whole jet set crowd tonight."

"Because I'm not. It's exhausting."

"Yeah, I can imagine."

"But it's an important cause. Penny and Sebastian asked us to be here, so I came. Besides, it was a good chance to see you dressed up. I would have hated to miss it."

I laughed and shook my head. "There you go with the flattery again. I'm starting to think maybe Sebastian and Penny are right; you have been replaced by a pod person."

He frowned then. "Is that what they said?"

I laughed and nodded. "Yup. Hell, even Elena said something similar."

He ground his teeth then. "I'm just trying to be... I don't know, better."

I shook my head. "Oh, I don't think it's about today or anything, it's just... everyone's noticed you're not being a hundred percent jackass."

He lifted a brow. "Oh what? Just 80%?"

"Hey, the 20% matters."

He laughed. "Fair enough. Maybe it's you."

I flushed, the heat creeping up my neck making me too warm. "What, I have given you a personality transplant?"

"Well, you're calling me on my bullshit, and now there's less of it."

"Hey, who knew I had that kind of power? If I'd known, I would have been using my powers for evil."

"I'm pretty sure you're already using them for evil." He winked as he spoke, and I nearly choked on my ganash. What a waste that would have been.

"You might be right about that."

I took another sip of my champagne and noticed how closely he was watching me. Direct and clear. No wavering. "Zia."

"Theo," I murmured.

His eyes fluttered closed. "I really fucking love that you call me that."

I shifted on my feet. "Well, you asked me to, right?"

"Yes, but you didn't have to listen. I know it's weird that you know about the trouble between me and my dad. The level of disdain is real."

"Trust me, I get it. I mean, if you want, you can have your name legally changed. But if it was that unbearable, I figure you'd probably want to change the Arlington part."

He shook his head. "No. I sort of like you being the only one who calls me Theo."

"Careful now, *Theo*. Someone might think that you're flirting with me."

His grin was brief. "Well, I'm doing a piss-poor job of it if you didn't notice."

I swallowed hard then. "You probably shouldn't be flirting

with me. What is it they said in that movie? 'Relationships based on intense situations never work out.'"

"Oh, the girl is quoting *Speed* at me. I think I'm in love."

"You fall in love too easily."

"That's probably true."

"What's this? Derrick Arlington falls in love easily?"

"Well, I never have before, but I'm pretty sure the right woman could work her magic on me and completely ruin me."

I swallowed hard. I don't know what game he was playing, but part of me wanted to play.

Yeah, you do.

The other part of me wanted to run.

Brain: That's a better move.

"So... ah, we should get back inside."

He took my arm and led me into the shadows. "Not before I break the rules again," he whispered, voice soft.

I froze. Holy hell. He was going to kiss me. Tamsin had been right.

Libido: Hell yes.

His lips were firm but soft as they grazed ever so gently over mine. He hesitated, pausing, giving me a chance to back away. Giving me an opportunity to say no. Giving me a way out. Did I want it?

God, no. I did not want a way out. I wanted to feel the full press of his lips. I wanted him.

You'll get hurt. He will hurt you and it will be bad. Just like Garrett was bad. This will be catastrophic.

I was already at that point where I would do anything to have his hands on me. I would do anything to feel his lips over mine. I would do anything to stay in the moment. His lips dipped over mine and I couldn't breathe. I couldn't function. I was kissing him back, sliding my tongue over his and losing just a little bit of myself.

Theo slid his arms around me. His lips were gentle but demanding. A spike of the electricity flared between us, scorching my lips when his tongue dipped inside. With a low groan, he shifted our angle, kissing me deeper and ripping a moan from me as my body started to melt.

I didn't have the defenses to fight off these feelings. Somewhere in the far recesses of my mind, alarm bells rang, starting as a low buzz, but quickly intensifying to a sharp clang.

But just as the sirens started to wail with impending doom, Theo dragged his lips from mine and stared at me. His muttered curse echoed my own feelings.

I was toast. This man could own me.

I told myself it was only a small part. I told myself that I could recover. I told myself all the things so that I could have this moment with him. But even as I told myself those lies, I knew what would happen. Derrick *Theo* Arlington was going to break me.

With my lips still burning and my mind spinning, Theo led me back downstairs, comm unit back on and broadcasting. My emotions were complete mush because he'd proven just what kind of expert kisser he was.

The gala organizers had so many people they wanted him to meet. Every time he spoke to someone, he was charming, confident, clever, while pulling me along and introducing me. It was hard to study the crowd from any vantage point. Luckily, I had my team in my ears.

"You look so pretty, Zia." Tamsin said.

Trace coughed as he muttered. "Oh yeah, because that's

CHAPTER 16

what matters to Zia right now, how pretty she looks in her dress."

I could almost picture Tamsin scowling at him. "Shut up! She does look pretty. And I happen to know she's deadly. How are those knife sheaths working out?"

I smiled at no one in particular and muttered through my teeth. "They're working just fine. Now can you please shut up so I can focus?"

Trace just chuckled. Tamsin grumbled about it, but they went back to what they did best. A tall brunette approached as we were talking to the former minister. She seemed to know Derrick right away. She beamed a smile at him and wrapped her arms around him. I fought the urge not to rip one of the arms off her and beat her over the head with it, because that was irrational. None of this was rational.

She leaned in and whispered something I couldn't understand, and Derrick stared at her as if he'd seen a ghost. Then he was pulling me through the crowd, but at the same time, someone announced that it was time for us to be seated and there was a surge in the crowd. The next thing I knew, my hand slipped out of Derrick's, and there were people between me and him.

I tapped my comm. "Trace, Tamsin, can you see him? The crowd is too thick."

Tamsin's voice was clear, not panicked, but tense. "Nope. No vantage."

"None yet. Hold," Trace added

Fuck. Oh God, I need to get to him. I started shoving my way through the crowd, pushing, pushing, though even in my four-inch heels I was barely five-six. Many of the men were tall, and every single one of them in a black tuxedo. It was difficult to see and pinpoint my target. Trace's voice was like a balm in my ear. "I have him. East exit with a tall brunette."

"Son of a bitch." I started shoving through the crowd. And when the people in front of me didn't move quickly enough, I started assisting them along. I had to get to him. I couldn't fail. Not again.

His life was on the line. And so was a little piece of my heart.

Theo...

FUCK. Fuck. Fuck.

How are you going to get yourself out of this one Mr. Billionaire?

My heart raced as I tried to think my way through this. There was still a way out.

But is there a way out and a way to still protect Zia? They'd threatened to hurt her if I didn't go with them.

And you think she needs saving?

Yes. No. Fuck, I didn't know, but either way I had to protect her or at least try. I was too damn close. So much for keeping her at arm's length.

You are two weeks too late for that.

Who the hell were these people?

The beautiful brunette who had come to say hi had leaned in as if she knew me. Or as if she knew Derrick. She gave me a standard double kiss as I tried to place her face with one of the names in the dossier. She hadn't immediately come to mind. I didn't know why. Her voice had been cool when she whispered.

CHAPTER 16

"Mr. Coleman, so fantastic to see you. I'm going to need you to let go of your girlfriend's hand and come with me. Mr. Arlington would like to speak to you."

There had been some small sliver of hope on my part that I was finally going to hear from Derrick and that he was here at the event. There had been a small flare of hope that we could just switch out and that with a snap of my fingers I could go back to my life. That I could tell Zia the truth. Would she still want me?

But something hadn't felt right. As the brunette led me through the crowd and then filed in behind me, cutting me off from Zia, I knew. When I halted, she beamed up at me with a smile, the mask covering only a part of her eyes. Dark brown, but not warm and vibrant like Zia's. Hers were cold and flat.

"Mr. Coleman, I wouldn't do that if I were you, or you'll meet the same fate as Mr. Arlington. Keep walking."

"The hell I will." I tried to move back.

"Now, I'm not going to threaten you with violence. That would be so uncouth. But while I can tell you're wearing body armor, the very handy bulletproof vest you have on, I'm pretty sure that Miss Barnes isn't wearing any. I have men in the crowd right now, and they will kill her. Or maim her. They can get so inventive with acid these days."

My heart squeezed and then stopped.

I tried to turn my head back to find Zia, but the brunette tagged me along. "Uh-uh, come with me. You, Mr. Arlington, myself, and my associates need to have a very long chat."

"Screw that."

"Walk, or she's dead. Trust me, my friends in the crowd do love their knives. Her beautiful face and that body will be carved up. She's wearing black. No one will even be able to tell she's bleeding until it's too late. There will be no help for her. Walk."

So with a hard swallow, I started forward.

"Oh, thank you so much for listening and sparing me having to get my hands dirty. I'm wearing white, you know."

I scowled at her as we walked arm in arm through the east doors and then to the left. Down the hallway, there were far fewer people. Then we made a right into another darkened hallway lit only by a few ambient lights from lamps in the corners. "We're out of the crowd. Now what the fuck do you want?"

The smile she gave me was beautiful... beaming. As if I held the answers to the universe. "Walk through there."

I scowled at the double doors she was attempting to shove me toward. "I don't think so."

"Move."

I shook my head.

She tapped her ear and then muttered something in what sounded like Russian or something Eastern European, and then two big men emerged out of the far door. The kind of men that looked like Arnold in his old days. Hulking. Massive. Unrelenting and deadly.

"Fellas. I don't want to hurt you," I mumbled. I'd always believed a little bravado went a long way.

"You don't have a choice. You can go with them quietly, or they can drag you out of here. Then when they're done dragging you out of here, they'll go and find your friend. As dates go, she's okay. Pretty. Uncomplicated. But I feel like you can do better, Mr. Coleman."

I scowled as the two hulking forms came forward.

The brunette headed back toward the ballroom and I called out after her. "Where are you going? You don't want to watch?"

She smiled. "Oh, don't worry. They will tell me when you're in the car and if you behaved like a good boy. Because if you don't, we will kill her."

She was right. I wasn't going to fight. Not if it meant keeping Zia safe. I turned back to the guys. "I don't suppose you want to tell me where we're going?"

They didn't even look at each other. They just came forward for me. Who were these people? Why did they know who I was? And for the love of God, what had they done to Arlington?

Stop being noble. Zia dispatched one of these guys all by her lonesome. She is badass and doesn't need you to protect her.

As they got closer, I could see that the one on the left was the one from the wedding. Zia had dropped him like he was a bad habit. *See, evidence she doesn't need your protection. Not to mention her team is here. And low-cut neckline or not, there's no way she'd leave the house without body armor.*

I had to remember the things I knew about her. She was hyper about security. That wouldn't just extend to her sister, but to me too. So, I could be an idiot and go with these guys, but then when she eventually found me, she'd kill me herself. Or I could fight.

And expose yourself.

At that point, there was no real option. It was fight or die in some horrible way later. I nodded at the familiar guy. "Hey man, good to see you again. How are you feeling after my girlfriend beat your ass?"

"When I'm done with you, I'll finish her."

I stuffed the simmering rage down at his mention of hurting

Zia. That was his bravado. She could take this twat. None of what he said mattered. What mattered was he looked like an ass, and it reminded me once again that Zia didn't need anyone to take care of her. She could take care of her damn self. Besides, she was my bodyguard. I wasn't hers. That meant she didn't need me trying to ride in on a fucking white horse and shit.

Put up a fight, asshole. That's what we're doing today.

"Guys look, I don't want to kick your ass. It seems unfair. We're not evenly weighted. Do you have another friend, maybe, that we could add to this?"

Oh yeah, taunt the Terminator rejects. That seems like a good idea.

But I knew what I had to do. I had always been mad at my mother when I was a teenager. She'd put me in everything from judo, to jiu jitsu, to Krav Maga. I had been more than a little wild, needing some kind of male influence in my life. I was bright but bored. And I had let the world know of my displeasure. My mother had found a way for me to channel that, and it was finally going to come to good use.

When they both stepped forward, I stepped to the right, avoiding the first blow and putting dumbass number two between me and dumbass number one, which was good. I landed my first blow, sending him back only about half a step.

I knew the rules. When on the offensive, stay on the offensive. Keep moving. One opponent between you and the other. Unfortunately, the assholes attacked back at me. Knees. Elbows. Fists. Elbow number two landed right on his temple. It should have been lights out. Honestly, it should have felled the two hundred and twenty pound, six-foot-three giant.

He was big, but I was mean.

When he didn't go down, his friend tried to come around

the other side. I shook my head. "Uh-uh, we're not going to do that. One at a time. Wait your turn."

The one I was fighting threw a wild punch, which I blocked, leaning into it and counter punching with a fist to the nose. The satisfying crunch was everything. And then, left arm still blocking his right one, I leaned in with an arm bar across his throat, my hand digging into the flesh of his shoulder and the other sliding under his suit jacket and into the cotton fabric of the shirt he'd been wearing. Then I dug in, making sure to grab not just shirt but flesh, bone, muscle, skin. Then I applied all the pressure I could on his throat. He coughed and choked and tried to remove me. But before he could, I landed a knee. Then another, dragging him forward even as I drove my hips forward. Knee. Land. Knee. Land. All the while using my arm to control his movements and placing him between me and the other guy, even as I delivered the blows.

Knee. Knee. Kick. Another elbow to the temple and an elbow down the back of his neck and he finally went down. I didn't give myself a chance to enjoy the victory. I hopped over him. "Opponent number one, I don't suppose you want to tell me what all this is about. Where have you put Arlington?"

"Arlington can't help you now," he muttered under his breath, and then he came forward, a wild swing coming. I lifted my right arm, bending it at the elbow and bringing my elbow all the way up past my head to block the blow.

These guys were more about brute strength than finesse. They probably spent most of their time battering their opponent as opposed to actually having to learn and fight. They were big. Bigger than me. I was tall but lean. Quicker. Deadlier, as it turned out. I landed a quick knee and was out of range again.

He came with another wild swing of combos, and one

landed on the kidney, but I went with it, ignoring the searing pain slicing through my lower back and up my spine. When I stopped, I landed a front kick, which brought him forward, and then I launched myself at him. My thumbs pressed into his eye sockets. He tried to reach for me, but I kept pressing. As he clawed at me, he got one hand lose. *Son of a bitch!* So I started landing blows, elbows, hammer fists. I could feel the anger rising in me. The fury I kept buried was taking over and taking control.

Fury is not the answer. With fury, you have no control.

I could hear my old trainers beating that into me. I had to regain it because fighting like this wasn't going to work. When he finally stopped moving, I knew better than to take the moment to rest. I had to get the hell out of there. I had to get to Zia, but not before I patted them down.

No wallet. No identification. There was a gun though, which I took and shoved into the back of my pants. Honestly, that was the worst place to put it. Same with his partner. There were two weapons but no documents. I couldn't very well walk back into the ballroom with those, so I just took the magazines and the bullets, shoved them in the hidden pocket of my tuxedo, and then stood and turned.

Zia was at the end of the hallway, gun raised in one hand, fingers of the other pressed at her ear. As I approached, she stared at me. "Who the hell are you?"

SEVENTEEN

ZIA...

I HAD QUESTIONS. ALL THE QUESTIONS.

Questions like, who the hell was he? What the hell had I just seen? Jesus Christ, how had he learned to fight like that? Those were at the top of the pile as my brain tried to make sense of all of it.

Theo had been exempted from military service because he was technically a British citizen, so he wouldn't have learned those moves in the Royal Army, despite being the king's cousin. Either way, he shouldn't have known how to do any of *that*. That was the stuff of serious time spent MMA fighting and training.

Whoever that woman was that took him out of the ballroom, and whatever the hell had happened there in that hallway, he should have been gone. Instead, he'd kicked all the ass, knocked out two giant men, and confiscated their weapons. If he could do that, then what the hell did he need me for?

I ran up to him as he stood slowly. "Are you okay?"

His eyes were glassy but slowly came into focus. "Yeah, are you?"

"I'm not the one that went all MMA on the tanks just now." I tapped my ear comm. "I have him. East exit. Let me know when you have the car." I couldn't help but search him over with my hands.

He's fine. Relax. Barely a scratch.

Not really true. There was blood on his knuckles, and he had a cut on his head. But mostly he was no worse for wear.

My eyes went wide when I saw the same guy from the reception pushing to his feet. His eyes were bloody, and his nose was broken. There was blood seeping out of his temple, but he was attempting to stand.

I did the only thing I knew to do. I shoved Theo behind me, and then I raised my gun. "Listen, jerkballs, I know you don't want any of this. I flattened your ass once. He has kicked your ass once. Walk away."

He gave me a toothy snarl and charged. I lowered my center of gravity and then hip checked Theo out of the way. It was the only way to get his big body to move.

As the asshole charged at me, I lowered even more, directing the full effects of my Taser straight to his groin. Once I made contact, I dug in despite his body looming over me, threatening to crush and pound me onto the ground. I held on to the Taser, delivering electric sperm scramblers, and didn't let go.

Finally, he sagged to his knees shaking. I still didn't let go until he fell on his back, eyes rolling to the back of his head.

When I stood, Theo stared at me. "Fuck me. Where have you been hiding that thing? Also let me point out that I totally softened him up."

I pointed at my hair even as I rolled my eyes. "Up there. Come on."

In my ear, Tamsin's voice was clear. "Car is here."

CHAPTER 17

I went and took Theo's hand and tugged him over the two bodies. "Let's go."

I didn't have to fight him. He came easily, but he was quiet.

When we got outside, an SUV screeched to a halt. I opened the back door and grumbled, "Theo, get in." He shook his head. "I know. This isn't how it was supposed to go. I understand. But I need you to get in the car."

His gaze lifted to mine, and he nodded. "Okay." And then he slowly climbed in.

I hopped in the passenger seat, and Tamsin gave me a nod. "Let's go back to the penthouse." The roads were quiet, and Tamsin's driving was as crazily reckless as ever, but she got us there in record time. Theo was able to walk in on his own, but his reflexes were sluggish and he didn't say a word. Shock. It had to be.

We stepped in the private elevator to find Jax was already in position. He gave us both a nod and watched Theo warily. "Do you need help getting him in?"

I shook my head. "No, I have him.

Once we were inside the penthouse, he started toward his office. "Theo, I need to check you out. Or at least call in the doctor or something."

"I'm fine."

"You are *not* fine. The last thing you are is fine. Jesus, are you going to start listening to me now?"

He turned. "What do you want me to say? You were right? I shouldn't have gone tonight? Or maybe you want to ask me a slew of questions. Who are those people? I don't know. Why do they want me? I don't know. Why is this happening? I don't know."

I inhaled a deep breath. "I get it. You've just been through something traumatic. But let me do my job. Let my team do its job. If you fight me at every move, Theo, this only gets harder. You and me, we need to be a team. If we're a team, great! We can handle anything that comes our way. But your insistence on doing things the hard way and going off on your own has to stop. That *has* to stop. Someone is trying to kill you. You have to understand that."

He swallowed hard and ran his hands through his hair. "I understand. I just—"

I frowned. "What? This is serious. Your life is in danger."

"This is the last thing I thought would happen."

I nodded slowly and suspected he wasn't talking about the kidnapping attempt. "Do you want a drink?"

He nodded slowly. "Yeah, I think a drink is in order."

I followed him to his office and grabbed two tumblers from the cabinet on the bookshelf. There were all kinds of liquor available. "What do you feel like? Scotch?"

He nodded again. "Yeah, scotch."

I grabbed a bottle of Lagavulin and poured. "You clearly knew how to handle those guys."

He shrugged. "I guess so."

I handed him his glass and watched him take a long sip. "Why, Theo? Why go with them? Does someone have something on you? Is there something you're not—"

"You."

I blinked. "What?"

He waved his glass in my general direction as he planted that very nice ass on his chaise lounge. "That woman, she said she had people in the crowd that could get to you. Hurt you. So I went with her."

My heart rate ticked up, and I swallowed around the lump

forming in my throat and threatening to cut off my air flow. "But why? I can take care of—"

He lifted his gaze, and stormy gray eyes met mine. "I finally remembered that. So I fought back."

He was trying to protect me? But why? I wasn't anything to him.

Lady parts: *Don't be daft. He wants to do more than bone you.*

He cleared his throat. "I remembered just in time that you don't need anyone to save you. You do the saving, so, yeah."

I shoved the feelings I couldn't sort through properly to the side. "You certainly were very efficient in your ass kicking. MMA?"

He drained the rest of the scotch in his glass. "I could give you some bullshit about anti-kidnapping training, but the truth is, I started learning to get some control. I was... a handful as a kid and needed an outlet for my emotions and aggression."

I frowned as I watched him, looking for the lie or the evasion, but no. This was the truth. "So, do you still train?"

"Just as a workout. I, uh, have better control over myself now."

Still the truth. "Did they say anything, Theo? Did they give you any hints as to why they wanted you?"

"No. I don't know why they would want me."

That. Right there. That wasn't the truth. It wasn't an actual lie, but he was holding something back. Tamsin would say I was too suspicious. I was always looking for a reason to not believe something, but I had to be suspicious. I had to make things safe for everyone, including Theo.

I let it go for the moment. "Look, you're safe now. We'll have a team meeting. I think the penthouse is still safe. But I don't think outside events are. So for now, the office and the penthouse are the only places you go. But we'll get the whole team on this. We've never lost a client, Theo. We're not starting now." He nodded slowly. My phone beeped, but I ignored it. "Come on, let's get you to bed."

His gaze lifted as he sat in the chair slouched like it was his job. He lifted his gaze to mine. "Are you joining me?"

Heat pulled in my core. I knew what this was. He had just fought off some people who were trying to kidnap him. That was survival instinct. After a big fight, I almost always wanted to be in close contact with someone. Usually sex, not that I got it, but I understood the desire. "You're going into bed. I need to debrief with the team, and then I'll take the couch. Probably better if tonight of all nights, we don't do something stupid."

He stood, his gaze piercing into my soul. "Just so we're clear, I want you because I want *you*. I've been fighting off a constant, persistent hard-on since I saw you at the wedding. This isn't an adrenaline thing."

Holy hell. What did I fucking say to that? *Dude, you have to say something.* "I—" My phone beeped again.

He lifted a brow. "Do you want to get that?"

I shook my head. "No, not particularly."

"Just get the damn phone."

"No, I'm on duty and she needs to learn."

His brows lifted. "Deedee?"

"Yes, it's my sister. For her everything is emergency. One of these days I need her to learn what an actual emergency is."

He nodded slowly. "I get it. Just answer the phone."

When it beeped again, I groaned and then yanked it out of my clutch off the table."

"What, Deedee?"

CHAPTER 17

"Zia, oh my God. I—I screwed up. I need your help." Her voice was timid, and she was crying.

"What happened?"

"I messed up. I messed up bad."

"We've been through this. Not to mention, I'm working at the moment. I can't just drop everything for whatever little emergency you have."

"It's not a little emergency. It's a real one. I need you."

"Well, I'm with a client, so it will just have to—"

Theo pushed to his feet and shook his head. "What's wrong?"

I adjusted the phone with the microphone down past my lips as I spoke to him. "It's my sister. She claims there is an emergency."

His brows snapped down. "Let's go."

My brows snapped down in reply. "What?"

"Your sister called three times in a row. Even I can hear how upset she sounds."

"There is no emergency. I was serious last time. She'll never learn if I always bail her out."

He lifted a brow. "She sounded upset. Let's go."

"We don't have to."

Theo stepped forward and then took my hand, placing his over it. "You just saved my life. Now it's time to save yours. I'm just going to change first."

I stared after him as he walked out of the office toward the bedroom. Why was he suddenly even hotter?

"Zia? Zia, are you there?"

"Christ, Deedee, I'm on my way."

"Oh my God, thank you. Thank you. I'm so sorry. Thank you. Just get here as soon as you can. I'm at central booking."

"What? Tell me you aren't in jail right now."

"Sorry. Just come please." And then she hung up.

I charged into the bedroom to change and caught Theo shirtless and in nothing but boxer briefs. Holy Christ on a cracker.

"I uh..." what was I going to say again? Oh yes. "I need to change. Deedee is at central booking. She's been arrested."

He muttered a curse, but quickly dragged on his jeans. "Change. I'll call the lawyer in the car."

"But Theo..."

"But nothing. I swear to God if you tell me you don't need my help, I will not be responsible for how hard I spank you. Now change."

Oh.

Well.

Then.

Why was the thought of that so hot? He wasn't exactly Theo now. And he wasn't exactly Derrick. But why did that somehow make him even more appealing?

I'd have to explore that later. Right now, I had to save my sister... again.

EIGHTEEN

THEO...

I couldn't lie. I was rattled as hell. Someone trying to kill you would really do that to you.

After the wedding, I had known that there was danger. I could sense it. It was why I had bodyguards. It's why I'd listened to my damn cousin. *Derrick's cousin.* Fine, whatever. Derrick's cousin. But then having them actually come for me in public like that, and having to actually defend myself against it, that shit was real.

Very fucking real. And on my goddamn doorstep. I had no idea what to do, because from the sound of it, they had Derrick. That meant there would be no answers coming. No guidance, no response, no nothing. I was on my own. And I was wearing someone else's life. It wasn't just about the skin or the clothes that I had to embody and inhabit. And I didn't have a fucking clue how to keep making it work. I was out of options. But this, this I could do.

Zia was clearly stressed, so I'd taken care of what I could. The lawyer had beaten us to the precinct and already had

Deedee at home, so Zia didn't have to worry about that. But she was still pissed off.

My experience was that she was always the first one to jump into a fray, the problem solver, the one with solutions. Why did she look so lost now?

When we pulled up, as usual she didn't wait for the driver to open the door. But I took her hand before she stepped out. "Are you okay?"

Her brows lifted. "Someone tried to kill you today and you're asking *me* if *I'm* okay?"

"Your shoulders are tense. Your jaw is tight. That beautiful mouth of yours hasn't attempted to cuss me out in at least an hour, so are you okay?"

She blinked rapidly. "I—I don't know. I don't feel okay. I feel like I have no idea what I'm doing. That's how I feel."

"Okay. That's probably normal. We all feel like that in this kind of situation."

"No, you don't understand. You know those days when you just don't want to deal? You just want to be someone else, be somewhere else? That's how I feel right now."

"Well, you're not alone."

Her dark gaze searched mine. "Thank you, Theo."

The bloom of heat in the center of my chest was new. Jesus Christ, I didn't think I could take it because the use of her voice saying my name was like molten heat and slow-moving lava through my extremities. I wanted to hear her say it again and again. Preferably on her back, lying spread open, my mouth on her.

Dick: That shit is not helpful if you don't want me commenting. Easy does it. Focus on the task at hand.

We walked to the apartment. She pulled out her key and

CHAPTER 18

then thought better of it, shoving it back in her pocket. She knocked. A petite girl answered the door, and I was struck again by how much she looked like Zia. Slightly taller, but somehow younger in the face. Which was ridiculous, because Zia barely looked twenty-five. "Oh my God, Zia, you're here. Derrick." She glowered at me. Apparently, she wasn't over our last conversation.

The lawyer, Ames, stepped forward. "Miss Barnes was arrested for public indecency and intoxication. I managed the bail process, and she has to appear before the judge tomorrow, but I'll make a deal and it will go away."

I shook my head. "No, she'll do the community service option."

Ames lifted his brows. He was Derrick's fixer. My understanding was he'd kept Derrick out of many a scrape.

Deedee was still glowering. "What the hell? How are you even in my business right now?"

Zia's body sagged as she stepped forward, "Deedee—" She started to respond but looked like she had no idea what to say.

Fuck that. I wasn't letting her shoulder any more responsibility on her own.

"That's enough Deedee. Let me assure you that I am not your sister. And I have only met you twice, but I've had enough of your bullshit. I got you out of jail. I also generously paid your lawyer, so you will do as he tells you. And no, we're not having your sister get you someone else so that she has to pay for your mistakes. This is your lawyer, and he's staying your lawyer."

"Who gave you the right, you pompous prick?"

"I care about your sister, and you are draining her. Jesus, look at her. she's exhausted. She is so tired of dealing with your bullshit. For once think of someone else."

In that moment I could tell Deedee loved her sister, because her gaze flickered to a still silent Zia. "Z, are you going to let your new boss, boyfriend, whatever he is, talk to me like this?"

Zia's gaze ping-ponged between us. Then she inhaled a deep breath. "Yep, because while you don't like him a lot, you actually seem to respect him. And seeing as you have zero respect for me, he gets to be in charge right now."

"No, wait, that's not true," Deedee protested, but Zia wasn't done.

"And while we're at it, you're also going to move out of here. You're going to get a roommate and pay rent."

"But I don't have a job."

"Well, you have thirty days to get one. And what's more, I will continue to pay for school, but the moment your grades dip below a B average or you take an incomplete, you're on your own. I'm done. I'm tired. I love you, but clearly, rushing in to fix life for you hasn't worked."

Deedee's eyes went wide. "Do you even care that this wasn't my fault? Yes, I was drunk. I'd been at a party, but there was this guy there who stole money from my boyfriend, Toby."

Zia frowned. "Toby? The dufus from the roof incident?"

"Yes, him. So anyway, this guy took money from Toby, and we were just trying to get it back and the cops got involved."

I lifted my brow and muttered. "Toby?"

Deedee slithered her gaze to me. "Yes, Toby. Why? What's wrong with Toby?"

Zia was losing patience. "Look, I don't care what his name is."

"Look, he doesn't do drugs, okay? But he owed this guy money, and then this guy came to get Toby and said that I have to cough up two thousand dollars. He was going to hurt Toby, and I didn't know what to do. And then this guy's muscle or whatever shows up and takes three hundred from Toby, so we were fighting with him with the cops showed up."

Zia stared at her sister. "So your boyfriend is a low-level campus drug dealer? Are you fucking serious right now?"

"It's not what it sounds like."

"So you lied to me?"

I could see this was getting out of hand fast. Zia was probably feeling some crazy level of betrayal, and I wanted her to feel the things she needed to feel, but at the end of the day, I wanted to help. However, being Theo, I realized I couldn't help. But as Derrick, I could. I stepped between the women when Zia took a step toward her sister. I gave Zia a sharp shake of my head. When I turned to Deedee, her eyes were wide, and she backed up several steps. "How much does Toby owe this dealer?"

"HE—HE said Toby owes him two thousand dollars."

"Wait, so Toby says he owes this dealer two thousand dollars, and if he doesn't pay, the dealer is going to hurt him?"

Deedee nodded. "Yeah, and I don't have it."

I put out my hand. "That's not what I'm asking. Who gave you this information, Toby or the dealer?"

"Toby."

"How is the dealer involved?"

She shrugged. "He approached Toby when we were out one night. They had heated words, and then the dealer told me that I'd see my boyfriend again when he was done with him. The next day, Toby came back and said that he had to pay and that he needed my help. So I've been slowly trying to get it from Zia, because I knew if I came and asked for two thousand dollars, she'd say no."

"As she should." I ground out.

"You don't understand, he's going to hurt him."

"Is anyone threatening to hurt you?" I asked.

"No, but I—"

I put up my hand. "Call Toby and tell him to get his ass over here."

Her eyes went wide. "What?"

"Jesus Christ, call Toby and tell him to get his ass here now."

That made Deedee scramble. When I turned, Zia looked shell-shocked, confused. "Are you okay?"

"I've been giving money to my sister to take care of her, and she's been giving it to a drug dealer or a drug dealer's friend. I don't know."

Oh, geez. She was going to lose it. "Look at me. You're okay. Everything is going to be okay."

"It's not okay. My sister, she's— God, she's naive and spoiled... so spoiled. After all this time, everything I do for her, she just pisses it away."

"Look, I don't know anything about raising anyone. I think you've done a great job."

Her breathing came in shallower pants. "I haven't. Clearly, I haven't. God, how does she always manage to do the exact wrong thing?"

"It's okay, we'll deal with this." I waited for her to say that she didn't need me to deal with it, but the words never came.

Deedee came back with the phone on her ear. "Just come over here. There might be a way out." She hung up and turned to face me. "What are you going to do?"

"Oh, you'll see." I said.

CHAPTER 18

It took ten minutes for Toby to turn up. When Deedee answered the door, the kid tumbled in looking like every slacker frat boy I'd ever seen. His hair was a shaggy, greasy mess. His button-down shirt hung open over a T-shirt with some graffiti graphic on it. His leather jacket looked expensive as hell.

This kid was just playing the part, but he was playing it poorly.

"You're Toby?"

He scowled at me. "Who the fuck are you?"

I had no patience for this. Somebody had tried to kill me today. And Zia was still upset, looking shell-shocked and exhausted. All I wanted to do was get her back to the penthouse so we could both crash the fuck out. I didn't need shit from this asshole. I crowded him. "Let me ask you again, are you Toby?"

The kid's eyes opened wide. "Yeah man. What? What do you want?"

"Listen very carefully, you are done fleecing Deedee over here. Deedee, you're done with him."

Both of them complained. "What?"

I slanted Deedee a look that told her to shut the hell up, and then I turned my attention back to Toby. "You see, you're done fleecing her for money. You're done making her feel sorry for you. You're done booty calling her. You're just done."

He scowled. "You don't know me."

"Oh, but I do. So, here's how it's going to go. How much money have you already taken from her?"

The kid had started to sweat. "I haven't taken anything from her."

Deedee wasn't having that. "What? I've given you two thousand dollars."

"You wanted to give that to me. That was for us. For us to enjoy ourselves."

I rolled my eyes. "Fuck, you're a piece of work, aren't you?"

He gave me a narrow-eyed glare. "Who the fuck are you?"

I stepped into his space. "I'm the motherfucker that's going to get you out of her life. If you come near Deedee Barnes again, I will know. If you talk to her again or even mention her name, I will know. And then I will do very bad things to you. Do you understand?"

I let the menace slide off my voice. The part of me I kept at bay, hidden. The part of me I kept behind a nice façade of the kid who just wanted to make a philanthropy app.

I usually didn't show that part of me that wanted to seek and destroy. I rarely let that person out to play, but after today, it was already so close to the surface. I snatched him up by the front of his jacket. At first Zia tried to intervene, but the look I snapped at her kept her in place. "I'm going to give you the money, and then you're going to vanish. If I so much as hear her even say, 'Oh my gosh, I wonder whatever happen to that guy named Toby,' I will find you, and I will end you. Do you understand?"

Toby's watery blue eyes started to leak. "Shit. Right. Okay. Fuck."

I reached inside my pocket and pulled out my phone. "Now, do you have Venmo or something like that, because that's how we're going to do this, nice and simple."

The kid's eyes went wide. "Venmo?"

"It's an app. Jesus Christ, I thought you kids were the forefront of technology."

When he pulled out his phone, I grabbed it, downloaded the appropriate app, and made the transfer. I stared at him. "If I

CHAPTER 18

hear so much as she's even thinking your name, I come for you. Do you understand?"

He nodded his head like a bobblehead doll.

His gaze didn't even flicker over to Deedee, which told me what I needed to know. He'd been using her. I opened the door, and he scrambled out.

Zia stared at me. "Did you seriously pay him—"

"I'm not done yet," I cut her off.

Her jaw snapped shut. I turned my attention to Deedee. "Now, Deedee, this stops immediately. First, you're going to get a job. Any job. I really don't care. Your sister assumed ownership for this place, so you're going to start paying her rent."

Deedee started yammering. "But I can't afford rent without a job making enough to pay."

I put up my hand. "You don't pay for anything, so you don't respect it. I'll let your sister determine how much rent you're going to pay her. It doesn't have to be what this place actually costs, but you're going to pay something. You're going to do it monthly. You're going to do it without complaint, and you're never going to be late. Do you understand?"

Deedee opened her mouth and then shut it again.

"I'll take that as a yes." I sighed. "And I swear to God, if you ever call your sister asking for money again, or to bail you out of jail, or to get you out of a jam of your own making where it's not an actual emergency that requires a hospital, you'll hear from me, and it's not going to be good."

"But how am I supposed to take care of myself, working and going to school?"

"That's the funny thing about a job. You get a job that pays enough to allow you the extras. If you don't have the money for it, then you don't do it. Make a budget. For the love of God, you have to learn to take care of yourself. You're fucking twenty."

I rolled my eyes, and then I turned my attention back to Zia. "Are you okay?"

She just stared at me with her dark eyes. "I think I'm too numb to know."

I stroked a thumb over her cheek. "Let's go home." But before I led her out of there, I said loudly, "Oh, yeah, Deedee, apologize to your sister."

"Apologize? You're the one who barged into my house and got rid of my boyfriend and..."

Lord, how had Zia dealt with her for all these years? At my worst, I was never ungrateful. Just angry. "The appropriate phrasing right now, Deedee, is thank you."

Her jaw fell open. "I—"

"I'm waiting."

"Thank you," she mumbled.

I turned to Zia. "Are you ready to go?"

For a moment, I thought she would argue and tell me to go fuck off and that she didn't need me. But then she nodded. "Yeah, I'm ready to go."

For the first time since she'd gotten the call, I watched the tension roll out of her shoulders.

Once we got back in the car, she slid into the driver's side and buckled up. "You didn't need to do that. I didn't need you to *solve* it for me."

I tried not to clench my jaw, and I leveled a look on her. "You take care of everyone else. I see you. Even though Olivia is a total bitch to you, you still don't fuck with her coffee order. You get it right. And I see you sharing your little Oreo cookies with her, even though she's terrible to you. For the last week or so, I've watched you tense every time you get a text message. I assume they've been from Deedee. You've been taking care of that too. For once, let someone take care of you."

And Jesus Christ, I wanted to be that person to take care of her in all the ways that mattered.

One little problem, she has no idea who you are. And when she does, she's going to hate you.

NINETEEN

ZIA...

It was late when we returned to the penthouse.

This fucking night. I was wrecked. And after what just happened at Deedee's, I had no idea what to say. All I wanted to do was crash and get a redo.

But there would be no redo. For once, Deedee had been put in her place. I dared a glance at Theo as we rode the elevator. His jaw was tense. He hadn't said a word. Granted, he'd said so many at Deedee's.

Inside, he marched toward the bedroom. At that point, I was exhausted. I'd been hungry earlier, but I was too tired to bother with chewing now.

When we finally reached the bedroom, I had no idea what to say. "I'm not even sure how to say thank you. I'll pay you back"

He stopped. I could visibly see the tension in his shoulders. They were bunched and tight, all the muscles coiled. He turned slowly as he took out his cufflinks. "You think I want you to pay me back?"

I frowned. "I— Look she's my responsibility and I—"

CHAPTER 19

His brows snapped down then, and he planted his hands on his hips. "Seriously? This is what's happening?"

I frantically tried to blink away the tears that threatened. God I was so damn tired. "I'm trying to say thank you, I've never—" My nose stung. Shit. I had to stop this conversation before I cried in front of him. I spun away. "I'm just going to—"

Before I could flee to the sanctuary of the bathroom so I could cry in privacy and peace like a normal person, strong arms wrapped around me like a vice.

"Shit. I'm sorry. I'm sorry. Please don't bloody cry. I'm here. You're not alone." His voice was barely above a murmur. It was gentle and soft and made me crack even more.

He turned me slowly in his arms. For the first time in a long time I felt safe and not alone and I wanted to stay here. I never wanted to leave the cocoon of this safe space. I tucked myself against the firm muscle of his chest. He'd almost been kidnapped again tonight, and he was holding me, comforting me.

This is dangerous territory, Barnes.

It was, but I didn't care. I just knew I wanted him. His fingers threaded through my hair as he soothed me. The low timbre of his voice set me in a trance and the tension ebbed out of my muscles. And for the first time, I wasn't worried about someone trying to kill him and I wasn't worried about my sister. All that mattered was us. Right now, in the moment.

I tilted my head up to meet his gaze and that silvery gaze was stormy. It was as if he was fighting something. His body was still tense against mine as his gaze dipped to my lips. His thumb brushed over my cheek and he groaned low.

"Theo..."

His voice lowered to something akin to a purr and a growl

combined. "I fucking love how you say that." And then he slid his lips over mine.

Theo...

SHE TASTED LIKE CHAMPAGNE. And just like bubbly, one taste of her went straight to my head.

I couldn't breathe; I couldn't think. I couldn't focus on any of the good reasons I had not to touch her. Because if she tasted this good, how could this possibly be a bad idea?

She doesn't know who you are for one. That sobering thought was just the bucket of ice water I needed. I started to pull back, but she made this whimpering sound at the back of her throat. Then with shaky hands, she started with the buttons on my shirt.

You're weak.

Yes, yes, I was. But she was in my arms and I couldn't stop unless she asked me to. And given how she was fumbling with my buttons and tugging on them impatiently, she wasn't asking me to stop.

She finally managed to get them undone and slid her hands inside my shirt over my skin. The feeling of her bare fingertips over my too hot skin was like a series of electrical charges over my nerve endings.

Her feather-soft fingertips scorched a path of heat from my waist to my pecs. She pulled me to her, and Christ I went willingly.

It wasn't quite a kiss, just a whisper of lips meeting, really. But as I breathed out, she breathed in, and vice versa. It wasn't long before I started to feel like I might die without her to supply me with air. "Zia?"

"Hmm?" Her fingers were busy setting my skin on fire.

"Is this what you want? Are you sure?" She had been upset a minute ago. I didn't want to take advantage of her feelings.

"You have been making me ache."

And what do you know, my dick liked the sound of that. I had already been steel-hard, but the fucking guy was throbbing now, begging for her touch.

She had barely touched me, and I was already so close to losing it. I wanted to pick her up, back her up against the wall, and bury himself so deep inside her that we couldn't separate ourselves for a week.

I should have been gentle. I *meant* to be gentle. But she slid her fingers into the hair at the nape of my neck and electricity kicked through my whole body. Lust chased away every flicker of doubt.

Zia moaned as I licked into her mouth, and my cock jerked, her throaty moans driving me crazy. I dragged her closer as lust coursed through my body, and Zia molded herself to me.

There was no hesitation in her kiss. When my tongue chased hers, she met the demand, sliding hers against mine, tempting me into a wicked game.

Lust tugged on my tenuous control. Fuck. Coming was the only thing my dick was interested in at the moment. No fucking way was I coming inside my pants. *Get yourself under control.*

As I devoured her lips, I backed her against the wall of the bedroom. I wanted to hurry and to bury myself inside her as deep as possible as quickly as possible. To chase that bliss and get straight to the bloody orgasms already. But when I kissed her again, she slowly melted into me. Her tongue teased and stroked and drove me mad.

She had the power in her touch and in her kiss to burn me.

Without breaking our kiss, I slid my hands down her arms and brought them up to wrap around the back of my neck. I pulled back momentarily. "I have wanted to know what you tasted like from the moment I laid eyes on you."

In some darkened corner of my brain, an alarm bell rang warning me that this was dangerous territory. That I couldn't have her how I wanted. I was trapped in a web and it was only going to get worse. But I didn't care.

Zia arched into me. The curves of her full breasts pressed into my chest. I slid my hands over the silk of her dress. I teased the edge before tugging it down, exposing her fullness. I pulled back and watched her carefully as I lightly palmed the soft flesh.

Shit. She was stacked. "God, your tits are so fucking perfect." She pushed up her breasts as if offering them to me, and I desperately couldn't swallow around the sudden mouthful of sawdust.

I reached behind her undoing the clasp on her dress. The fabric fell, skimming over her hips, then her calves, and she was naked except for a thong.

Perfection. So lush. So full. Taking advantage of her arched form, I lowered my head and hovered my mouth over a puckered bud for a moment. Zia's fingers threaded through my hair and she pulled me to her.

Pressing my lips over the raised peak, I sucked her gently. Her answering moan was low and throaty, and I tugged harder, trying to taste every rich flavor of her skin.

"Theo..."

Hearing her say my name made my cock jerk against my fly,

urging, begging me to bury myself in her and get lost. "Fuck, Zia, you're killing me."

She reached for my belt, and I eased back. I had to get control and quick before I did something stupid. I tried to slow down the frantic kisses and the pace as I carried her to the bed.

I laid her down in the center and stared down at her. Fuck, where did I want to start? Everywhere. With her lips, her toes?

She frowned up at me. "What's wrong?"

Wrong? Was that what she thought? "I'm having a hard time deciding where to start. Do I want the slide of your tongue against mine again? But then that would mean I'm not licking your tits. And damn, woman, I've had every single fantasy there is to have about them." As I spoke, I shucked my shirt, then my trousers, leaving only my boxers. "I've dreamed about fucking them, sucking them. Making you come by just licking them."

Before leaning over her, I reached into the bedside table and grabbed a condom then tucked it into the waistband of my boxers. Her smile was saucy as her gaze landed on my erection. "I see you've given this great thought."

I crawled over her. "Oh yes. I've pictured you on my desk, on your desk, on the floor of my office, in the shower, on that couch. Hell, every flat surface from here to the palace and back."

"I see you are inventive."

"Oh, I am."

"So tell me Theo... where did you decide to start?"

I slid a brief, chaste kiss on her lips. I wasn't getting distracted, because I could get caught up doing nothing but kissing her. At her breasts I paid homage to the distended tawny peaks. Just a brief caress with my tongue.

I kept kissing until I reached the promise land. "Spread your legs for me sweetheart."

She lifted her head to meet my gaze. "I—"

I lowered my voice and gave her my bossiest command. "Open, Zia."

She complied almost immediately, and I made a note to use that voice again. My gaze on hers, I slid my finger under that tiny scrap of fabric she called a thong and shifted it out of the way. "Good girl. Now I'm going to make you come. You okay with that?"

"Oh, fuck."

I gave her a smile. "I'll take that as a yes." And then I planted my open mouth on her clit and refused to let up until she screamed my name.

I was prepared to spend all night on my task if I needed to. I was ready to settle in and never come up for air. I had my arsenal on lock. But it turned out I didn't need the whole arsenal, because she was writhing in seconds.

One slide of my tongue on her clit and her legs pressed in around my head. "Oh my God, Theo."

Yes. God. Yes. She tasted sweet, so sweet as she melted on my tongue. Licking and stroking, I did my level best to make her forget anyone who came before me. But it wasn't until I stroked two fingers inside her with my tongue on her clit and my pinky grazing her tight bud of an asshole that she started to shake. She threaded her fingers into my hair again and held me against her hard. All the while muttering. "God, yes. Right there. Just like that. Theo, please. Please. More."

But the real satisfaction came when my pinky slid in past that tight ring of muscle and I gently fucked her with it while I alternated between sucking on her clit and sliding my tongue as deep as it would go. Gently I stroked her ass and grunted as I feasted, completely unable to contain the feral beast I'd held back for so long. Her legs started to quake around my ears. "Yes, that's it. Let me make you feel so, so good," I muttered against her flesh.

I increased my pace, and all I heard were her muffled pleas of, "Please, please, please, please, please, please, please."

When she finally broke, her body went hyper tense, then she jerked in my arms, the convulsions taking over.

Christ. I was going to die from this, and I was completely okay with that. I eased my fingers away and kissed my way back up her body. When I reached her breasts, I dipped my head, grazing first one nipple, then the other with my stubble. I followed up with my tongue and with playful tugs with my teeth.

"Theo, Jesus." Her body continued to jerk.

As I feasted on her nipples, I whispered, "You taste like heaven everywhere."

She answered with a rotation of her hips, and my cock strained, insistently desperate for her heat. I slid a hand between us, searching for her center again. She bucked as I withdrew my finger then slowly slid in again.

I buried my lips in her neck. With each gentle slide and retreat of my finger, I whispered against her skin. "You feel fucking amazing. You taste better than I ever could have imagined, you know that? Now that I've had a taste, I'm not sure I can stop. I'm dying for you to grip around me."

Even though she dug her nails into my shoulders and softly whimpered, I took my time. Never mind that I was on the verge of spontaneously combusting. I kept up the slow, lazy retreat and entry.

She rocked her hips into my questing hand. Hell. She was so hot. "Theo, please stop teasing me."

I smiled against her flesh. "This is called seducing."

She gave a little frustrated growl, and I chuckled. Finally, I reached between us and snatched the condom from my waistband.

I dragged my head back to watch her. With trembling hands, she took the condom from me, then tore the foil and discarded it. She met my gaze levelly and reached into my boxer briefs, freeing my cock.

Fuck. I'd underestimated the impact of her soft fingers on my dick. I was going to blow. Dragging in deep breaths, I tried to think of anything that would keep me from coming. As it was, pre cum leaked out of the tip. *Oh fuck. Oh fuck.*

Her sure fingers froze my brain synapses for several seconds. Not once did she take her eyes off of mine. She pumped me slowly, then again, and I bit back a strangled choke. "So good. Oh, God."

Still, she didn't take her gaze off of mine. Instead, she sheathed me before smiling. That simple, confident smile had an orgasm chasing partway up my spine.

Hell. If that didn't wreak havoc with my self-control. I eased my fingers out of her and tugged my boxer briefs all the way down. My cock nudged her slick folds, and her eyes fluttered closed.

Her rocking motions caused her sex to rub against the tip of my cock, and I had to clench my jaw to ward off the orgasm.

I shuddered. "I don't know what you're doing to me."

"Same thing you're doing to me."

With slow, tilting motions of my hips, I slid in to the hilt.

She moaned and threw her head back while I gritted my teeth and yelled out a curse. "Fuck."

Taking advantage of her exposed flesh, I nipped at the column of her neck even as I drove forward. On my retreat, she milked me with the tight sheath of her core. Volcanic heat pulsed around me as she dug her nails deep, scoring tracks of fire into my upper back and shoulders.

As she moaned my name, I knew the danger.

This would never be enough. I would need this like a drug.

I would *crave* it. She was already under my skin.

Her eyes went wide. "Theo, I—"

Reaching between us, I stroked her clit with my thumb in slow circles as I picked up the pace. "Zia, God, you feel incredible."

Her body clamped down tighter around my aching cock as I drove her higher and higher. With a shuddering breath, her legs tightened around me, and her delicate fingers twined into my hair, tugging me to her.

She whispered my name, and her body clamped tightly around me just before breaking apart in my arms.

I ground my teeth together. The tingle in my spine morphed into molten fire. I couldn't hold back. "Zia." Her name was on my lips as she branded me.

TWENTY

THEO...

I FUCKING WOKE ALONE. SHE'D RUN.

Well, do you blame her? You were a dirty boy.

I rolled over only to discover that half the covers were on the floor and we'd lost two pillows. When I sat up in bed and noticed her laptop on the couch, I realized she hadn't left.

So she didn't exactly run. She was still in the apartment. But the message was loud and clear. No lazy morning wake up. Did she regret it? Had she changed her mind?

Once I was dressed, I marched out to the living room, expecting to be able to question her about why the fuck she'd gotten out of bed. But she wasn't alone.

Jax was leaning against the counter eating a croissant and taking up far too much room in my flat. I knew he was married. I'd read that in the dossier I'd been given on the company. And I'd seen him and the woman I presumed was his wife at the wedding. They were clearly in love.

But it still irritated the fuck out of me to see Zia so comfortable with him. Happy, smiling. I stopped short. "What's wrong?"

Elena bustled around clucking at him about how a guy as

big as him needed more fuel. And that she should make him some eggs.

He declined with a polite smile, but when his gaze landed on me, he narrowed his eyes slightly. "Nothing. His Majesty has requested your presence at the palace."

Shit. What misstep had I made?

You mean besides sleeping with a King's Knight?

"Fine. I'll get Tim to—"

Jax shook his head. "No. Sir." The sir was added as an afterthought, I could tell, and was said through clenched teeth. "His Majesty has requested I drive you. If you don't mind, I sent Tim to the office. He'll meet you there for your later appointments."

My gaze darted to Zia and back to Jax. "I have a series of meetings this morning. I don't have time to see the king." I'd already noticed that she wasn't meeting my gaze. So it was regret then.

Jax lifted a brow. "You're going to say no to the king?"

Fuck. Fuck. Fuck.

"No, of course not. I'll have to rearrange my schedule. Let me call my assistant."

Zia's voice was quiet. "Already done."

Jax's gaze still read like a big brother's face of 'I'll kick your ass the moment she's not looking,' but he excused himself to the car.

Elena came bustling out with one of those Bento boxes. "Are you attempting to leave without breakfast?"

I tried to contain my frustration. "Elena, Thank you. I'll make sure to eat."

She rolled her eyes. "King's cousin or not, you're still mine to take care of for the time being. You need to eat.

I've never gotten to fuss over you. Let an old lady do it now."

I frowned. "You fuss over me all the time."

Her gaze met mine and held. "You know what I mean."

Jesus, the look she gave me was direct, slightly narrowed, as if she *knew* I wasn't Derrick. As if she knew I was Theo. There was no way. No way. I'd kept out of her way for the most part. She'd be the one person who would know. Is that what she was trying to tell me now?

Zia went into the room to pack up her bag, and when she returned, she led the way to the elevator. When we were alone finally, I turned my attention on her. "Did I fuck up somewhere?"

She exhaled and sagged against the wall. "No, but I think Jax knows. He had been texting all morning, and when I didn't answer, he came looking. He knocked on your door and it took me a minute to answer, because I had to throw on clothes. It feels like he knows."

I reached for her. "He doesn't know anything."

"He does I'm telling you. He gave me this look that was pure disappointment."

"Bollocks. He can go fuck himself." I tugged her close and she relaxed against me. "You sleep okay?"

She giggled into my chest. "You mean in spite of the sex maniac who woke me several times to administer orgasms?"

I grinned. "Yeah, besides that."

"I feel like I'm walking funny."

Like the idiot caveman I was, I wanted to thump my chest. "You might just be, but it's sexy to me." I leaned in and nuzzled her neck, inhaling her fresh clean scent. "Do you have any idea how much I want you right now? Think he'll notice if I stop the

CHAPTER 20

elevator for a quick taste? Thank you for wearing a skirt today. It will make having my breakfast much easier."

She giggled and swatted at me. "Stop, we have four more floors." She ran a hand through her dark locks. "I don't know how this is supposed to work."

Fuck, neither did I, but I couldn't stop myself from touching her. "We'll figure it out. The world thinks we're dating already, so it'll just be more real."

She tilted her dark gaze up to meet mine. "Theo, this feels like a really bad idea."

She's right.

I kissed her nose. "Don't overthink it. Right now, you want me and I want you. We'll figure out the rest."

Like how you're lying to her? The guilt wormed its way in, chasing away the warmth and happiness I'd woken up with. By the time the elevator dinged, we were in separate corners of the enclosed space. She stepped out first, leading the way to the car. After I climbed into the car, she got in the front with Jax. So no possibility of molesting her undetected.

Get your head in the game. If you're being summoned to the castle something is wrong. Focus on that and not the tempo of how Zia likes her clit rubbed.

I was a goner.

I was in the backseat, but it wasn't like I was being chauffeured. It was more like I was in the backseat of a cop car. Lord knew I'd become familiar enough with the feeling back when I was a kid. "Listen, is anyone going to tell me what this is about?"

Zia looked back at me, but she didn't say anything. She only shook her head. Oh, that was helpful.

Fair enough then.

As we drove up to the palace, I did my level best to contain my awe. Oh yeah, I'd seen it at the wedding, but I hadn't come at it from this angle. It looked like something out of Camelot with the beach at the foot of the mountain. Fucking paradise. And now I was actually going inside the walls of the palace. Last time, we'd been at the chapel and then the ballroom. Not anywhere near the inner sanctum.

I could consider myself lucky. *Or you're headed for the dungeons because they know who you are.*

As we pulled up, I typed a quick message to Kyle, letting him know where I was and what the problem was. Immediately, four texts came back.

Kyle: *Oh shit.*
Kyle: *What the fuck?*
Kyle: *What did you do?*
Kyle: *Do they know?*

My response was terse.

Derrick: *I know nothing right now. I'll call you later.*

He'd twist in the wind about that a little bit, but it was all I could give him right now. I didn't know anything else.

When we parked in VIP parking, I could visibly see Jax and Zia relax. Neither one of them was as tense or as tight as they'd been at the penthouse. Was it because the palace was protected?

All I could hear in the gilded hallway we took to see the king were the clips and clops of our shoes on the marble. My mother would love this place. She had a love of art. This place would be like a candy store for her.

We stopped in the outer office, and Jax knocked. I recognized the voice immediately. The one from Saturday, the one I wasn't supposed to talk to. "Come in."

CHAPTER 20

Jax opened the door for me, and I went in alone, without him and Zia. *Shit.* This couldn't be good. When I entered, Sebastian was at his desk frowning over a laptop. He glanced up and saw me, then he gave me a broad smile. "Derrick, thanks for coming to see me."

"I wasn't aware that was a choice."

He frowned. "Shit, did they give you the 'the king has to see you now' face?"

"That was pretty much the one I got."

"Fuck. I have a new admin. We're still getting used to each other. Every time I say something, she assumes I mean right the fuck now. I'm sorry. It's nothing urgent. I just wanted to check on you and see how you're getting on with Royal Elite."

I blinked. "Not urgent?"

He shook his head. "No. I just wanted to catch up and remind you about the basketball game."

I frowned. "Game?"

He rolled his eyes. "You never come, fair enough, but I thought you would at least remember."

Derrick had given me nothing to go on. "Uh, remind me."

"Look, I know we haven't been close lately, and I'd like to change that. I was surprised you came to the wedding. And seeing you reminded me that we should make an effort to see each other more often. So the prince's basketball tournament... It's for charity, and it's next month. I've got our other cousins, Alexi and Xander, coming in. I actually managed to get those two out of London for once. They act like that city is all there is. We're going to have a practice. You should join us."

He was saying lots of words. Basketball. Princes. Tournaments. My mind tried to grapple with all of his words. "You want me to play basketball?" I was treading in choppy waters here.

Sebastian folded his arms. "Yeah, you know. Dribble a ball, shoot some bricks. I won't give you any shit about not being able to play, but I can't guarantee Lucas won't be an asshole."

Lucas was his brother. "I'm still confused. You want me to play basketball with you?"

He chuckled. "Did your brain get scrambled by those motherfuckers who are trying to kill you? Yes. Say yes."

"I—"

"Are you going to say no to your king?" He folded his arms.

"How does that go over with the queen, all that kingly bravado?"

He smiled sheepishly. "She could give a shit. And these days, I'm fucking terrified of her. You ever see a pregnant woman in a mood? Yeah, I talk really slow around her and try to give her whatever she wants whilst not pissing her off in the process."

"You know I had meetings this morning."

He shrugged. "Well, it's good to be king." His voice was light, and I almost laughed. "Look, honestly, I mostly just wanted to check on you."

Way to overreact, Theo. "I'm good. The uh, the Royal Elite team is everything they are cracked up to be."

"Zia's one of the best. She got a bum deal."

I frowned. "You know her well?"

He shrugged. "I do. She's one of my personal knights. But yeah, she was in the military. Good soldier by all accounts. But picked a real winner for a guy. He screwed with her, then essentially blackballed her in the Guard. To this day I'm not sure if

CHAPTER 20

she knows he sabotaged her chances of getting into Intelligence."

"Sounds like a twat."

"My sentiments exactly. It worked out better this way anyway, but still. She's gun shy for obvious reasons."

Was it me or was he watching me a little too closely? "Yeah, of course."

"I don't know. I sort of look at her and Tamsin as the younger sisters I never had. I'd do anything to protect them from twats who don't deserve them."

I swallowed. I certainly didn't deserve her. "Right. Of course."

He lifted a brow. "You're not taking the guard-your-body thing to heart, are you cousin?"

Fuck, I was starting to sweat. "Uh, what do you mean?"

He shrugged. "Your reputation precedes you. I saw you guys at the ball. You know, you looked... intense."

I swallowed. "Nope. Not intense."

"Uh-huh. You've never been the kind of guy to stick. If you're dicking around, she's not the one to dick around with."

"You her father now, cousin?" Stupid stupid stupid. Why the hell did I say that?

"Nope. I just care about her. If you know you're not planning on sticking around, don't do it. As a personal favor to me. I like this one, and she doesn't deserve that."

Fuck. Me. He suspected. And I got the warning signals loud and clear. I never should have gone there with her. Not because I was the playboy Sebastian thought I was, but because I was a liar and an imposter, and she deserved better. "I hear you." My gut twisted and knotted into something ten times tighter than a sailor's knot. I'd fucked up. I knew it and he knew it. He just thought I was a fuck-up for a different reason.

"Good. So are there any leads?"

I shook my head. "No, not yet."

"Well, the good news is the team is tenacious, so they'll uncover it. In the meantime, come play basketball. Prove me wrong. Show the others you aren't a colossal dick."

"Such a glowing rep I have."

He nodded. "Yeah, well. Up until that wedding you had been. Good to have the old you back. Look, if you need anything, just tell me. We never get to spend much time together, so I really do want to fix that."

"Okay. I will. But I do need to get back to the office."

He nodded. "Right. Tell your Dad I said hi."

"Yeah, I'm pretty sure I'm not the person to tell him that."

He grinned. "Glad to see some things never change."

"Well, what are you going to do? I am the prodigal son."

"And I know a lot about that. But you know, you probably don't have to be the prodigal son if you don't want to be. Life is funny that way."

"That's a good point. If we're done here, I'll see you later."

"Yep, I'll see you for basketball."

When I left Sebastian's office, I only found Zia in the hallway. She blinked in surprise. "It's time to go."

"You're done already?" Her smile was sweet, and it made my heart ache.

"Yeah. Apparently, it wasn't urgent."

She frowned. "Jax said his assistant made it seem like life and death."

"Yeah, well, I guess she doesn't understand that. I don't know. It's fine. Let's go."

CHAPTER 20

"Okay. Jax has something to do, so it's just us. Want to make out in the car?"

Yes, yes, I did. But I wasn't going to do that. Because Sebastian was right. "So, can we get to the parking lot through the garden?"

"Yeah, sure." She led the way down the hall and to the right to the North Garden. When we were out of the palace, she leaned close, our fingertips brushing. I eased away.

A crease marked her forehead. "What?"

"Zia, listen, I think—"

Her frown deepened. "Why are you giving me a douchbag morning-after face?"

I rubbed at the back of my neck. "It's not like that. You know how much I want you. I was never supposed to touch you in the first place."

Her eyes went wide. "You're serious?"

I swallowed and nodded. "I'm not what you need. You deserve better. And I—"

She blinked rapidly. "You're serious right now?"

"Zia. It's not what you think. This has nothing to do with how much I want you. It's killing me not to touch you right now. But it isn't a good idea. Last night I knew I shouldn't, but I did it anyway, and you're going to get hurt if I don't get this shit under control."

She stopped and stared at me as she blinked rapidly. "You're really serious?"

"Last night was amazing. Incredible. Soul-shattering. I could say those things. They'd be the truth. But then I'd be faced with the fact that I can't have you again. So maybe I shouldn't say those things. Maybe I shouldn't tell you that you leaving the bed this morning twisted *me* up. Maybe I shouldn't tell you I feel more than I should. But this isn't right. I'm going to hurt you." *Hey, look who's capable of being honest.*

"I'm not hurt. I'm irritated that you're telling me what can and can't happen. I'm a grown woman. I know what I want."

She didn't understand. "This has nothing to do with you."

"Whatever. Don't worry, I know your type. I know how this goes. Now that you've had me, you're not interested. I get it. But you're still stuck with me. We're short-staffed, and there are no more bodyguards available. So, let's go."

She tried to get past me, and I grabbed her elbow. "Would you stop it? Don't you have any idea how much I want you?"

"You know what, the words don't matter. It's the actions that do. I knew you were going to go full asshole. I knew it and I slept with you anyway because I felt open and vulnerable. I knew you were going to pretend none of it had ever happened. Never mind what *did* happen last night. Never mind how close I felt to you. You've put the mask back on."

"Zia, please..." I wanted to stop her. But what could I say? I couldn't have her. She had no idea who I was.

TWENTY-ONE

ZIA...

I.

Was.

An.

Idiot.

What the hell did I think would happen? Like after the best sex of my life, Theo would want me to stick around? God, I really hadn't learned my lesson. I deserved this strange burning in the center of my chest.

Somehow, I'd managed to get myself caught up with a man I couldn't have... again. One who was powerful and gorgeous and completely out of my league. And even after I'd made myself a promise that I wasn't going to go there, I went there... several times. And it had been outstanding.

But this feeling was *not* outstanding. Last night once he'd kissed me, he'd been like a dam breaking free, like everything he'd wanted to say and do was finally burning all the fucks down and just going for it. He didn't have that tight leash of control. He had been all fire and destruction, and now I was broken.

No lie, I had passed out. Legitimately passed out. I don't remember anything that happened after orgasm number four until Theo woke me up with his mouth on me sometime in the wee hours of the morning. Was it the exhaustion, or was it the orgasms? Maybe a combination of both.

It was one hell of a way to break a year-long dry spell.

The only problem was now he wanted to go back to buttoned-up Derrick. When I called him Theo last night, he melted in my arms. He gave me the most tender kiss, as if he was giving me all of his secrets, giving me everything of him. Now, he was Derrick again. Telling me all the reasons why he did not want to go there again.

Fine by me. I wasn't going to beg. I had already been down this road with Garrett. It was horrible.

Because Theo hadn't just *said* all the right things; he'd shown me. He'd come with me when I needed help. For once I'd had someone's support. For once, I'd had someone backing me instead of the other way around. So he'd gotten me good, and now I was going to pay the price.

Fair enough. I needed to pay this particular price, because like a fool, I'd jumped in headfirst without any thought to consequences or the penance. The penance was, apparently, a very sore vagina and the best night's sleep I'd had in months. Either way, it wasn't happening again. I wasn't going to fall again. I was going to project what I wanted to happen. I was going to accept it. Hopefully, we could determine what the hell was going on with him soon, then I could go back to my life where it was safe and there weren't gorgeous men telling me that they wanted to take care of me and that I just needed to let them. Because listening to that, was a recipe for disaster. And I had learned my lesson.

CHAPTER 21

When we arrived at the office, Olivia was already in a mood. She had a stack of papers on her desk, things to be delivered, which I ignored, things that needed follow-up, which I managed, and personal things she wanted done for her, which I refused. It was our dance. She had yet to grasp that she wasn't my job. Theo was. I did not have time for her requests, but I had to deal with him. Lucky for me, it was technically my day off.

Theo had a round of meetings with Kyle concerning something about the board. Once I took care of those things, I'd be in the office of the Royal Elite trying to figure out what we were dealing with. I considered not telling him that I was leaving, but I wasn't a brat. I was a grown woman. I could deal with him. I knocked on the door. His response was terse, "Come."

I swallowed hard and pushed the heavy glass open. "Hey, I'm just letting you know Jax is on duty. You need to notify him if you're going anywhere. I'll be back at the penthouse later tonight."

He nodded, his gaze not leaving mine. "Zia—"

"I have to go." Then I turned around and left him. I wasn't going to blame him. I'd screwed up because I had wanted to believe. That had been my fault, not his, so it was me who needed to pay.

When I walked through the door of Royal Elite thirty minutes later, Tamsin found me in my office. "Hey, welcome back stranger."

"Hey. Was anyone able to sift through the information I sent back from Derrick's office?" I asked Tamsin.

She nodded. "Ariel and Jameson are on it. We were able to determine from the information that you gathered that something is up with that acquisition. There are several board members on the defensive about it, but senior management is all for it. Up until recently, Arlington has been full steam ahead himself. But you said that in recent meetings, he didn't seem to want to do it. And there might be a good reason for that. Word is Inline Tech's numbers don't add up. I don't have the forensic accounting background that Jameson does, but the more she sees the more she thinks the company is built on a house of cards. And anyone with half a brain would know the finances are bogus. I mean, they're buried, but anyone looking at acquiring the business should be smart enough to dig deeper. If they dig deeper, things don't add up."

"Maybe Derrick is just starting to dig in. He only became CEO six months ago." It was easier to call him his real name at moments like this.

She shrugged. "It might make sense, but why wait this long? This acquisition has been planned for a year."

"So what's changed in the last month to make him want to put the brakes on?"

"Well, maybe the rumors are true. Maybe he has been some kind of despot, only now he's starting to pay attention. I mean, he's clearly not an idiot."

I leaned back in my seat. "No, but he's up to something or hiding something. I just wish I knew what it was."

She narrowed her gaze at me. "What's with you?"

I lifted a brow. "What do you mean?"

"I mean, what's with you? You are... I don't know, tense. Watchful. Something is up."

"Nothing. I just really want to figure out what's going on."

"Uh-huh. Spill. What's happening?"

I shook my head. No way was I getting into what happened between us and explaining how I humiliated myself. "I don't know what you're talking about. I'm fine."

CHAPTER 21

She watched me with another narrow-eyed gaze, and then her mouth hung open. "Oh my God, you slept with him."

I blinked. Blinked again. "What the hell do you mean?"

"Oh my God, I knew I could see something different about you. Oh, yeah. You have that look of someone who has been fucked thoroughly."

"Would you keep your voice down? The walls are not that thick."

"Yes, they are. Ariel had this place renovated herself. So, are you going to tell me what happened or not?"

I shook my head. "No Tams, it's already too humiliating."

"Come on, you've had billionaire dick. I need to know everything about it."

"Oh my God, I am not telling you about it."

"Obviously, you want to talk about it, otherwise, you wouldn't have come back here. You could have gone back to the cushy penthouse and relaxed, but you came here. Which means there's something to talk about."

I swallowed hard. Was that right? I could have just called to check on their progress. Instead, I had come to the office on purpose. I hadn't wanted to be in the penthouse and forced to see the evidence of my screw up last night. I covered my face with my hands. "I just— It shouldn't have happened. It's such a nightmare."

"It happened after the gala? Makes sense. The adrenaline and all."

"That's what I thought too, so I stopped him at first. But then Deedee called saying she was arrested, and I had to go save the day... again."

"I swear to God I'm going to kill your sister."

"You don't have to. Arlington gave her a harsh spanking last night. And not in a fun make-you-tingly way." I filled her in on what had happened with Deedee.

When I was done, she sat back. "Wow. So he walked in and saved the day for you for once."

I nodded. She got me. "And it was hot. So hot... like brain-cell-killing hot. I'm pretty sure what that man does with his tongue is illegal in the islands. But then today, he's telling me all the reasons why he can't have me. He's gone back to being cold and remote. It's like there are two of him, and I'm not sure which is real."

She shrugged. "Well, he could be both guys."

I frowned. "I need consistency."

"Well, maybe he's like you and doesn't open up easily."

"I'm not closed-off."

Tamsin laughed. "No, you're not. But you're suspicious of people, and you keep things close to the vest. But if anyone needs you, man, you ride to the rescue with your bag full of tricks. Birthday kits. Double-sided tape. All the things. It's pretty amazing. How you even carry around double-sided tape is beyond me. I'm just saying, you deserve someone who's going to, you know, look out for you."

"Yeah, and look what I got. Today, of course, he was full of regrets. He started spewing, 'we shouldn't have done that,' and 'you don't understand how bad this is.' I'm not putting up with that again. I've done it before, and it's not worth it. I'm not that person. I can't be someone who second guesses myself and be somebody's secret. I don't deserve that. I deserve better than that."

"Hell yes, you do. And he's an asshole if he doesn't see how awesome you are."

"Yeah, well, he's an asshole. I agree."

"He's got the T-shirt and decorated his man cave with posters that say *I'm a giant douchebag.*" She bit her lip. "Just one question though."

"Shoot."

"How was it?"

My body flushed as I thought about how he put his mouth on me this morning, worshipped me, and then held me. I'd almost felt I was cherished, but then I felt like I'd been had, because where was *that* guy? "He's next level in bed. The kind of guy who makes you want to slap the guys you were with before because they clearly had no idea what the hell they were doing. He's that guy."

"Even if he is a dick, I'm so jealous. I guess every woman should be shagged at least once by someone like that."

"How can I ever be with anyone else who doesn't give me five orgasms a night? I have standards now."

I wasn't kidding. Derrick *Theo* Arlington had ruined me. Just like I'd known he would.

TWENTY-TWO

THEO...

I HAD NO CHOICE. AFTER WHAT HAD HAPPENED AT THE charity event, I'd been running my options over and over in my head. It was time to throw in the towel. At least partially.

I found Kyle in the office down the hall. Zia had tried to come with me before she left for the day, but I'd waved her down. She didn't want to talk to me. And it was too difficult trying not to touch her, so having her in close proximity was a problem.

I knocked on his door, and Kyle looked up, frowning, surprised that I'd come down to see him.

I closed the door behind myself, and he studied me closely. "Theo, what's up?"

"Listen, I need a favor."

He nodded. "Anything."

"Protocol H. I need you to go home."

Kyle's brows lifted. "What?"

"I need you to go home, man."

"Why? What's happened?"

"Someone tried to grab me at the charity event."

He blinked once, twice. "Then why the fuck aren't you coming with me?"

"Because, I still have things to do here."

"Jesus Christ, Theo. Are you out of your fucking mind?"

"Yeah, probably. But I've got to see this through. There's two million dollars on the line for us. For my mother. I need to do this."

He shook his head. "I have told you, stop trying to do this for me. Stop trying to do this for her. Look, your whole I'm-not-worthy shtick," and he stopped. "You're worthy. You don't have to do this. Those motherfuckers tried to grab you again? It's time to go. We can both be on a plane tonight."

"I hear you, but I can't. If I leave now, I'll be looking over my shoulder for the rest of my life."

He sighed. "Jesus Christ, Theo. How did we end up here?"

"I don't know. But can you do it? Can you go back to Jersey and look out for her? She's staying with my aunt. I just need someone to make sure she gets the treatments and that she's safe."

"Look, you know for you I'll do anything. I just—"

"I know. I know."

He ran his hands through his sandy blond hair. "I feel responsible. I was joking. I hope you know that. When Arlington walked in, and I suggested you body-double him, I was kidding. I didn't know you'd take him up on it."

"I know. You were just mouthing off. I mean, how many times does an identical stranger walk into your life? I thought it was the craziest shit ever. It just turned out that it was a lot more complicated than that."

"Jesus Christ, if you're sending me home to your mother, it's bad."

"Look, I'm still in one piece, I have a damn bodyguard. I'll be fine. But I can't do this *and* worry about her. If someone's in fact watching her, I want someone I trust covering her."

He nodded. "Okay, you got it. But listen, Theo, Inline, Timothy Arlington, you're in a whole nest of vipers. None of this shit is safe."

"I know. Right now, I trust no one who isn't you."

"You need someone else to trust. Because it's going to get lonely and complicated. You can always call me, of course, but someone on the ground."

I knew what he meant. "I'm not bringing her into this. I need to keep her safe."

"You might not have a choice. And guess what, she's a bodyguard. She knows how to deal with this shit. These dudes mean business, Theo."

"I can't with her. This isn't her mess. Besides, I have to stay away."

Kyle frowned. "What? Why? Since when?"

"Since I had a conversation with the king. He warned me off of her, and he has a point."

Kyle groaned. "No, that is bullshit. The king actually told you to stay away from her?"

"Yep."

"And you're listening?"

Yep. Like a pussy. "No, it's not about her. It is, but it isn't. It's about the lies. She deserves better than this."

"You'll never know unless you give it a real shot. When this is all over, tell her the truth. Try and take her on a normal, nice date."

"You say that so casually. When this is all over. I don't think it is ever going to be over."

"T, you care about her, right?"

"It doesn't matter. It was never going to work. At least I got her saying my name."

He shook his head. "I won't bust your chops. Because I know you care about her."

"I care about her more than I should. And I'm terrified it's going to get her killed. So right now, I need you to go be in Jersey and cover my mom. Then I can focus on this stuff here." And try and forget all about Zia Barnes.

"Okay, if you say so. Look, I'll give you a call when I get there. I still think it's a mistake you're not coming with me, but I get it."

"I promise, as soon as I tie this up, I'll be back. And I'll have the money we need."

"Like I keep telling you, I don't need you to have money. We'll survive on our own."

"Yeah. I hear you." But I didn't hear him. I was doing this. Seeing it through. I had to or the people I cared about would never be safe.

Theo...

IT HAD BEEN two and a half weeks since Royal Elite had been assigned to me and three nights since I'd slept with Zia. Last night, she hadn't stayed at the penthouse. It had been her night off, so Trace had stayed in the guestroom. Elena hadn't even asked any questions as to who he was or what he was doing there. She just made him breakfast and was happy to fuss over him. She said he was too thin.

Today, Zia was back at the normal time, but it was as if there were a shield around her. One I couldn't penetrate. One I maybe *shouldn't* penetrate. We both thought it was a good idea to back off, so why did I feel like I'd been hurt? Or maybe she felt like *she'd* been hurt.

Crap. I didn't know what to say to her or how to make it better, but I itched to hold her, to touch her. God, I wanted her. Once wasn't anywhere near enough. And she was only days away from the end of her job. This shit wasn't getting any easier.

I had to figure out what I was going to do. In less than two weeks, two million dollars was supposed to transfer into my account. I would have what I needed. I could go home.

Yeah, but where the fuck is Arlington?

Those people who had tried to grab me hinted that they had him. Was that the truth? Was it a ploy? Was it just a way to make sure I went with them? I didn't know what the truth was. I hadn't spoken to Arlington since he'd hired me. I was still running his company as if it were mine.

And I was losing my goddamn shit.

There was a knock at the door. I expected to see Zia standing there, but instead it was Sebastian fucking Winston. I gave him a nod as I stood. "This is starting to be a habit."

He shrugged. "Well, I like you better now."

"You keep saying that."

"It's true. You got gym gear with you?"

I frowned. "What?"

"Gym gear. Do you have any?"

I nodded absently. "Yeah, I keep a set in the closet."

That was an understatement. I had a full wardrobe in there for any occasion. There was even a tux just in case I was at the office and needed to do black tie quickly. It sure was handy.

Sebastian nodded. "Good. Gear up. We're going to play basketball."

This again. "What if I can't play basketball?"

"Then you're going to get your ass beat by me, Lucas, Xander, Alexi and Roone. Tristan sucks at basketball. Football is his thing, so at least, you might beat him."

"So, what, we're all just going to hang out?"

Sebastian nodded. "Remember how we said we were going to do better? This is me doing better. Now, gear up. You look like you need to work out some shit anyway."

I frowned. "What does that mean?"

"What that means is that you've got the look of a man who has been beaten by something. Something nasty that won't let you go, and I guarantee you we've all been beaten by that thing."

"I don't even know what you're talking about."

Sebastian grinned. "Yeah, sure you don't."

I changed quickly. I didn't have any meetings until later that afternoon, and I figured I'd be back long before then. When I stepped out into the main office area, I stopped short. There were no less than six guards in there. All wearing black tailored suits, all clearly concealing their weapons.

Olivia was curtsying so low her knees nearly brushed the ground. Zia stood but she didn't curtsy.

"Your Majesty, should I join you?"

She gave me a beaming smile and sauntered around the desk. I watched that sway in her hips, and something tightened inside me. Sebastian chuckled when Zia sidled up to me and gave me a kiss on the cheek. "You want me to come with you, honey?"

Honey? I had no idea what she meant by that. Was she still pissed at me? Did she want me again? Christ, my dick was all about that action. Would she accept my apology? Because if she would, I was not above groveling. I wanted her more than I'd wanted her before. How could it possibly be worse?

I was on a verge of kicking everyone out of my office when Sebastian suggested, "Why don't you come? You've never seen the palace, have you Zia?"

Oh, this was about the role she was playing. Her undercover job.

"Oh wow, Your Majesty. Nothing would make me happier."

"Join us."

Sebastian turned to Olivia. "I'm sure Miss Tullman can hold down the fort?"

Olivia blinked up at him, eyes wide at the use of her name. "Yes, Your Majesty. Of course."

I marveled at how he'd done that, taking the thing that would make her feel left out, and making it seem that she was doing an important job for the crown.

I'd have to remember that trick.

When we arrived at the palace, Zia excused herself. "If you don't mind, I'll go visit with Queen Penny."

Sebastian gave her a smile. "Sure. She's painting. You know where to find the studio, right?"

Zia nodded and vanished around the corner.

"I guess she's been here a lot."

Sebastian gave me a smile. "She's one of our best knights. One day, she's going to be as good as Ariel."

"I don't doubt it."

Sebastian watched me for a moment. "So, you've been beaten, huh?"

I followed him down through the gardens toward the sports complex. "Beaten by what?"

He just laughed again. "If you don't know, I won't tell you. You'll figure it out for yourself."

I frowned. "Are you suggesting I have a thing for Zia?" A thing would be an understatement.

"I'm not suggesting anything. I'm using my eyes, and they tell me you are desperate for Zia. And right now, she's got you by the balls."

He had a point.

"She does not have me by the balls."

He chuckled. "Okay, if you say so. But I see how you're watching her like you can't keep your shit together. It's clear. It's apparent. I'm just wondering if you love her or not."

"I don't love her. I barely know her. We just— fuck, I don't know."

"Yeah, we have all been there."

Every time I came to the palace, I marveled. This basketball court was set on the hillside with a backdrop of azure blue water in beautiful pristine white sand. "Jesus Christ, this is amazing."

Sebastian grinned. "Let's see if you still say that in thirty minutes after you've had Roone check you hard."

"I'm pretty sure, I can hold my own."

"What, cousin? Did you pickup basketball along the way?"

I shrugged. "I've got some skills."

Holy shit I was about to play basketball with the royal fucking family. There were a couple of other guys I didn't recognize. When I approached one of them, he smiled. "Hey, what's up? I'm Trevor. I'm usually Tristan's guard." He introduced me to two more royal guards.

Tristan. I'd seen him at the wedding too. He came over and

shook my hand again. "Hey, Derrick. I haven't seen you in ages."

"Different game for you. Are you ready mate? How's your basketball?"

"Uh, let's just say professionally I'll stick to football." Tristan played for the Argonauts, the Winston Isles' soccer team.

I grinned. "Yeah, I hear you."

Lucas, I knew from a couple of events before the wedding. He gave me a nod, even as he watched me closely.

"Lucas."

"Are you still a dick?"

I frowned. "No?"

He lifted a brow. "That sounds like a question."

"Well, I guess that depends on what you consider dickish."

He rolled his eyes. "Whatever."

The big guy was the one who'd gotten married. Roone. He came over to shake my hand, and I took it and said, "Congratulations are in order."

"Yeah well, I feel like you shouldn't be congratulating the luckiest son of a bitch alive."

"It must have been a short honeymoon."

"Yeah, our longer one will be two months from now. Jessa had some work she had to do."

I still didn't understand how the Princess of the Winston Isles actually had a job, but whatever. It wasn't my business.

Xander and Alexi were brothers and also Derrick's cousins. Alexi was the quiet one of the pair. Xander, well he was a character. Flashy and brash. He was easy to like.

When we started playing, I was on a team with Sebastian, Roone and Trevor. To say the game was athletic would be an understatement.

Lucas didn't like to lose. I'd learned from a little information

CHAPTER 22

in the car ride over here that Lucas had been all over the world, but he and Sebastian had synced up in New York. He'd also been a conman in his former life. Maybe it took one to recognize one.

You're not a conman, you were hired.

Yeah, yeah. Semantics.

Lucas, apparently, wasn't buying anything I was doing. He rode me hard. Every turn, every jump, every shot I attempted, he wasn't having any of it.

He dogged me.

Maybe he thought I was going to lose my shit. Maybe he thought I was going to let up, but when he pressed, I pressed. When I shot a jumper over his head, he whistled low. "Okay, Lebron, have you been practicing that?"

I shrugged. "I prefer Curry to Lebron."

He lifted a brow as if he respected that. "Okay, so you're not too bad."

"Same goes for you. You're okay."

He chuckled. As the game continued, I began to sweat. I enjoyed the jokes and the jest between the guys. Sebastian gave it as good as he got, and Roone always called Sebastian on his bullshit.

Lucas still blocked every chance he could.

Alexi was surprisingly sneaky. He kept fitting in tight spaces and catching rebounds. He put in the work and hustled for every ball.

Xander, unsurprisingly, talked the most shit.

Lucas has his own style of playing. He stole the ball, fought calls, and ran more than any of us. When he was called on it by Tristan, he just laughed. "Why do you guys always seem to forget that I'm a thief and a hustler?"

Both Sebastian and Roone said, "Former."

Lucas laughed. "Okay, okay, former. But honestly, I used to steal things. Stealing from you chumps is easy."

I laughed. "Oh my God, you guys are intense."

Sebastian clapped me on the back. "See? This is what it's like to have family. Maybe you should stop being a stranger."

Fuck. I'd like to. He was all right. Even Lucas *felt* like family.

Sure. Just not yours.

When we were done, my muscles ached. And that worry and trepidation I had about my time coming to an end eased some. I had to go back to my life. I couldn't stay. I couldn't live this life as if it was mine to have. But still, I couldn't help wishing for it. I liked these people. Even Lucas. I liked being here, I liked the island, I liked the water.

Most of all, you like Zia.

Yeah, I did like her. The problem was, I was lying to her through my teeth. I wanted my fucking life back. I want to tell her who I really was and have her still want me. I needed her to know.

You can't tell her.

I had signed a contract, a full-on NDA. I'd cheated a little with the Theo thing, but when she found out, either way, she was going to hate me.

It didn't matter. I still wanted her.

You should have thought of that before. Liking her could get you killed. Liking her could get her *killed.*

I didn't know what was going to happen, but falling for her was most certainly going to get my heart broken. Let alone what it was going to do to her when she found out the truth.

TWENTY-THREE

THEO...

My phone rang, and I answered on the first ring. But since my mind was still on the conversation with Zia that morning, I was in a fuck of a mood. "What?"

"Okay, dickhead, who shit in your chocolate pudding?"

I relaxed marginally when I heard his voice. "Sorry. Just a long a fucking day."

"I called earlier, but you didn't pick up."

"Yeah. I was in a meeting. How's Mom?"

"She's good man. Her color is better than when we left, and she's eating. I think the CBD stuff you got for her is working. Or it might be the pot I snuck her."

"You gave my mother pot?" I pinched the bridge of my nose.

"Relax. It's sanctioned for medical use. But I got her to my guy with the best grade stuff."

"Jesus, Kyle."

"Relax. I've got this. She's good. You gonna worry that I'm scoring pot for your mom or be happy that she's eating?"

"I'm not opposed to pot. Clearly you remember college, but for my mother?"

He chuckled. "Well, you should see her high. It's hilarious. She's a giggler."

"Christ." I might kill him when I got back.

"You all right man? You don't seem like yourself."

I automatically glanced around to make sure no one else could hear me. I shook my head. "I don't know. I feel like, I don't know, like I'm him. Or I'm not. I don't know. It's all fucked."

"I've been saying, maybe it's time to pull back and come home?"

"How am I suppose to pull back, Kyle? These fuckers know where my mother lives. You think I can just go back? It's hitting home that I can't just slide back into my life. Exactly where am I supposed to go? How am I supposed to hide?" There was no going back to my life until I found Arlington.

There was a beat of silence. "I don't know. But maybe hiding in plain sight is the thing. Once you're injected back into your life, they'll have to leave you alone. I hear it in your voice, dude. You're underwater. What bad thing happens if you just walk away? Even better, if you just stroll up to the king and tell him everything?"

Kyle had known me longer than anyone. I wanted to tell him he didn't know what he was talking about, but obviously, he did. He could see I was struggling.

"The king? That would likely mean jail time. I don't want to be locked up abroad, Kyle. With Arlington missing, this looks bad. Really bad. Every avenue, every option, seems like a dead end. I'm not just frustrated; I'm angry at myself, at you, at—"

He gave a humorless laugh. "What are you angry at me for?"

Fuck. "Forget it."

"No, dude, you said it, I'm not gonna forget it. Out with it."

I ran a hand through my hair. "I'm not even really angry

with you. Mostly, I'm just pissed at myself. Because while you wanted this to happen, while you thought this was a good idea, I still had to be the one to say yes. And like an idiot, I said yes when I never should have. This being in someone else's skin is too much. I'm not this person."

Kyle sighed. "What makes you think you're not him? You've been doing a good enough job so far. Better than he ever did."

" I can *pretend* to be him. But I'm starting to *become* him. Don't you get it? I'm not just acting. *I am him.* I'm running his company, staying in his house, eating his food. I have taken on his personality. The more I do it, the less I feel like *me.* I'm doing shit I would never do. Hurting people. Look, we were supposed to go home soon. This was all supposed to be work. Something is very, very wrong. I haven't been able to talk to him since I got this job. It's like he vanished off the face of the earth."

"Yeah,, I've been meaning to talk to you about that..."

"What?"

"That phone number he gave you, it's never been active. As in, it was never turned on."

I frowned. "The fuck?"

"When you call, what happens?"

"It says 'out of service area.' I just figured he was out of range or something."

He shook his head. "It was never turned on. He bought it a week before you took over. Activated but never once accessed."

Fuck. I rubbed my temples in frustration.

"You've done everything you needed to. You can walk away in a week. None of this has to affect you. None of this has to *touch* you. On your turf they won't touch you."

I shook my head even though I knew he couldn't see me. "I started this. I have to finish it."

"Theo, look at yourself. I doubt you've had any real sleep in over a week. You're testy. Exhausted. I mean, you've taken on this merger like it's real. Like it's *your* actual merger of *your* company not someone else's. You are not him. None of this is your job. You don't have to take on any of the shit that you don't want. You don't have to be what everyone needs all the time. You owe these people nothing."

"That's easy for you to say."

"Maybe, but at the same time, I know you. I get it. It's tempting. You get a do over. You can run any company you want. You were on that track. You were headed that way, and then things changed. I mean, if you walked away, maybe all of this reminds you of that?"

"No. Maybe. I don't know. I just know that I don't like who I'm becoming. I'm keeping secrets. I'm lying. I just want to tell the goddamn truth." Mostly I wanted to tell the truth to one person.

"Or maybe you want to tell a certain brunette who you are."

I frowned. "She'll hate me." *She already does.* "It's a moot point."

"Well, man, you can't pretend she's not a factor."

"She's not a factor." She couldn't be. I didn't get the happy ending and get the girl.

"That's not even anywhere near the truth. She's absolutely a factor. In case you don't know it, you're in love with her."

Fuck. "I'm not." *I couldn't be.*

"I think it's fucking great. For the last two years, you've just been focused on the company. You haven't done anything for yourself, working these nutso eighty-hour weeks, they were going to put you in an early grave. You have feelings for her and you can't even be yourself. I think that's fucking with you. Because you don't know if she'd want Theo."

He was right. I *knew* he was right. There was no getting around it. I'd bought into my own bullshit, and now it was coming to bite me in the ass.

I had someone I wanted to care about, *actually* care about. I couldn't tell her who I was because she thought I was someone else. In a matter of a week, I'd have all the money I needed to have the life I wanted. I could take care of my mother and move my company forward with Kyle, but I wanted to stay.

I had to get myself back. Which meant I was going to have to leave. I was going to have to walk away from this, from Zia, from the Winston Isles, from the new relationships, from everything.

This wasn't my life. Eventually, the real Derrick Arlington was going to come back, and he was going to want his life back. And Zia was going to leave because she was going to find out who I really was. I might look like him, but I had a completely different lifestyle, and well, I'd lied to her. *Was* lying to her. And would continuously do so until this was over. So that didn't make me a great candidate for a boyfriend.

"I'm in way over my head, aren't I?"

"You know you need to walk away."

"Yeah, I know."

Question was, could I?

TWENTY-FOUR

THEO...

"Mr. Arlington, did you want me to get pastries for your meeting?"

I'd just finished my run. My ankles had started to act up, so I finished earlier than planned. Olivia had followed me into my office as I marched in to take a shower.

"What meeting?"

"Your eleven o'clock. Some of the board members are here, your father, Brian Cohen... Would you like pastries? You usually tell me, and the meeting is ordinarily on the schedule before the day, but I didn't notice it until this morning. But I can still get pastries from the place downstairs in a hurry. It's on the main calendar of the conference rooms. Not your personal calendar."

I lifted a brow. "Eleven, you say?"

She nodded. "Should I get pastries? I wasn't sure."

I shook my head. "No Olivia, don't worry about it. Is Zia at her desk?"

"I sent her to go make coffee. Let's hope she at least gets that right. That girl, she's such a mess." Then she shut her mouth abruptly. "I'm so sorry sir. I know that you and she are—" She shut up.

I lifted my brow. "She and I are what?"

"I'm sorry sir. It's not a secret that you're dating her, but as an assistant, she's not great."

I nodded slowly. "That's all, Olivia, thank you."

She scowled and scurried away, closing the door behind her. I checked the time. Those motherfuckers were trying to perform a *coup d'etat* behind my back.

That's how coups work. You're not allowed to know until it's too late.

I had ten minutes to shower and get down there and find out what the fuck those motherfuckers were planning.

I didn't so much think I needed a bodyguard as I needed someone to hold me back. Just what the fuck were they doing, and why wasn't I included?

I'd never showered so quickly in my life. In five minutes, I was showered and dressed casually. Not in a suit. I wore a long-sleeved shirt shoved in a more casual pair of slacks. My hair was still wet, but I combed it back. Yes, I knew the look was kind of fuck-boy, but it was the farthest I could get from my supposed old man, I guess.

When I opened my office door, Zia stood and was ready with her laptop and her phone. "Everything okay?" Her gaze searched mine, and there was a level of warmth there, but not like before.

Not like when she trusted me. Not like when she wanted me. Which was fine, because that's not what this was about at all. She followed behind me without saying anything, but when we stepped in the elevator with just the two of us heading down, she frowned. "Is something broken? Is someone trying to kill you? A little insight would be terrific."

"No one is trying to kill me. At least not yet. But give it ten minutes."

Oh shit. She pulled out her phone and sent a quick text to Trace and Jax, who were downstairs in the van. "I'll need backup inside the building."

"Are you calling off the merger? I should probably have more guns."

My gaze slid over her trim frame. Another pencil skirt. Jesus Christ, this one had a kind of flutter-skirt thing at mid-thigh, so when she walked, the fabric swirled around her a little bit. Where was she even hiding that gun?

When the elevator dinged, I stepped aside and let her out first. Her perfume wafted into my nostrils, trying to distract me. I followed, and sure enough, in the large conference room sat Derrick's father, Brian Cohen, and six other board members who presumably might still be sympathetic to my father.

I gave them a broad smile. "Gentlemen. What, no ladies? Ugh, tsk, tsk. We really should work on our gender equality."

My father sputtered. "What are you doing here?"

"Well, it looks like you're having a board meeting without me, so I figured I'd join you since this is my company now."

Brian stood up. "Okay, everyone, calm down. Take a breath. We're just having a friendly meeting with some board members over some concerns that they were communicating."

"I would be delighted to answer any questions they may have."

I sat next to Timothy Arlington's chair and smiled at him. "I'm pretty sure this seat is for the CEO, right?"

He shoved down a bit. "Why, you piece of shit."

"Tsk, tsk, Dad. Not in front of our investors."

I took the seat he vacated and met each of their eyes. "I understand you have some concerns. I would be more than happy to answer any questions you have in my office."

Brian tried to interrupt again. "Well, yes, but since you're really busy, we figured we'd take that off your plate."

I gave him a smile that was all teeth. "Next time someone has a question about something the CEO should know, make sure you call me."

Behind me, Zia took notes, grabbing for a spare chair to put her recorder on. Olivia had turned on the recording feature of the conference room as well. I could have just listened in, but I wanted the full show. And I wanted to make Derrick's father squirm.

I smiled at the board members. "So, if you have questions, let me answer them."

I didn't know how I did it. Question after question about any delays, why we would have delays, what we were trying to accomplish, and why I had reservations. I answered them with efficiency and a clarity I didn't feel. I had no choice. I had my one big directive; make sure this damn merger went through. And these people were dicking with me. I answered their questions, listened to their concerns, gave them examples, and let them know why I was waiting.

One of them leaned forward. "You've never given a moment of care about this company or the business we do. Why should we believe that you care now?'

I leaned forward with my elbows on the desk, my hands clasped. "I'm not asking you to believe what I say. Of course not. That would be ridiculous. I'm sure there are lots of things over the years that have given you pause or concern. But what I'm asking you to pay attention to are my recent actions. What have I been willing to do so far? In the last month or so, what have my actions said? I know you're all eager for this merger. I know how important it is for this company, and I will deliver. But what I want to make sure you know is that I care enough about our company and the Arlington name to not do a bullshit job. If there are discrepancies, I want them addressed *before* the deal goes through. If there are questions, I want them answered. If there is anything that isn't right, I'm willing to walk away. And you all should know that by now. It is my job to take care of your money. Take care of your investment."

I talked fast. I worked the magic. The former me came out, the former me who had looked forward to running my own company, and I loved every fucking minute of it.

I wasn't even Derrick at that moment. I was *me*. *Theo*. Theo owned Arlington Tech, and Theo knew how to run it. Theo knew what was best for its people, and I loved every second of it. When I was done, the board members were on board with my direction, which was to find out what the hell was going on with Inline Tech, who was hiding money, and what the discrepancies were before moving forward.

The deal was worth a lot of money to both parties. But I wasn't going to shove through this bad deal just because Derrick Arlington had told me to. He fucked up enough to leave all of this behind for me to deal with. So that might have been his move, but I had a different one.

Zia...

CHAPTER 24

I FOUND Theo on the rooftop balcony. He'd stormed out of the conference room and hadn't waited for me. There was no point arguing that fact now. Besides, he'd been clearly upset.

The balcony had been made with the designated green spaces in the city in mind, overlooking the expanse of the island. It was filled with lush bougainvillea, and birds of paradise, lemongrass to keep the mosquitos away, and, of course, the ever-present hibiscus. It was an island oasis.

One tier below us a party was happening for one of the companies. We could see them clearly, but they couldn't see us.

"You want to tell me what just happened down there?"

He loosened his tie and pulled it off as he leaned on the balcony. "That," he paused to toss the tie in a waste basket, "was a failed coup."

I frowned. "Your father? But won't they only look worse if they don't include you in this deal. You are the CEO."

"That was my father posturing. He was trying to rattle me. He can't stand being a relic."

"You think he's capable of going through with it?" Why did I care? He wasn't mine. Wasn't going to be mine.

He shrugged. "Maybe, but now I'm untouchable. The board will have to see he's actively sabotaging me."

"At least you have what you want."

His gaze snapped up to mine. "No. I don't."

Liquid heat pooled in my core. No. I wasn't going down this road again. "Don't, Theo, this morning you said—"

"I know what the fuck I said. And I was an idiot. I was trying to hold on to something. Something that isn't mine to hold onto."

"I don't understand."

He shook his head. "No, of course you don't. Look, Sebastian spoke to me and warned me off."

"He what? You what? Of all the stupid—"

He shook his head. "That's not why I backed off. But he had a point."

I pointed my finger at him. "You gave me something and then you ripped it away. Do you know how that feels?"

"I do. But I didn't back off because of the king. I backed off because of me. You deserve someone better than Derrick Arlington. Sebastian was right. There are things I can't tell you. You want an open book. You want someone who can give you guarantees. I can't. I'm not who you think I am."

I frowned. "I remember once you said maybe I didn't see myself clearly enough. Maybe you don't see yourself clearly enough. I watched you march into that conference room an hour ago hell bent on making things right, not just for the board but for the investors. You didn't know me from a hill of beans, but you've bent over backward to help me, my sister, that kid, Peter. You helped him, a total stranger." I dragged in a deep breath. "My whole life, I've been around people who gave lip service, saying that sounds best. But when you need them, they're not there. I now know what it feels like to have someone show up for me."

"Zia—" He shook his head. "I have things you—"

I didn't let him finish. "I don't care. I know who you are. I've seen it. That's more important than what you can't tell me. Maybe one day you can. I would rather have someone real who turns up. That kind of loyalty. To be secure in the knowledge that there is someone I can count on. That's more important to me than anything."

CHAPTER 24

"I'm afraid I won't be able to let you go when you change your mind."

"Good luck getting rid of me."

He was on me in three strides.

His lips were a brand. I could feel the need coming off of him in waves.

He lifted me and placed me on the corner balcony and stepped between my legs. "God, you are so unbelievably sexy. I need you."

His kiss was hard and a little rough. With his big hands, he scooped me up by my ass and tucked me right up against his erection. "See how much I've missed you?" he mumbled against my lips. "Three days was too long."

I gasped as his thumbs traced circles over my nipples. "God, Theo."

"Mm, baby?" He traced a pattern of kisses from my ear to my clavicle. "I like it when you say my name. Can you do it again?" He rolled my nipple with his thumb and forefinger through the thin fabric of my top.

"Jesus." I let my head fall back.

"I'm not quite the second coming, but I'll do my best."

"Theo, I—"

With one hand, he held my ass in place as he rocked against me. "I know what you want."

"Theo, there are people having a party down there."

Through gritted teeth, he touched his forehead to mine. "I know."

My skin was hot, and the light breeze from the ocean did nothing to help cool me off. My breasts swelled as I drew in a shuddering breath. My whole body coiled tight in anticipation of his hands on me.

But we couldn't do this here—in public.

My rational brain shouted all the reasons we couldn't.

But when Theo circled my nipple once more with the pad of his thumb, I forgot all those reasons.

I slid my arms over his broad shoulders and dug my fingers into the muscled flesh.

He bunched up the fabric of my skirt so it was just above my knees, then he met my gaze. "I'll give you what you want." Theo kissed me again, this time taking his time and pulling a response from me. His hands continued on their path until he reached my panty line. "Sweet fuck."

"Theo, hurry."

"Don't want to hurry." He slid a finger inside my center, and we both moaned.

"Theo, please. Someone's going to see us."

He nipped my neck, then soothed the spot with a light flick of his tongue. "Right now, I don't really care."

He slid another finger inside me, and I let my head hang back as I moaned. He knew exactly how to touch me to get me to melt. And I was addicted to him. His smell, the way he moved. What he could do to my body.

As his fingers retreated, I gasped. "Wait, more." I could almost hear the smug, satisfied, smile in his voice.

But he complied. "See, I know what you like." His thumb circled my clit, and my breath hitched.

"Jesus."

He brought me to the brink with his deft fingers. Sliding into me, stimulating me just so, then pulling back as I teetered on the edge. He dragged down one shoulder of my blouse along with the strap of my bra. With his thumb, he circled my nipple, causing it to form into a tight little bud. I felt every movement and every caress in my core, and I wanted to scream with frustration when he wouldn't pick up the pace. "Theo."

Removing his expert thumb, he braced my upper body with his hands and tipped me back, replacing his thumb with his mouth. He suckled and tugged and nipped once, which was enough to send me so close to the edge that he stopped teasing me. " I don't want you to come yet. Wait for me, sweetheart."

I squirmed in his arms. "Theo, I don't want to wait."

"Now look who's impatient."

He held me still as he removed his fingers. Briefly kissing a path down my sternum, he lifted the fabric of my dress out of the way.

Oh, no, he wasn't. Not here, not... *Oh, God.*

The moment his lips touched my pussy, I trembled. Unlike last time, he paid very little attention to my clit, only pausing long enough to trace a circle around my most sensitive spot, then move back to his slow licking. I had no other choice but to hold on for the ride.

And I did. I threaded my fingers through his hair and held on tight.

"Shit, Zia..."

All it took was one slow lick, and I knew what was next. I started to shake in his hands. Hot, electric currents started in my spine and poured through my body. The orgasm tore through me with no mercy.

Theo shifted up my body, and I bit my lip. I knew what was coming—what I wanted. He grabbed a condom from his wallet and made quick work of it. When he was sheathed, he met my gaze. "You're incredible." When he drove in, I groaned and tossed my head back.

The full length of him was almost too much to take. He held

me still and panted, his harsh breath tickling my ear as he whispered, "God. I could stay inside you forever. I need you to do me a favor and be quiet, okay? I think I might die if we get interrupted."

I smoothed my hands down the back of his shirt and smacked him on the ass. He rewarded me with a grunt and drove home again.

"Theo, hurry."

He grabbed my hips with both hands and held me tight as he drove into me again and again, each stroke tickling my g-spot. "You're so goddamn sexy, Zia. I want to bend you over this balcony and slip into you from behind. Maybe play with your ass a little. Tell me Zia, would you like that?"

"Oh God, Theo, yes."

"God, you make me so damn crazy. I can't let you go."

I had officially lost my damn mind. But God, it felt so good. I became so lost in the sensations of Theo driving into me and tugging on my nipple that I didn't care who heard us.

Theo chose that moment to clamp a hand on the back of my neck and angle my head back to kiss me and muffle my cries.

He knew my body so well. The tingles in the base of my spine had triggered a chain reaction in my body. My toes had started to curl, and my breasts ached, and my pussy felt like it was riding a wave of heat and fire.

"Theo." His name was a breath on my tongue as I came apart in his arms.

"God yes, Zia." He drove in once more before clamping his teeth on my shoulder and cursing.

He held me tight as his body jerked, then he sagged against me, exhausted. "Damn it, Zia, you're going to kill me."

TWENTY-FIVE

ZIA...

I was fooling myself. I was in way over my head with Theo. After what we'd done on that balcony, I knew there was no protecting myself from feelings. I'd told myself one thing and completely done another.

I hadn't meant to break my no-more-sleeping-with-Theo rule. I really didn't. After all it was a direct order from the king.

Also none of his business.

But I was too far gone now. I didn't just want him.

That itch I had to make everything safe and perfect? I couldn't do that here. Nothing about him was safe or perfect and I wanted him anyway.

It doesn't matter who he is. All you have to do is keep someone from killing him.

This was true, but I wanted this job to be so much more than that. I could stop someone from killing him. I just thought he'd be different. I felt it in my bones he was the kind of man that I could trust.

Then why the niggling doubts?

He was the first man who would talk to me, wanted to be

right by me, wanted to take care of me. Not that I need anyone to take care of me, because God knew, I could take care of myself. I'd been doing it for so long I didn't know how to accept help most times.

I'd left him in bed, and I needed to soothe my restless sleep with something sugary. I went straight into the kitchen. I opened the freezer and found pints of every flavor of ice cream imaginable. Jesus Christ, I didn't ever see him eating ice cream, so whose was it?

I took a pint and after three tries finally found the spoons. I also grabbed graham crackers. I scooped out some rocky road, crumbled Graham crackers on the top, and then sat down.

"Oh, goodness, I am so glad to see someone eating."

I jumped. "Oh my God, Elena." I twirled around, my mouth full of ice cream. "I hope this is okay."

She waved me off. "Of course, it's okay. I bought all that extra ice cream hoping you and I could have some girl chat."

I laughed. "Well, if you want girl chat, you just have to say the word. I happen to have time to talk to you."

She nodded. "I figured at some point my boy was going to do something stupid and then you'd need me."

I shrugged. "Well, you know better than anyone that of course, he's going to do something stupid."

Elena laughed and made her own bowl of vanilla ice cream and candy canes.

"Candy canes? Really?"

She shrugged. "I wish I could explain it. I really love it, the combination. It's delicious."

We ate in companionable silence for a moment, but then I finally had to ask, "What was he like as a kid? Was he always so secretive?"

CHAPTER 25

Elena laughed. "Derrick was spoiled from the moment his father showed up with him."

I frowned. "Where was Mrs. Arlington?"

She huffed. "If you ask me, it's not the way things are done, but Mrs. Arlington, God bless her soul, was at a private retreat. She'd gone there to give birth. Rumors floated around that she was having a difficult time with her pregnancy and the new baby and needed some R&R. They struggled to have a child of their own for so long, and finally, the pressure got to be way too much for her, you know? Just too much on her mind, so she'd gone away to get herself well while pregnant with Derrick."

I frowned. "Was that her choice?"

Elena's brows furrowed, and she watched me closely. "That is an interesting question, young lady."

"Is it?"

"I mean, Timothy Arlington certainly had enough money to put her anywhere he wanted."

"Who cared about a woman's choice back then, right?"

Elena shrugged. "You know, honestly, I don't know. But when she came back, she swore up and down that it had been the best place for her and the months away had served her well. Those months away had given her the space and love to get well so she could love her beautiful baby boy, which was all she wanted."

"Well, at least she got well. Postpartum depression can really rock a new family to its core."

"I just wished I'd been able to be there for her when she was pregnant, but Mr. Arlington insisted that he had staff to do that. And then Mr. Arlington brought home that little baby boy. God, his head was so full of thick, dark curls. That boy had so much hair. But he was miserable. Oh, so miserable."

"Being separated from his mom?"

She shook her head. "Nah. Even when Mrs. Arlington came home, he never took to his mother, you know? Whenever she'd hold him, he would cry. When she tried to feed him, he would cry. When she tried to put him down, he would cry. He was only ever reasonable for me."

"I see. Well, I'm glad he has somebody he's close to that he can talk to."

She shook her head. "Oh no. I'm just a surrogate for his mother and the one he gets to use as a punching bag when he's mad at his father."

"It must have been so hard for her."

Elena shrugged. "It was. That poor baby was struggling too. He was so small. At first, you know, he wouldn't eat. He wouldn't sleep."

"I never imagined he had it so hard."

Elena nodded, taking another bite of her ice cream and chewing on peppermint. "Yeah, he did. But he also had it way too easy in a lot of ways. His father overindulged and underparented."

"Well, that I can see. The man is clearly spoiled rotten."

"Oh, he was."

"What happened to Mrs. Arlington?"

"Car accident when Derrick was seven."

Jesus. "That poor kid."

"As a child he was dragged along on business trip after business trip, mostly with me following behind trying to keep him entertained. The only time I saw him actually happy was one time when we were in New York. The whole time he was holding Mr. Arlington's hand. There were lots of business meetings, of course, so I had to take Derrick to the park and show him all the sights. He was a baby, of course, he doesn't remember that now."

"Mrs. Arlington stayed behind?"

Elena nodded. "Yeah, she didn't want to go. As a matter of fact, that's when her depression really took hold and she never believed she was free of it."

"That's so sad."

"It is, but the point is Derrick can be tricky. But lately, I don't know. He's been like that sweet boy that I showed around New York all that time ago."

"He must have been such a sweet kid though."

Elena shrugged. "He had his moments. You should have seen him. There was this little baby in the apartment we stayed in. I still remember the mother. She was this sweet, timid thing, and she had a baby the exact same age as Derrick. Oh, gosh, those two got on like a house on fire. Looked a lot alike too. When we would take the little ones to the park, everyone asked if they were twins. It was the first time I'd really seen Derrick happy. I knew he needed friends, or family, or something. Mr. Arlington didn't approve, of course, but when we returned to the islands, I made sure he had friends, you know?"

"Did that help?"

"Some." She finished her ice cream. I looked down and realized I had finished mine too. Then with quick, efficient movements, I stood and gathered the bowls, rinsing them before putting them on the top rack of the dishwasher.

"You don't have to do that."

"I wanted to do it."

"Nah, let me get you a hot chocolate so you can tell me about all your Derrick problems."

"Look, I'm not having Derrick problems. I just—" I stopped

myself. No one was supposed to know I was his bodyguard. To them, I was just a girlfriend having a fight with her boyfriend.

"Uh-huh. I know woman problems when I see them. This is the kind of problem only a man can cause."

"Okay fine. This whole time he's been trying to make this merger happen, and I assumed it was to make his dad proud or something. But lately, he's been different. He's really concerned about the work he's doing and wants it to be right. And he's just acting so different compared to what I saw before."

Elena nodded slowly. "And let me guess, you confronted him?"

"Well, I figured talking to him about it might be the best way to understand."

"The thing is I raised Derrick. I know he is spoiled, sometimes baffling, and he can be self-serving. He's always taken the easy way out. That's basically the man in a nutshell. No surprises there. But lately, in the last month or so, he's been different. It's like he's a different person entirely."

"What does that mean?"

"Now he's caring. I see him with you. He wants what's best for you."

"Yeah well, I know from the outside it looks like that, but I can't take anymore lying. I can't be with someone who isn't truthful with me."

"I understand, but maybe there are some things he can't tell you yet."

I considered that. "I don't know. The truth always seems difficult at the moment, but in the end, it's easy. It's the right choice."

"You know, Derrick; he's complicated. But who he is now is the man I have always tried to raise him to be. He is caring and considerate and respects other people and pursues the right things. I have to tell you, I haven't seen this Derrick in years. So, whatever is changing him—and honey, I think it's you—whatever is changing him, I'd like it to *keep* changing him. Because the Derrick I know wouldn't usually care about other people. He'd have to be told why it was important and be convinced. But now I see him becoming the man I always raised him to be. And it makes me so proud."

She reached over and gave my hand a warm squeeze before turning in the direction of the staff quarters. "Oh, and Elena, can I ask you a question?"

She turned around. "Yes, sweetheart. Of course, whatever you need."

"The name, Theo, he said his mom wanted to name him that. I can't find any instances of the name in the family. Do you know why?"

Her eyes went wide. "He asked you to call him Theo?"

I nodded. "Yeah. But he says it's only for when we're alone and that it's important to him."

Her face flushed red, and she held her hands to her ears. "Oh my God. I never suspected—" She took a deep breath. "If he wants you to call him Theo, then call him Theo. That name means a lot to him. I can only say it will be the fastest way to get through to him. That man cares about you, even if he doesn't know how to show it."

"Thanks, Elena."

Did he care about me? And did it matter if there were things that he was still hiding? Things I needed to get to the bottom of because I did care about him. I'd already been burned once, and I needed to know whether or not I could trust him.

TWENTY-SIX

THEO...

I WAS A GONER.

I knew it. She knew it. And I was powerless to do a damn thing about it.

Are you powerless?

I wanted to keep her. *I wanted to make her mine.*

I watched her as she curled into me. Tiny. Soft. This woman had bent over backward and run into danger to protect other people. No one ever did that for her. And I wanted to be the one to do that.

She doesn't know who you are.

If I just told her the truth, it would all be okay.

Are you insane? You are bound by a contract. You can't tell her the truth.

Which meant I'd have to keep lying to her. But I would tell her as much of the truth as possible. She already knew my name. Maybe I could tell her other bits about me. The parts that were true. Like about the PhilanthroApp and my friendship with Kyle, and how much I love my mother.

CHAPTER 26

Maybe I could show parts of myself to her. And when the truth came out eventually, maybe she wouldn't hate me. I'd have to show her that even though I might have my secrets, it didn't change how I felt about her.

You're going to get hurt.

I almost didn't care at that point. I pushed out of bed. I didn't want to fight with her. She had some good points, points I needed to text to Kyle. I grabbed my phone and headed into the kitchen. Elena was up, and she smiled at me. "Good morning."

I gave her a grin, not caring that I was shirtless in my pajamas. And she was grinning at me like an idiot. "So, I see you and Miss Zia made up."

My lips twitched. "Ah, I'm working on it."

"What are you doing in my kitchen, Derrick?"

I winced at the name.

"What, you don't like your name?"

"No, it's fine." I shifted my gaze so she wouldn't see my annoyance with it.

"Okay, I'll call you Theo."

I frowned and whipped around. "What?"

"Oh, you didn't think I'd remember. When you were little, we took a trip to New York. We met a little boy named Theo. You liked that name so much better than Derrick, so you insisted I call you Theo for weeks."

I frowned at that. "How old was I?"

"About two. You kept saying, 'Me, Theo, me, Theo'. Of course, that just drove your father insane, and your mother, well, she thought it was fine at first, and then she was exasperated by it."

I didn't know what to say. I didn't know how to act. I didn't know what the response should be. "I, um, call me what you want."

She gave me a warm smile and then patted my hand. "How about when it's just you and me, I'll call you Theo."

Fuuuuck. Did she know? Did she have any idea? Instead of asking any of those questions, I asked, "Do we have eggs?"

Her eyes went wide. "Yes, what would you like? I can make you scrambled eggs, or maybe an omelet."

I shook my head. "No, I'm going to cook for Zia."

Elena blinked at me, and then she stepped forward and looked at me. Really looked at me. She brought a hand to my face. "This is good. This is very, very good." She studied me again. "I'm happy to see you this morning."

I frowned. "Uh, you saw me last night."

She inhaled deeply, making a long soothing sound. "I know. Indulge an old lady. What are you making?"

"I was going to keep it simple. Eggs benedict?"

"Simple? Where did you learn to make hollandaise sauce?"

"Elena, there are YouTube videos for that." I pulled out all the ingredients, and the old woman kept me company as I cooked. I made her breakfast too.

She blinked back tears. "Theo, you've never made me breakfast before."

I winced and frowned. "I should have made you breakfast a long time ago. After all, how many breakfasts have you made me?"

Her smile was warm. "I'm not keeping count. As far as I'm concerned, we're even."

When she ducked into her room thirty minutes later, I figured it was a step toward repayment. I'd make it a point to buy her some tickets to some shows that were coming to the island soon too, because something told me the real Derrick was never going to make that happen.

I carried a tray into the room. Zia had expanded into a starfish shape. How did someone so small sleep so big?

"Sleeping beauty, wake up."

She frowned then reached for something under her pillow. When she turned around, I was facing a Taser. "Well, you know, I'm not really into the painful kinky foreplay, but if it really rocks your boat, I could try."

She scowled. "What are you doing out of bed?"

"Well, I went to make you breakfast."

She blinked, and then her nose took over. "Is that hollandaise?"

"Yep. I made Eggs Benedict."

She sat up, putting the Taser back under the pillow before scooching her ass up until she hit the headboard. "You made breakfast?"

I nodded. "Yeah, so eat up. We're going to spend the day together."

"Uh, Theo, that's—I don't even know what to say."

I grinned at her then kissed her nose. "First, start with thank you."

She grinned. "Thank you. This looks amazing. How much did Elena help?"

"She didn't. I can cook."

Zia watched me. "Are you telling me the billionaire knows his way around the kitchen?"

"Yeah. I like to cook. It relaxes me."

"Did you even know where all the utensils were?"

I rolled my eyes. "Everyone's a comedian. Eat up. I'm serious. We'll spend the day together."

She took a bite and moaned. Suddenly, I wasn't thinking about getting her fed, but rather keeping her naked and never leaving the bed again.

She swallowed a mouthful and then groaned. "Oh, crap. What's today?"

"It's Saturday."

"I wish I could. But after our scolding, Deedee got her own apartment. She moves in today."

"Oh, really."

"Since Deedee, of course, refused to pay for movers, she still needs my help."

That sister of hers. "Okay, I'll go with you."

She stared at me. "Have you ever moved someone into an apartment before?"

The real answer was yes, of course, many times. But I had the feeling Derrick never did anything like that. "Well, how hard can it be?"

"You don't have to do this."

"I don't have to, but I want to. So, eat. I'm getting a shower."

"You're not going to eat?"

I shook my head. "I ate with Elena. I wanted to bring you breakfast in bed."

She shook her head. "Sometimes I don't even know what to do with you."

"Well, I have a few ideas." I shifted the tray out of the way, making sure to move the orange juice I'd squeezed to the bedside table so it wouldn't rock. And then I pounced, catching my weight on my arms so as not to crush her. She giggled. "Oh my God, you're impossible."

"I know. Listen, I'm sorry I've been such a twat. Let me take care of you. Let me help Deedee move in."

She met my gaze with wide dark eyes. "Okay. Maybe I'll join you in the shower."

"Yes, now you're talking my language."

TWENTY-SEVEN

ZIA...

It was official. Derrick Theo Arlington was a Chupacabra.

Oh sure, they may be called mythical creatures, but I was certainly looking at one. This billionaire playboy was loading boxes into the moving truck for my sister. He didn't hire someone to do it.

Oh no, he was moving them himself, carrying them down the stairs and then up a little platform into the truck. He was dusty, he was sweaty, he was dirty. Still, every time he placed a box in the truck and hopped down from the platform, he gave me a winning smile. Like he was posing for the goddamn cover of a magazine. He was stunningly gorgeous. Those are the only words I had to describe him. I couldn't say much about anything else. Honestly, though, he was everything. Where did he come from?

Nope, you promised you wouldn't do this. You promised you would enjoy yourself, have fun and not worry about it.

This is true. I could do my job and protect him. I didn't need to know anything about him. He was right. I just wanted to know everything, which was different. When he could tell me, he would.

Are you sure about that?

All I knew was that he'd woke me up with kisses and food. The man had cooked. I'd snuck a peek at Elena and asked if she'd made the breakfast, but she shook her head and said he'd done everything himself. She also said it was the first time he'd ever cooked for her.

And then in the shower, he'd kissed me until my legs were jelly. When we'd gotten dressed and ready, we left together. It was my off shift, so Trace and Jax were nearby. Which meant they also were moving boxes because they had muscles.

And of course, Deedee and her friends who'd come to help were really just sitting around sipping mimosas and ogling. Not that I blamed them.

"If you keep smiling at me like that, I'm going to have to do something bad." Theo's voice was low and mumbling. I could feel a vibration against my back as he spoke.

"Well, you keep moving these boxes and I won't be able to help myself."

"Is that the key to your heart? Move some boxes around?"

"Well, in theory, I could move back into this place. I mean, I do own it. And then we wouldn't always have to stay at the penthouse."

His smile lingered for a moment. "You don't like the penthouse?"

"No, of course, it's uh, beautiful. Lord knows, I've never seen a view like that before. But we could have real privacy, you know, with no one around. We can't stay at Royal Elite, obviously, because that's where I work, so everyone's around."

He nodded. "So, what you're saying is you want me all to yourself, with no staff, just like normal people?"

I bit my lip and blinked through my lashes. "Kind of. I thought maybe it would be nice, you know."

He nodded. "I think that would be fantastic. When do you move?"

"Um, I want this place to be sanitized first. By professionals."

"We could clean it. It's not so bad."

"Are you serious?"

He shrugged. "Yeah. I mean, I'd be down for that." I grinned at him like an idiot and he added, "Look, however I get to spend time with you is how I want to spend time with you. It doesn't matter if we're at the penthouse, or at Royale Elite, though that's awkward for you, or if we're at your place here now that your sister is moving out. I could get behind this."

"Why are you being so..."

"Awesome? Handsome? Fantastic? Sex god-like?"

I laughed. "You're insane."

"About you."

The words were true. I could tell in his eyes. There was no deviation from the truth there. He was telling the truth. So how come there were so many times when he *wasn't* telling the truth? He wrapped his arms around me and held me tight, and I wanted to stay in his arms forever. As soon as the door swung open to my flat, he let me go and stepped aside. So far, I hadn't really told the guys, or anyone else for that matter, that we'd become a thing. Tamsin knew, of course, but she was respecting my right to to keep it under wraps for the time being.

Not that I really wanted to, to be honest. I wanted to tell them what was going on. I wanted everyone to know.

"How about I call someone to see if they can come clean this place tonight?"

I blinked at him. "Oh, you're serious?"

He nodded. "For this kind of thing, I'm more than happy to put in the hard labor. But if you won't move in here until it's spic and span, I'll make that happen in an hour."

I grinned. "I don't have any furniture. I don't have anything."

"You just let me take care of that."

"You think I'm going to let you furnish my apartment?"

"I think that you could let me do *something* for you."

I shook my head. "I don't want anything. I don't want money."

"I'm not saying you do. I'm saying that I could be of use. I'm saying that I could perhaps just do something for you. Stop worrying about how it looks or what it means. Just let me do something nice, okay?"

"Why are you being so sweet?"

"That's who I am. And sooner or later you're going to realize that."

"I guess I am."

He kissed my nose and jogged back in the house. I couldn't help but stare at his behind as he moved.

Deedee came jogging over. "Oh my God, you guys are the cutest."

I wrinkled my nose. "I don't know what you mean."

"I mean, I see him looking at you. You guys think you're slick with the secret touches, but I see them. Mostly, I see that you're actually happy. And not that pretend happy you always put on, but the real one. The real smiles, when he looks at you, when he talks to you, and when he gets me out of trouble."

"Could you do me a favor and *stay* out of trouble for a while?"

"Yeah, I'm working on it. But I like him for you. Also, he's a billionaire, so he can buy like the biggest house on the island."

"I don't need the biggest house on the island. I just need someone to love me. Someone who's going to stick around and be there."

She shook her head. "He's all well and good now, but if he fucks up, he'll have me to contend with. You don't deserve just the bare minimum. You deserve everything. You're my big sister, and you looked after me. Maybe I haven't always said it or showed my appreciation, but you are the best. Better than I deserve, for sure. So don't accept anything less than actually fantastic."

I pulled back and stared at my sister. When had she grown up? In the last few weeks, when Theo had handed her her ass? I didn't know, but somewhere in the last month or so, she'd become the grown-up I'd been trying to make her all these years. And she was the one who had smart words for me. "I hear you."

I glanced back at the house where Theo, Jax, and Trace were laughing together. My stomach flip-flopped again. I really, really hoped this was going to work out because I didn't think I could survive another broken heart. Not by him.

TWENTY-EIGHT

THEO...

THE SOUND OF BUZZING WOKE ME UP WITH A START. When I checked my surroundings, I wasn't quite sure where I was at first, and then it hit me. I was on Zia's air mattress that we had basically destroyed last night. The thing was only semi-inflated. Unlike me, who was fully inflated. I didn't think after last night I could possibly go again.

I groaned as I patted around for my phone. When I flipped it over, I frowned.

There was a photo of a bloody temple. Derrick Arlington's bloody temple.

Unknown Caller: *Come to the beach. Alone. Lose the bodyguards, or your mother will have a premature death.*

My stomach fell as I bolted up in bed.

Me: *Who is this?*

Unknown Caller: *Someone who is done fucking around. You want your mother and your girlfriend to live, you come to the beach now.*

Fuck. I slid my gaze over Zia's naked back, and I knew I was going. I knew I had to walk away and leave her.

There was a window in back I could use, and then I could jump the fence and grab a cab further down.

Shit. I didn't want to leave her.

You don't have a choice. Move.

The choice I hadn't wanted to make had come to a head. I shoved my phone in my pocket and made my decision.

ZIA...

I woke up and patted the bed next to me. It was still dark in the room, and I had to blink to let my eyes adjust. "Theo?"

His side of the air mattress was cool. I felt around, but he wasn't there. When I moved, the mattress moved with me, which meant we had certainly been enthusiastic and deflated the bed some.

I sat up properly this time, holding the sheet to me. "Theo?"

There was no sound. There was no light coming from the bathroom. Maybe he'd gone to sleep out in the living room. Had he gotten a call?

I climbed out of bed. I had no clothes in here. All I had was a sheet, and I wrapped it around myself as I padded out into the other room.

"Theo?" With every step forward, my heart hammered. My belly slowly clenched itself into a tight knot. He wasn't here. Oh, God.

I whipped around, glancing all over again, making sure I hadn't missed anything. My clothes were there, but his were not. He was gone.

CHAPTER 28

I grabbed my underwear and bra, tossed my t-shirt over my head, and was stepping into my jeans even as I pulled my phone out. I dialed Tamsin quickly. "Derrick, did you see him leave?"

Tamsin yawned. "No, he was with you. Did you accidentally kill him?"

"No, Tamsin, he's gone."

Tamsin's voice went alert immediately. "What the hell do you mean he's gone?"

"I don't know. I woke up and he was gone. His clothes aren't here. He's not here."

"He didn't leave. I've been watching the front all night."

"What do you mean? There's no other exit."

"He did not come out of that door."

I frowned. And then I cursed. "Jesus fucking Christ, he must have gone out the window."

Now it was Tamsin's turn for curses. "Jesus fucking Christ is right. You call Ariel. I'll see if I can activate his tracker."

I had wanted to be the one to activate his tracker and go after him, but I knew protocol. I wasn't on duty, but I was the last one to see him. So it was my job to call it in and explain to my boss how I'd failed, how I'd fucked up. How the one job I had I hadn't done well.

I hung up with Tamsin and dialed Ariel using the various protocols we had.

She answered sleepily. "Hello?"

"Ariel, it's Zia."

She still had a little confusion in her voice. I could hear her shifting around and a whispered, 'Hush, stop it.' "Zia, what's wrong? You're not on duty."

"I know, but the client was with me. He's gone."

Just like that, Ariel was alert and awake and all manner pissed off. "What the fuck? Where are you?"

"My old place. I moved my sister out today, so I moved some things in."

"Why was Arlington with you?"

Yeah, just the question I needed. "Uh, we were here together."

There was a beat of silence. Another muttered curse. And then Ariel was all business. "Okay, who's the guard on duty?"

"It was Tamsin, but he didn't go out the front. He went out the goddamn back window."

More muttered cursing under her breath. "Fucking Christ."

"I know. Tamsin is getting his tracker up."

"I know he's not going to have his phone on. He's been too bright for that," Ariel muttered.

I hesitated for a moment. "Uh, that's not where I put his tracker."

There was a pause. "Okay, well done."

"With all due respect, Ariel, none of this was well done."

"You and Tamsin go. Track him and alert the team when you have a location. Do not engage."

"Yeah, on it."

I didn't have nearly enough weapons. Just a Taser, a gun, and one clip. That wasn't going to do anything. Because once I caught Theo, I planned to kill him well and good.

I only brought my light jacket. I slid it on even though it wasn't really that chilly. And then I was out the door, barely closing it behind me, and in the van with Tamsin. "We have a location?"

"Yeah, nice tag, because he turned off his phone. I didn't think we'd be able to find him."

"Yeah, I figured if he ever decided to do a burner, he knows enough not to use his phone. But his wallet though, you can't separate a billionaire from his money."

"That was smart."

"Yeah, basically the only smart thing I've done."

Tamsin tapped the monitor and started the engine. "Looks like he's headed toward the beach."

I frowned when I saw which beach he was headed to. "But why would he go to Queen's Way Beach? That's right next to the shipping pier. There's nothing to see there."

"I don't know why, but that's where his wallet is going," Tamsin said.

"Okay, fine."

I typed a message to Ariel to let her know where we were heading and threw my seatbelt on as Tamsin peeled out of her spot.

"Are you okay?" Tamsin asked.

"No, I am not okay. But I will be. I messed up. I can see that."

"You didn't mess up. You deserve to have some fun. You deserve to enjoy yourself."

"The thing is all my instincts told me to ask questions, be wary, demand more from him, but I just wanted to believe. And because I wanted to believe, I overlooked the most important things. He's hiding something. He has been since we started his case. I've already tried to unravel it, and he has no idea what to do so he's running. Even after I told him how much I care about him, he is still running. He chose to run instead of tell the truth."

"Look, I get it. You feel betrayed. Hear him out. Maybe he really had a good reason."

"He left me, knowing what I would have to explain."

Tamsin pressed her lips into a firm line. "Look, I admit it doesn't look good for him right now, but I will hold off on judgment until you can talk to him."

"There really isn't much to talk about."

We pulled into the parking lot, and I scanned the beach. I saw a dark figure on the sand about four hundred meters away, and I pointed it out to Tamsin. "Over there. That way."

She revved the engine and sped over there as fast as she could. I hopped out before she could even stop the car. She yelled my name and tossed another clip my way. I was shoving it in the back of my jeans pocket when I came across the figure kneeling on the sand. Gun at the ready, I called to him. "Theo, what the hell are you doing? You're making it real hard to trust you."

He didn't move.

"Theo, I am armed and approaching. You have to talk to me. Why did you leave? Why this chase? I do have backup. So if you plan to hurt me—"

He turned his head, and I could see his profile but not his hands, and there was blood streaked down his face. He was holding something in his lap. No, not his lap. He was doing chest compressions. *What the hell?*

When I realized that Theo wasn't going to hurt me, that he was giving chest compressions to someone on the beach, I ran for him. All I knew was that something was very, very wrong.

I approached, and he just kept up the chest compressions. When I finally reached him, I could see there was a man on the sand as if he'd washed up that way. "Theo, what is going on?"

His gaze flickered up to mine. I could see him counting his compressions.

I leaned down next to him, ready to assist in the first aid. I

CHAPTER 28

pulled out my phone and called Tamsin. "Tams, body on the beach. We need help."

I hung up and started mouth to mouth. He just kept up the compressions. I didn't look, *really* look at the person I was giving mouth to mouth resuscitation to until the body started to move.

It started to cough and convulse, and then I stepped back. Theo moved back as well, removing the shadow from the man's face. And the moment he was unobscured, I scrambled backward.

Holy shit.

Theo held up his hands. "Zia, I can explain."

And then suddenly, all of the pieces of the last several weeks slid into place, and I understood. The man on the ground was coughing and moaning. His hair was longer, and he was bearded and bloody, but I would know those eyes anywhere. Stormy gray.

His nose was smoother. It hadn't been broken before. His lips were covered by a mustache and beard, so they were hard to discern, but I knew the shape well. I lifted my gaze to Theo.

"So, which one of you is really Derrick Arlington?"

To be continued...in The Billionaire's Secret...

THANK you so much for reading BODYGUARD TO THE BILLIONAIRE!

I hope you've loved Zia and Theo! Find out what happens now that Zia knows the truth. And find out who's behind the plot to destroy the royal family.

Order THE BILLIONAIRE'S SECRET now so you don't miss it!

And you can read Nathan and Sophie's story right now! Find out what happens when a seductive, jaded playboy with a filthy mouth meets his uptight neighbor and they strike a little ex payback bargain.

One-click MR. DIRTY now!

> "Mr. Dirty is a ***fun and flirty romance*** with complex characters and a great storyline." - Amazon Reviewer

Need another sexy filthy rich playboy to get you going? The sexy billionaire fake fiancee book, SEXY IN STILETTOS is FREE on all retailers!

Download SEXY IN STILETTOS now!

Turn the page for an excerpt from Sexy in Stilettos...

ALSO BY NANA MALONE
SEXY IN STILETTOS

Come on, Trudeaux. Shoulders back, chin up. You are amazing. Jaya was well aware of the impact the three of them made in the crowded lounge. They weren't the typical San Diego girls, tall, blonde and leggy—but they were stunning in the way they stood out from the crowd with their brown skin and dark hair. Or at least, she could be made stunning just by standing between her friends. With Ricca's curves and Micha's striking looks and hair, nobody could help but look twice. For once though, she didn't bask secretly in the glow of secondary adoration. But maybe Micha was right. If she faked it, she'd start feeling better.

They selected the booth by the bar. It had easy access to drinks, a great view of the dance floor, and was close to the side exit in case the place was packed and they didn't want to go through the lobby of the Westhorpe Hotel to get out.

Jaya slid into the booth, careful to keep the skirt of her dress bunched. The damn thing was so frothy and flirty, every time she moved, the skirts threatened to lift up and expose her ass to the world. The top was no better. The neckline was so daring, she hadn't bothered to wear a bra with it, putting her goods even more on display. But at least she was comfortable in the shoes. They felt like padded silk and they looked amazing. The perfect complement to the dress.

Once their drinks arrived, Jaya raised her glass as she tried to shake the feeling that someone was watching her. Though, given the Do-Me shoes and the Look-At-Me dress, she should have been more surprised if someone *wasn't* watching her.

"Okay, listen closely, ladies, because this is the only time you'll be hearing this from my mouth. You were right." She paused for effect. "I do feel better. Thanks to you guys, I'm not pulling the death-by-cookies-'n'-cream routine. And—I have a plan."

Ricca raised her glass and clinked it with Jaya's.

Micha's grin was broad as she spoke. "I knew we'd see the old you eventually—Planning and everything. Soon you'll be making one of us a to-do list. You're on the road to recovery." She took a sip of her Lemon Drop, her ruby-red lips closing around the rim of her martini glass. "So, what's the plan? Should I get my shovel? Will this require a trip to the desert and a body burial?"

"As much as I would love to throw Derrick in a ditch, I've got something else in mind." With the hairs on her neck standing at attention and making her take furtive look around, she continued in a softer voice. "I'm going to finish my drink. Then I'm going to get my job back—and oust the interloper from my family."

Micha and Ricca exchanged wide-eyed looks. "I prefer the desert idea," Micha mumbled.

"Well, okay. As soon as I *legally* get rid of him, I'll don the sexiest of cat-burglar-chic and help you dig." Jaya sighed cheerily as she took another sip of her drink. "I will be back on top in no time."

Ricca's happy face went from friendly bolstering to wary concern. "Exactly what *is* the plan?"

A shot of adrenaline zinged through Jaya. Now that she had a strategy, the tension was already rolling out of her shoulders. "First things first. I'm going to get a date to Tamara's wedding. There's no way I can show up alone. It just screams 'I'm a jobless loser who can't even find a boyfriend.'"

Micha slapped the table top. "At last. Now you're talking sense. I told you all that *I'm-strong-enough-to-go-to-the-wedding-alone* nonsense was bullshit."

"Yes, you were right. There's no way I want to show up alone." She shrugged. "Besides, it won't hurt to have somebody hot as a fixture.

Someone who won't think Tamara is the most beautiful woman on the planet and the sun shines out of her ass."

Micha snickered. "Is *that* what a sunrise looks like?"

Jaya chuckled. "Once I have a date to the wedding, my real work begins. I know for a fact Dad has invited some of our largest clients to the wedding. And I'm sure they'll win the conference bid. When they do, Dad will be beside himself to invite Brett James to it. He loves to schmooze and give an air of family at Trudeaux."

"But how do you plan to get close to him?" Micha asked. "Won't Derrick try and keep you away?"

"Probably. But I'll figure a way around it. I just need to speak with the client. I know I had Brett at that pitch."

"You two are on a first-name basis now?"

Jaya grinned. "You'd better believe it. Once the client starts grumbling that he wants me back on the project, Dad won't have much of a choice but to reinstate me."

Ricca shook her head, sending her glossy black hair waving around her shoulders. "I don't know, Jai. Sounds risky. What if the client doesn't demand to have you back?"

Jaya waved a dismissive hand. "I have that covered. I know this client inside out. I'm a comic-book-reading, superhero-loving, self and publically professed nerd. They won't want a substitute. I know what I'm doing."

"Okay, so when do we start trolling our contacts for Mr. Perfect?" Micha pulled out her phone, apparently ready to get on the case. "You only have two weeks. And we'll want to help you audition them, shirts off of course." She waggled her eyebrows.

Ricca giggled. "You could always take Beckett."

Jaya shook her head. "No go on Beckett. I've known him since college. It'll be hard to pass him off as my boyfriend, since Dad and Tams know him too. You must have some male model types you use for Fantasies, Inc."

"Yeah, we use an agency. I suppose we could hire you someone. But why pay if you can get a real date?"

Micha tapped her phone. "That'll be our last resort. In the meantime, I have a couple of guys I've been dying to fix you up with."

I've done it now. Now that she'd opened the floodgates, her friends would be all over this.

Through the crowd, she noticed Beckett's broad shoulders making their way over to the booth. Most people got out of his way— something she'd never understand because he was harmless. His blond good looks and lazy countenance should have put people at ease, but instead, he made people nervous. Ricca especially. Maybe it was his eyes. They were shrewd. Never missed anything. That and his six-foot-five build.

As he joined them, Jaya put on her best brave face smile. But he saw right through it. "Cut the shit, Jaya. You're a terrible liar."

She flashed Ricca a look. "Did you tell him? I know you two work together, but is there no loyalty?"

He rolled his eyes. "She didn't have to tell me anything. I called your office. Then your secretary—who's now your sister's secretary, by the way—told me you were fired. What the fuck?"

Jaya cleared her throat. "Yeah, long story. Pretty much the old man lost his mind and I'm out of a gig. Oh, and did I mention I'm still expected at that stupid wedding?"

He winced. "If you want, I—"

She cut him off. "Already been through that. And no. But thanks."

To avoid the uncomfortable shift in emotion, Jaya scanned the crowd. The usual glitterati were out in full force. Short skirts, bleach-blonde

hair and teetering heels. Her eyes shifted to the bar area and she froze.
No. It couldn't be.

Alec. Leaning against the bar. Staring at her. The way she saw it, she had two options. Duck under the table and hide, though not the best choice because, given the skirt, everyone would see the color of her thong. There was the option of shuffling out of the booth and making a break for it. But Micha was quick and Jaya would never make it out without having to explain herself.

As he approached, her whole body tensed, every beat of her heart wearing a more permanent pattern into her chest cavity. *Shit.* With every step he took, he looked like a predator. The sexual approach she could handle. A kind-hearted, hey-aren't-you-the-girl-who-cried-on-my-jacket? thing she couldn't do. If he showed her pity, she'd cry and ruin Micha's excellent makeup job. Not to mention he'd probably think she was crazy for real.

All of his tall, dark and delicious frame paused at their booth. "I got tired of waiting for you to come to the bar, so I figured I'd brave the crowd."

The velvet voice melted into her center making her core contract. The broad chest didn't help either. Talk about a sexy, make-your-panties-drop kind of body. She whipped her head up to meet his gaze.

If anyone asked her later, she would swear up and down she tried to form words—

Intelligent words. Instead, all she managed was the flap-jaw routine. Open, close. Open, close.

"Cat got your tongue?" He grinned at her.

Damn, that smile should be illegal. "I-I—Uh..."

Clutching his hand to his heart, he added on the extra charm. "I'm wounded. It's worse than I feared. You've forgotten my name *and* my face."

The giggle escaped before she could corral it. "I haven't forgotten your name, *Alec*. You're the one who forgot to call me about your shirt."

"Ahh, you remember me then. It's a start. And I did call you. *You* forgot to mention that you no longer worked at Trudeaux Events."

Heat suffused her face. "Well, since they were the reason I ruined your shirt, I figured they should pay."

"And if I told you I didn't call about my shirt?"

Great. A charmer. Derrick had been a charmer once. "I'd say you had no other reason to be calling me." She felt Micha nudge her with her foot.

Alec put his hand over his heart. "Ouch. Shot down by a goddess."

Jaya fought not to roll her eyes. "Does this approach ever work for you? The whole I'm-sexy-and-have-more-charm-than-brains thing?"

"So, you think I'm sexy?" He winked at her. "I'm just going to ignore the rest."

"Are you going to introduce us to your friend, Jai?" Micha made no bones about her open admiration as she eyed Alec up and down. "Even better, is your new friend going to introduce me to his friend at the bar?" Micha turned and waved to the tall man at the bar with the sandy brown hair.

Jaya could feel her skin grow hot. She wasn't supposed to ever see him again. He wasn't supposed to be charming *and* hot. This wasn't supposed to happen. She had a plan to implement. "He's not my friend. He's—"

"Alec Danthers. Ladies," he said with a grin at Ricca and Micha, but only nodded at Beckett. Maybe it was some guy thing, but the two of them didn't speak and Jaya could sense the malevolence coming off Beckett in waves.

Ricca and Micha both traitorously grinned back at him.

"Allow me to buy your drinks for the rest of the evening," he said to them. "Maybe you can put a good word in with your friend for me."

Jaya rolled her eyes. Taking in the badge on his shirt that said Manager, she said, "Isn't it your job to make sure the bar makes money and not loses it?"

"And not hit on my friend?" Beckett grumbled beside her, but no one paid attention to him.

"I think the Westhorpe Hotel can handle a couple of free drinks for some beautiful women."

While Alec chatted with her friends, Jaya realized the carefree flirtation had vanished. Sure, he still smiled and complimented her friends, but something she'd said had turned off the light inside.

Damn.

"Thanks for the offer of drinks, Alec. But, if you'll excuse me, I'm headed to the dance floor." Walking away she could feel his gaze on her back burning her flesh.

Jaya joined the gyrating throngs on the dance floor and she closed her eyes and moved her body to the tune of Rihanna's "S&M." As Jaya moved her hips to the lyrics about chains and whips, a warm hand landed on her hip. Sharp zips of electricity jolted her flesh.

The deep voice at her ear was low and inviting. "Come see me when you're ready for a drink."

Alec kept his hand on her hip for a moment too long. His parting squeeze made her body yearn for a more intimate touch.

Even as she turned to face him, he had already moved toward the bar. When her friends joined her on the dance floor, she bit back a smile as Micha gave her a clear, girl-go-get-your-man look. Ricca just fanned herself and fake-swooned. Silly girls. Charmers are for morons. And this was not her first trip to the rodeo.

"Honey, if you don't go and get him, I will." Micha booty bumped her.

"You put on your moxy—borrow mine if you must—and go make me proud. I'm going to take on his friend."

Jaya turned towards her goal, her body jerking with adrenaline at the thought of her plan. Or maybe that was Micha's shove in Alec's general direction. Either way, Jaya's feet navigated the masses of the pretty and rich towards the promise of some serious sexual gratification. Though, the closer she got to him, she had a feeling she'd been ensnared rather than the one ensnaring.

Taking in his longish dark hair curling at the ends, she wondered how it would feel between her fingertips. Tousled as it was, it gave him a youthful appearance. Those eyes, though. They were by far his best feature. That unusual shade of blue framed by black, sooty lashes. As she openly ogled, she decided his eyes were not his best feature. Strong shoulders, flat stomach. Given the hard planes of his chest when he held her, she was pretty sure his black polo hid a pretty excellent set of abs.

Mr. Sex on a Stick looked just like the panacea she needed. She needed to flirt a little, secure the date, then move on with the plan. She reminded her libido that everything hinged on getting the plan to work right. *Focus. You can do anything.* She just needed to pretend she was a superhero.

When she reached the bar, he grinned at her. "If you'd waited another minute to come over, I'd have found a reason to come to you. I had wingmen standing at the ready to occupy your friends."

Jaya knew she must be blushing, but she held on tight to her borrowed pair of brass balls. "Micha's already secured one of your wingmen." She indicated the dance floor where Micha, pressed up against Alec's friend, worked her hips in time to Sean Paul "I fear for his life. Or his c—."

He barked out a laugh, interrupting her. "Do you always say what's on your mind?" He eyed the pair. "Besides, I think Caleb can keep up."

She liked the feel of the brass balls she wielded, not watching what she said. Not being so cautious. "No. I don't always speak my mind. But I think I'm starting to like it."

He reached out to brush a stray hair from her cheek. The contact had her wobbling in her heels and she placed a hand on his chest to steady herself.

His sharp intake of breath and the hitch in his heartbeat under her hand gave her the final boost of confidence she needed.

Leaning in, she pressed her mouth to his. She pulled back and murmured, "Let's go somewhere."

Those three words zinged around in Jaya's head, repeating over and over and over again. Had she really said that? She slid Alec a look from under her lashes and saw naked lust sprinkled with a pinch of curiosity.

Without a word to her, he took her hand and pulled her around the bar. Tossing a set of keys to the other man behind the bar, he ground out a command. "Lock up."

Download now!

ABOUT NANA MALONE

USA Today Bestselling Author, Nana Malone's love of all things romance and adventure started with a tattered romantic suspense she borrowed from her cousin on a sultry summer afternoon in Ghana at a precocious thirteen. She's been in love with kick butt heroines ever since.

Nana is the author of multiple series. And the books in her series have been on multiple Amazon Kindle and Barnes & Noble bestseller lists as well as the iTunes Breakout Books list and most notably the USA Today Bestseller list.

ABOUT NANA MALONE

Printed in Poland
by Amazon Fulfillment
Poland Sp. z o.o., Wrocław